A BEAUTIFUL, TERRIBLE THING

'Powerful and complex, it's a beautiful and compelling exploration of love and forgiveness. Bravo'
Louisa Reid, author of *Gloves Off* and *Handle With Care*

'Incredibly moving. Brutal, beautiful and ultimately hopeful . . . A deep look at love, loss, grief and all the emotions in between. A rare new voice'
Christine Pillainayagam, author of *Ellie Pillai is Brown*

'It is going to whip your heart out of you . . . joyful, broken and everything in between. Absolutely superb'
Fiona Sharp, *Independent Book Reviews*

'Heartbreaking but hopeful . . . beautifully written . . . an important book'
Denise Gale, Waterstones

'Exceptional . . . gut-wrenchingly compelling'
Cornerstones Literary Consultancy

'Beautifully written . . . very visceral' *Scottish Book Trust*

www.davidficklingbooks.com

A BEAUTIFUL, TERRIBLE THING

Miranda Moore

David Fickling Books

A Beautiful, Terrible Thing
is a
DAVID FICKLING BOOK

First published in Great Britain in 2025 by
David Fickling Books,
31 Beaumont Street,
Oxford, OX1 2NP
EU Rep: Authorised Rep Compliance Ltd., Ground Floor,
71 Lower Baggot Street, Dublin, D02 P593,
Ireland.
www.arccompliance.com

Text © Miranda Moore, 2025
Cover by Michelle Brackenborough

978-1-78845-368-4

1 3 5 7 9 10 8 6 4 2

The right of Miranda Moore to be identified as the
author of this work has been asserted in accordance with
the Copyright, Designs and Patents Act 1988.

All rights reserved. No part of this publication may be reproduced,
stored in a retrieval system, or transmitted in any form or by
any means, electronic, mechanical, photocopying, recording or
otherwise, without the prior permission of the publishers.

Papers used by David Fickling Books are from
well-managed forests and other responsible sources.

DAVID FICKLING BOOKS Reg. No. 8340307

A CIP catalogue record for this book is available from the British Library.

Typeset in 10/14.75 pt Sabon by Falcon Oast Graphic Art Ltd
Printed and bound in Great Britain by Clays Ltd, Elcograf S.p.A.

For you, whoever you are

Chapter One

Nathan

30 June, Edinburgh
The boy, he's dying.
He's dying in front of me, on the tarmac, and there's nothing I can do.
I've killed him.
I've killed a boy.

It's supposed to be the first day of the rest of your life. A new beginning.

When the teachers wish you all the best for the future, they wheel out all the clichés. They talk about unwritten books, new chapters, dreams, ambitions, opportunities, oysters. They talk about creating your own destiny. They don't pull you aside and say, 'Hey, Blakey, yours starts and ends tomorrow.'

My new beginning lasted two hours and thirty-seven minutes,

from the moment I woke up to the moment the world stopped.

So. I was driving my mum's car, feeling mighty chuffed with myself. I was off to meet Scotty at the shops. The morning haar was starting to burn off and there was a summer buzz in the air – you know, when the sun's shining and everyone's smiling and the whole world's happy – or maybe it was just me. I was fiddling with my tunes on my phone, turning up 'Starlight' – my favourite track on my favourite album – thinking: *Thursday, no Maths, no Geography. Freedom!*

I looked up, braked hard, roared.

Thud.

My body lunged, the seatbelt slamming me in the chest. Filling my vision, a boy, four or five years younger than me. His eyes were saucers, fixed on mine, his mouth open in a scream, head arcing back, then his eyes glazed and he slid down the front of the car, leaving a big scarlet smear. My mind pulsed to the backing track of my heart pounding, so loud – a thrash-metal beat inside my throat.

Everything was slow-mo, frame-by-frame. I unclipped my belt, opened the door, stepped out. A blizzard of noise and movement exploded and people shouted and screamed. A purple sari fluttered on a rail outside a shop, next to a red 'Kebabs' sign with the 'abs' hanging off.

The boy, pale, brown-haired, in skinny jeans and green checked shirt, lay slumped, earbud flung from his left ear, phone smashed on the tarmac; grey eyes open, unblinking. I stumbled backwards – the air spinning away from me like I was trapped in a vortex, all bass reverb.

A giant fist gripped my chest, squeezing, squeezing. I fought to take in a breath. The blue stripes of his Spezials jumped out at me. Same shoes as my little brother.

A man with a black crew cut was in my face, yelling, his own face twisted. I stepped back. Another man with white hair in a ponytail stepped in front of me to block the punch coming my way. Two men, three, held Crew Cut, told him to calm down.

'He needs to be locked up,' he shouted. 'Fucking wanker.' I took a puff of my inhaler.

I don't know how long I was standing there before the siren wail seeped into my consciousness. I heard them before I saw them: ambulance, police. The paramedic jumped out, checked the boy for a pulse, started chest compressions.

Nothing.

Another bottle-green uniform fitted a tube into his mouth and squeezed something, then pulled up the boy's sleeve and injected him with a syringe.

One officer cordoned off the area, another directed backed-up traffic and blocked the lane. It was all a mess of people and noise and blue flashing lights.

'Two minutes,' said the paramedic doing the compressions.

The other one stuck wires under the boy's shirt and checked the screen. She said something.

A patch of red soaked through the boy's shirt, pooling on the road. The face was grey, the lips draining of colour as I watched. The hand, flung out to the side, was white, dead-looking, small.

The bottle-green bodies blurred, pumping, waiting.

The hydraulic hiss of brakes of a bus then a lorry, and the drone of a motorbike growled in my head, like a defibrillator shock. I looked over and locked eyes with a wee girl with a Greta plait, on the top deck of a bus in the far lane, her jaw gaping.

'Four minutes. Adrenaline.'

They swapped places.

A policeman shoved away a man filming on his phone.

A car horn. Voices on phones. A kid, wailing.

A policeman spoke into his radio. He looked at me, shook his head, bunched up his mouth, more sad-looking than angry. He took my phone, asked my name, age, address and whose car it was, and I was breathalysed. I blew into the tube until it beeped. 'Pass.' I don't know why I was so calm. It was like watching someone else. I couldn't stop staring at the boy.

'Eight minutes.'

'Come on, son,' said a voice. The policeman. 'Come on,' he said again. He bundled me into the back of the blue and yellow car. I'd heard about people being 'bundled' into police cars in media reports. I hadn't ever considered the bundle might one day be me.

I stared out the window.

A moment of stillness, of surrender.

A small shake of the head.

The paramedic's lips moved.

On the car radio, a woman's voice: 'Fatal RTC, vehicle versus pedestrian on Haddington Place, Leith Walk, outside Gigi's. Ambulance on scene. Can the traffic sergeant and collision investigators be asked to attend?'

Fatal RTC.

The police officer climbed into the back seat beside me and recited his arrest spiel. I hadn't noticed a woman officer in the driver's seat. She indicated, pulled out. I felt cold, so cold; a marble sculpture of myself.

Fatal RTC.

Two officers with white tops and gadgets were doing stuff with Mum's car as we drove past.

It couldn't be real – none of it. Except I was in a police car. On the way to a police station. Real.

I'd only been driving four months. I'd passed my test first time.

The policeman talked into his radio. I could see him, didn't hear him though. I just saw him, the grey-black side of his head. Short back and sides. His mouth moved, but my head was crammed with silence. The streets were a blur. I had no idea where we were. All I saw was a series of stills, like some sick slideshow. The body, the neat, white jaw. The smell of blood. A red light. Hands – fine, like child's hands. Spezials. Earbud. What had he been listening to? My mind wandered, scanned, skirted round him, touring along the perimeter, avoiding the bit in the middle: the lifeless heart, the dead eyes.

The dam couldn't hold; the truth flooded in, choking me.

The boy – he was dead. I had killed him. I had killed a person. Silence gave way to thumping: the thumping of my heart, loud, louder, like a kick drum. Thumping out my existence.

Fuck. What was he doing, wandering across the road?

Too busy listening to his tunes.

Man, why did you do this to me?

Fuck.

The door opened. I hadn't noticed we'd stopped. I looked down: concrete paving stones, dotted with discs of chewing gum. Looked up again. Brown bricks. The policeman's black shoes walked three steps, through a door. I seemed to be following.

'Have a seat,' my policeman said, waving a muscled forearm towards a chair. He was medium-tall and looked like the sort that runs ultras for fun – classic copper's build.

A man and a woman sat behind a glass-slider partition. The man looked up and slid open the window a head's width.

'He's in for the fatal on Leith Walk,' my policeman said, leaning in, his voice lowered. He thought I couldn't hear him, but my hearing zoned in just on him, like it was making some monumental effort to filter out other sounds and follow the script. 'Best get him a cup of tea and a biscuit. Worst sort of driver, these young lads – think they know it all. Worse than women.' And he winked at the pretty, brunette officer, her hair scraped back under her hat. She pulled a face.

It's not funny.

'The lad killed – how old?' she asked.

'Thirteen. Poor lad.'

They nodded, shook their heads.

'And the lad that did it?'

'Just turned eighteen.'

They looked at me.

'Watty and Trish got the job of informing the family, poor bastards,' said the policeman – my policeman. 'They'll take them to ID the kid.'

The man and woman shook their heads again.

'Come with me,' my policeman said, leading me along a corridor and into a room where another officer was typing at a computer. A harsh, blue-white light buzzed overhead, giving a high-pitched hum. Everything seemed twice as hot, twice as bright, twice as loud as usual. The other officer glanced round then returned to her typing. I had to empty my pockets – house key, wallet, inhaler.

'Sergeant Spencer – the custody sergeant – will be with us shortly,' said my policeman. 'Do you want a solicitor informed, or we can arrange the duty solicitor?'

Custody sergeant?

Solicitor?

I blinked. He sighed.

A female officer entered the room. Straight, fair hair, tied back. 'Sergeant Lisa Spencer,' she said.

My officer – I'd missed his name when he told me – asked my full name, date of birth, place of birth, address, occupation. I told him I'd just finished S6 – didn't have an occupation. Grease stains from white tack shone from the four corners of a child's drawing on the wall. The foreground was green crayon. Three flowers – red, yellow and blue – stood to attention beside a stick man with a big round belly and a big U smile, a black suit and a black cap. Blue sky and sun in solid rays formed a band across the top of the page, above a big blank space – no man's land between earth and sky.

Sergeant Spencer sat down and swivelled to face me. 'Do you want us to contact another reasonably named person?'

I stared at the straightness of her fringe, a floating line.

She looked at the officer and back at me. 'I've got a son myself. Turns seventeen in two weeks. Desperate to learn to drive.' She leaned in. 'Will we call your mum – ask her to come?'

My officer bent forward in his chair, stared at the floor, his elbows resting on his knees. A smell of coffee, a trace of sweat.

Mum?

I didn't realize how nice the police were until the solicitor arrived. Seven feet tall, just about. Tall and thin. Pinstriped suit. Pink tie. He shook my hand. His was cold – long fingers that gripped my knuckles in a vice. He had narrow, black-rimmed glasses and his scalp shone, like it had been polished. It probably had, like his shoes.

'Stephen Jeffreys,' he said, with no human glint in his eye. His nose puckered in silent appraisal.

'I'm Nathan,' I said. 'Nathan Blake.' Inside my head, my voice sounded strangled.

My officer found a room for the solicitor and me, then left, pulling the door behind him.

The solicitor rummaged in his briefcase and gestured for me to sit. 'Can you describe exactly what happened, in detail?'

I tried. I told him anything I could remember.

'Where's my mum?' I asked.

'Pacing around in reception, asking why they're holding her son.'

I shivered, picturing her.

'Here,' he said, handing me his phone. 'Want to give her a call?'

How can I just ring her? What am I supposed to say?

'Mum?' I said in a low croak, shrinking back in the chair.

'Nathan?' she said. 'What's happened? Tell me you're all right.' Her voice was tight.

'I crashed the car.'

'But you're not hurt?'

'I'm not hurt.' My voice quavered.

'You're all right?'

Silence. I couldn't find the words, the courage.

'Why have they arrested you? Where's the car?'

'Leith Walk.' Or maybe on the back of some recovery vehicle. I didn't tell her it was smeared in blood.

'What is it, Nathan? Tell me.'

'I ran into a boy in the car. I don't think he was looking – he wasn't looking. He was listening to music.'

A pause. 'This boy – is he injured?'

I heaved a great sob that stole the air from my lungs – couldn't hold it in.

'It's OK, love. It's going to be OK.'

I couldn't speak, couldn't control my chokes and grunts. They burst out of me with a ferocity I'd never experienced. I heard Mum too, choked up.

'The boy's injured? How bad?' she said, in a voice that was quiet, flat, scared.

The dark blue of the carpet blurred.

'He's dead.'

Silence.

Say something, Mum.

Mum, you have to say something.

'He's what?'

'He's dead.'

'No,' she said. 'Are you sure?'

'He's dead, Mum.'

The solicitor looked up at me.

'Oh, God,' she said at last, in a voice that didn't sound like Mum. 'God, Nath, no.'

Then a silence, loud and frightening, from the receiver. I'd never had the shakes before.

'A child?' came Mum's voice, barely audible.

'Thirteen. I'm sorry, Mum,' I managed, after a rasping wheeze. The solicitor scribbled in his notebook.

I swallowed and gulped, echoed by Mum, still on the line.

'OK. Try to breathe.'

I hung up. She was here, on the other side of a few doors.

Scotty. I should have told her to ring Scotty. I pictured him, still waiting, texting me.

The solicitor stood up, filled a paper cup with water, handed it to me, pursed his lips in a sympathy smile.

A Cardigans song played in my head. 'Erase/Rewind'. The boy's big round eyes jumped out at me, pressed up on the bonnet staring right into mine in pure terror.

Where had he come from? How come I hadn't seen him?

I retched. The solicitor shoved a bin under my face. I puked, the bile burning my throat.

So this was my new beginning. A grim realization gripped my stomach. I would always be the one who had killed a thirteen-year-old boy. Twenty years from now. Fifty. No matter what else I did. No matter if I saved 10,000 lives. It was inescapable. My newly created destiny.

A blackness stretched before me.

He should have been paying attention. You don't just wander across the road. I was only fiddling with my phone for a second or two.

It wasn't my fault.

We were led into an interview room. The officer and a woman officer – the driver, maybe – sat opposite the solicitor and me. The solicitor breathed in my direction. Garlic breath.

My officer noted the time and listed our names. He fixed his brown eyes on mine. 'Nathan Blake,' he said, 'I am charging you with causing death by dangerous driving.'

Death by dangerous driving. The words rammed me in the chest.

I stared at the ceiling: a white blur that slowly turned black. My future had been ripped from me by some sick magician. A sleight of hand, like that tablecloth trick. I'd been sitting at the kitchen table drinking tea from my World's Greatest Son mug only a couple of hours before, staring at the shiny red apples of the tablecloth Mum liked, thinking: year out, travel maybe, get a job? Save up, go somewhere cool, learn to scuba dive. Voluntary work in Chile or something. Then see if I can get into uni. Some sort of engineering.

How had it happened? I'd only looked away for two seconds, three max.

Chapter Two

Cara

30 June, Tweedshaugh

I texted Si between periods, asked him to pick me up a pair of drumsticks and a decent card for Dad's birthday. Si always found a funny one. I'd already wrapped the garden shears – we always went halvers. Si normally texted right back a thumbs up or something. Maybe he was in the orthodontist's chair right that moment, having his jaw drilled into.

Double Psychology then double English – my best morning of the week. A text buzzed in as I put my phone back in my bag. It was Mel, about a girls' night out on Friday.

Since it was the last day of term, Miss Fernandez had us in pairs doing a collaborative summer poem. 'Have a bit of fun,' she said. 'Be free with it. Don't worry about fancy language or ideas. Just express how you're feeling inside.' She thumped her heart. The boys stared at her chest, the repulsive gits. Miss Fernandez was in a league of one.

Ava leaned over and shared the now-infamous legend of Roger Ferny's trip to Snipz, where he thought he was booked in for a Turkish shave. Shell and I had already heard it but it didn't matter – we drilled down into whether he'd booked it himself or whether it was a set-up by Dougie.

We were still wetting ourselves about Roger's back-sack-and-crack story when a knock sounded. The door opened and a face appeared in the gap – the depute head, Mr Thomas. I pressed the four fingers of my left hand tight on my desk, glanced at Shell, concentrated back on the desk, then ripped my right hand upward, in mock wax-strip removal. Shell let out a snort and buried her face in her desk, her shoulders quaking beneath her sheet of black hair. I reached over and poked her, and she sniffed and turned her face to mine. She dabbed at the tears with the backs of her hands.

That was when I noticed the eyes of the whole class on me. Even Piotr – beautiful, mysterious Piotr – with his big, brown soulful eyes. I looked up at Miss Fernandez and Mr Thomas.

'Cara?' said Mr Thomas.

Shit.

Shit-shit-shit, he knows about the glitter bomb.

I glanced at Shell. She gave me a one-sided grimace.

I looked back at Mr Thomas. 'Sorry?' I said.

'Could you come with me please, Cara?'

'Wohhhhhhh!' started up the slow-rising chant. I looked around at Dougie – always the ringleader – and narrowed my eyes at him, but he just kicked the back of my chair and laughed. I started to laugh, too. Surely, I couldn't be in too much shit for something as tame as glitter?

My cheeks blazed anyway as I fumbled to shove all my stuff in my bag.

Shell reached out to grab my arm. 'You OK, hon?' she whispered.

I shrugged. 'Maybe he's just after a crack wax,' I whispered back. Shell mimicked a retch. 'See you later. See you in the park?'

She flashed me her best bright smile.

Mr Thomas pulled the door closed behind us and Miss Fernandez's disappearing face imprinted on my mind, her head tipped to the side, eyes like Bambi's.

'Cara,' he said, all awkward. Me and Mr Thomas were besties, ever since my first day of S2 – the day he'd started. He'd seen me in the corridor outside the girls' toilets, and it was class time so it must have looked like I was skiving, but he didn't ask why I wasn't in class; he just pointed two fingers at his own eyes and then pointed one finger at me and grinned. From that day on, I'd always got on with Mr Thomas.

I looked at him. 'What's going on, Mr Thomas?'

He glanced at my face then looked away. 'Come on,' he said. 'Your mum rang the office and asked us to send you home. She's sent a taxi to pick you up.'

My stomach lurched.

What?

Nothing to do with glitter bombs?

'A taxi?'

Since when had Mum ever ordered me a taxi?

'Yes,' said Mr Thomas. 'I'm not sure . . .' His voice tailed off.

A wave of stone-cold dread swept over me, making a whooshing sound in my ears.

'Why? What's happened?'

What's she doing at home?

Mr Thomas gestured for me to go ahead of him down the

stairs. 'I've just been asked to send you home.' He hesitated. 'Your mum wants you home.'

'You don't know why, or you're not telling me why?' I asked.

'I'm sorry, Cara.' We were now at the office. Laura the nice receptionist clocked me and put her hand to her mouth. Even Sal, the psycho receptionist, blanched and resisted the usual sarky comment about my skirt belonging in the accessories department. Gordon the janny was there, too, and the other depute, Mr Mancini, and the headteacher's secretary, Mrs Patel, eyebrows steepled.

I scanned the faces. Why were they all looking so freaked out, so – *solemn* was the word that hovered at the edges of my awareness? There was never that number of people in the office. It was like walking in on some Greek tragedy, before they all get turned to stone. Some weird urge to laugh came over me and I concentrated on stopping myself. Mr Thomas coughed and ushered me out the double doors.

'Hi, Cara!' Mrs Curran, the PE teacher, said in her bouncy voice, slamming her car boot, engulfed by two big sports bags and a bag of basketballs. She saw Mr Thomas and the smile faded from her eyes – a conversation without words. A giant ice-cream scoop sliced through the air and gouged out my insides.

'Hello, Mrs Curran.' I kept my voice steady.

Mr Thomas slid by me like a car overtaking on the inside. The taxi was right there, humming away. He opened the door.

'Wait!' Shell came barrelling out the doors – a sergeant major in the body of a five-foot lassie.

'Milne?' called the driver.

'Yes,' said Mr Thomas into the cab.

'I'll come with you,' he said.

'It's OK,' I said. 'You don't need to.'

'I'll – go,' said Shell, to Mr Thomas, between breaths. She doubled over.

Mr Thomas considered her offer.

'OK,' he said. 'That's probably a better idea. I'll sign you out and ring your mum. Here—' He reached into his chest pocket and pulled out a tenner. Shell plucked it from his hand, giving a thumbs up instead of having to speak. She stepped into the taxi and tugged me in. Mr Thomas pushed the door closed and we pulled away. I saw him in the wing mirror, his hand still outstretched like he'd been frozen in time.

We sat in silence down the hill and along the high street, Shell's breathing slowing.

I turned my body ninety degrees to face Shell.

'I'm scared it's something really bad,' I said.

'Oh, hon.' She squeezed my hand. 'What did Mr Thomas say?'

'He just said Mum had sent a taxi to take me home.'

Shell gulped. 'Miss Fernandez seemed a bit . . .' She swallowed the thought then let out the breath she'd been holding. When you read about people looking 'drawn', that was it. Her cheeks and mouth were pulled tight by invisible threads. I imagined she was pale under the foundation. But mostly it was the eyes, under that make-up. They were wider, whiter, and if I wasn't mistaken, fucking terrified.

She leaned into me, squeezing harder on my hand. 'You've no idea what it's about?'

'No idea at all,' I said, searching the taxi ceiling for answers.

'I don't know, I hope it's just . . . just . . . something not . . . well, something not, like, really bad. I'm not helping, am I?'

'It could be anything.' My heart pounded. It was myself I was trying to reassure, and Shell knew it.

'Yeah, course. I'm just being silly.' She smiled, her lips pressed together.

Think of reasons why Mum would be at home.

Had someone—?

No. Good reasons.

Papa? Gran or Gramps? Gramps couldn't have had another heart attack – he'd had the all-clear for years. Cancer, maybe? I dreaded that one. Did Mum have cancer? Dad? Had our house burned down? I banished these thoughts from my head. Was I being self-indulgent, imagining these tragedies?

Good reasons. She's bought me a car as a surprise for working so hard for my exams. She's . . . She's won a million pounds in a prize draw – no, a luxury villa in Portugal – and couldn't wait to tell me.

No new texts.

No reply from Si.

Stop being a fanny. Maybe . . . maybe Mum had taken the afternoon off. Maybe some distant rellie had called in and wanted to see me before they left.

I rang home then cancelled it.

I rang Si – needed to warn him. It went straight to voicemail. Had they sent a taxi for him, too?

Shell swallowed and looked at my right eye, then my left, and back to my right. She was Snow White with a perma-tan.

'I'm just being silly,' she said again.

I didn't have time to think or talk, because the taxi pulled into our street. A police car was parked outside our house.

My body stiffened. Shell gasped and clutched my arm. She covered her mouth with the other hand and looked at me.

'Oh my God,' I said. 'Oh my God, oh my God, oh my God.' An incantation to keep calm. I gripped the leather seat.

We've been burgled, that's all.

'Number eighteen – this one here?' said the taxi driver, then registered all was not right. He looked round at me, then at the house. He waved his hand and shook his head when Shell thrust the tenner at him.

We tumbled out and Shell slammed the door.

'Wait there,' she yelled through the window to the driver.

She turned to face me and gripped me by the shoulders.

'Breathe,' she said.

I concentrated on breathing in.

I fixed on Shell's hairline, paused there, not wanting to look at the house.

Maybe Si had done something stupid.

I had to know, but part of me wanted to hold on to this Cara, this Cara whose world was happy and normal, this Cara before I learned whatever was the awful piece of news that was waiting for me. I closed my eyes, breathed in, held it a moment before I released the breath and opened my eyes.

To my left, Mrs Duke from next door retreated inside her house.

'D'you want me to come in?' Shell asked.

'No. Get back to school. Thanks m'love.' We hugged, an urgent hug. I hiccupped and we both laughed. My voice cracked. 'You're the best.'

I pulled away, sucked in one more breath, turned from her and placed one foot in front of the other on the gravel.

I stopped dead in the middle of the drive and looked up at the house. The shapes of Mum and Dad were silhouetted in the kitchen, slumped in a hug, the luminous yellow of a police officer further back in the room. It wasn't Dad, then. Cold sweat lined my armpits. Silence crowded into my skull. Then a car revving, the gear changes. My breathing. Short, shallow breaths. The urge to scream presented itself, but I controlled it. Dread branched inside me.

Mum looked through the window, straightened up to come to the door, her fingers splayed across her mouth, then pulled her hands away as her mouth burst open. Dad's arms flailed.

I forced my feet forwards.

The door opened, as though through a will of its own, and Mum and Dad were there, Dad a step behind Mum. My stomach lurched again, pole-vaulting into my chest.

I stared at them.

I dry-retched. I was a deep freeze.

'Tell me nobody's died,' I said.

Mum tried to speak but she was too choked up. Dad let out a seismic sob. I looked at them both, reached out.

It can't be.

It has to be.

No. Please, no.

'Who is it?' Terror gripped every cell in my body.

She held it together for a second.

'It's Si,' she said. 'He was crossing the road—'

I vomited over Dad's prize dahlia, its single bud bowed.

'Not—?' I said, a thin croak.

A microscopic nod from Dad, and I stepped back, gasping for air.

'No,' I yelled. 'No, no, no, no, no. Si. Mum. Dad.'

'Hit by a car. We've to—' A wail burst out instead of words.

She put her hands on her head, then thrashed her arms like someone drowning.

Dad had to finish her sentence. 'It's him. They have his wallet, his bus pass, his phone. We've to identify him – at the mortuary,' he said, his face grey and grim; every word an effort. He looked me in the eye once he had the last word out. Mortuary.

'No,' I said.

I launched myself towards them and we crumpled to the hall floor. My head was a jumble of sounds and images. Then, like a zoom lens, it crashed and crowded into focus.

My brother was dead.

Chapter Three

Nathan

30 June, Edinburgh

The taxi turned into our street, slowed to a stop at the kerb outside our drive. The air rolled towards me like the crest of a wave. I didn't want to get out.

The ground swayed. Mum, sunglasses forming a groove in her short, wavy hair, took me by the arm and led me into the kitchen. She dropped her handbag like it was weighed down with lead and watched me. I slumped into one of the kitchen chairs.

My World's Greatest Son mug was still on the table, the apples on the tablecloth every bit as shiny and red. I stared at the clementine crowning the mound in the fruit bowl. How could it sit there and shine? I stared at the rubber plant in the corner, beside the fridge. Mimi sauntered in, arched her back, rubbed her side against my leg. She closed her eyes and purred, then turned and stared at me, her ears shifting upward.

Mum just sat there, her water-blue eyes misted and puffy, her mouth pressed into a line. Damian passed me on the stairs – still in his PJs. He spun round, following me with his eyes. I had the longest, hottest shower. My knees buckled and I crumbled to the shower floor, racked with sobs, then crawled out. *Fuck fuck fuck fuck fuck fuck fuck.*

The walls pulsed and the floor swayed as I felt my way from the bathroom to my bedroom. Everything was as I'd left it – the covers flung back on my bed, my alarm clock sitting there, flashing away. Seven hours since I'd last seen them. Mimi jumped off the bed and slunk away.

Mum's voice edged up from downstairs, speaking in low tones to Damian. I didn't want to hear their conversation. Couldn't face eating, either. Food: giver of life.

I sat on my bed, listened to my tunes, focused on the rhythms and waves, the patterns they made in my head. I blinked. *Wide eyes – mouth open in a scream – head arcing back.* My teeth chattered and I blinked up at the ceiling. *Solitary earbud in a crimson lake.* Squeezed my eyes tight. *Earbud.* Stared at the ceiling. Tried not to blink.

Thud. I woke up at 11 p.m., roaring, back at the moment of impact. *Scarlet smear . . . lips turning blue.* My heart drummed. 'Starlight' played, the keys loud and tinny on my speaker. I hit stop. I took off my jeans and T-shirt, soaked with sweat, hurled them at the door and collapsed back onto my bed. Mum must have put my duvet over me. Peach light edged round my curtains – the afterglow from the setting sun mixed with streetlights. I shivered and hugged myself into a ball, like a foetus.

The boy was dead.

Dead.

On the edge of sleep, my mind threw up image after image on widescreen: a blur of motion, the boy's fine features, his wide-open eyes looking right at me, his white hand, the girl on the bus, traffic lights, the solicitor's sneer, his shiny shoes – all these images swimming around.

Mum came to check on me.

'My baby,' she said, and stroked my cheek. I closed my eyes, pulled myself into a tighter ball, shut her out. But it didn't get dark – not properly. I needed dark.

3.26 a.m. The new day nudged its way round the curtain.

An empty bed, somewhere.

I rubbed at my eyes, digging into the sockets.

Who are you? Where were you going? Why were you there?

I hid under my duvet, a hermit crab in its shell.

'Nathan, love? Can I come in?'

I sobbed into my pillow, thumped my fist on my mattress, let out a feral roar.

Barely toasted toast smeared with butter and cut into triangles appeared on a tray at my door. I gulped it down and crawled back into my shell.

Bing bong! A police car was parked in our drive. My blood ran cold – yep, cliché, but that's what it felt like. Glacial streams trickled through my veins. I yanked on jeans and a black T-shirt. It was two new officers – a bald guy with a big chin and a woman officer pushing six foot – piloting some intervention-support thing for offenders and offering to refer me for trauma counselling. *No thanks.*

I pictured a Venn diagram with overlapping circles for offenders and me.

The 'victim's' name was Simon Paterson, they told me. *Victim.* Tiny, invisible needles – thousands of them – pressed into my skin.

The fact he had a name made it worse. My teeth chattered again – weird. I kept apologizing. They said to expect a letter from the Crown, charging me with causing death by dangerous driving, and Mum wouldn't be getting her car back for a while. Me and Mum looked at each other – I was pretty sure neither of us wanted to see that car ever again. They left, and Mum walked me back upstairs like a zombie, sat me down on my bed. She kneeled on my bedroom floor, held my hands in hers.

'Love, we need to talk,' she said.

I blinked at the carpet, shook my head. She chewed her cheek, sighed, ruffled my hair, and pulled the door behind her.

He was a 'popular' thirteen-year-old from Drumleith. *Drumleith? Out in the country?* Going into second year? Not any more.

Simon Paterson, what were you doing?

I knew what he was doing – crossing the road, at a pedestrian crossing, so the police said. That bit still hadn't registered.

I checked social media on my old phone with the cracked screen. Some nutjob messages from people – trolls? – one saying I was a stupid fuck who deserved to die. I deleted my accounts – wasn't big on posting anyway. Couldn't bring myself to Google him.

A knock at my bedroom door. A pause. Another knock.

What day was it?

'Nathan?' It was Damian, in some sort of forced whisper. 'Let me in, would you?' He shoved the door.

I lay there, deciding. I kicked the beanbag and stuff out the way – my homemade blockade. He tumbled in, all gangly legs in black joggers and a grey T-shirt.

'You need to talk about it,' he said. 'You can't stay in your room. You need to do something. It's driving Mum nuts.'

'I don't want to talk about it.'

'Nathan, she just put a bowl of cat food in front of me.'

'She did?'

'Yup.'

There was a big, fat silence.

'OK, I get it, Damo.'

'You need to talk to someone.'

'Thanks for the advice.'

'I'm not trying to be . . . I just—'

'I don't want to talk about it.'

He flicked his eyes upward, blew out through his mouth and shut the door.

He was right, though. I couldn't stay cocooned in my bedroom for ever. Had to get up, if only to shower. I stared at my face in the bathroom mirror. Dark circles, puffiness. A smell of old sweat. My gaze dropped to the urchin that guarded Mum's jar of shells on the window shelf.

Thursday. One week – a whole week – only a week. Mum knocked on my bedroom door and sat on my bed. I wasn't up for talking. 'At least let me hug you,' she said.

An hour or two later she slid something under my door. An A4 envelope and, on top of the envelope, a postcard. I picked up the postcard. A cartoon frog sat cross-legged on a lily pad, its hands resting on its knees, its eyes closed in meditation. Another frog arm reached in from the side, holding out a mug, which Zen frog seemed oblivious to. I turned it over.

I LOVE YOU, NATHY.
YOU'RE A GOOD BOY.
Mum xx

The envelope was white and official-looking. It trembled in my hand. A lion with a crown sat holding a sword and some fancy stick thing, beside the words: 'Crown Office & Procurator Fiscal Service'.

I stared at it a long time, coldness wrapping around me. The lion had an impressive mane and looked like the sort of lion you wouldn't mess with. I opened it. All my details, unambiguous in Times New Roman, stared back at me from the white sheet: my full name, date of birth, address, and the charge in bold: causing death by dangerous driving on 30 June, with a summons to the Sheriff Court. My guts turned to mush and I started to sob.

'You all right, man?' A text from Scotty, like he was some sort of mind reader. He'd gone and buggered off for a week to Mull with his mum, hadn't he. I tried to tap out an answer but deleted it a few times then gave up. What words were there?

Mum came with me the to the Sheriff Court the following morning. The waiting room seats had hard plasticky cushions and creaked when you moved. The 'No Smoking' signs on the walls hadn't stopped whoever had made a pattern of cigarette burns along the left armrest of my chair. As if on cue, the man next to me coughed a spluttery cough that smelt of stale cigarettes. I leaned my elbows on my knees, cupping my hands over my nose and mouth. I snatched a look around, taking in the woman with the pink hair, chewing gum, a parade of piercings like staccato dots down her ear and along her nostril, raising her eyebrows, silently telling me to fuck off and mind my own business.

Mum ushered me into the courtroom. I hadn't heard my name being called. I was shaking, but it took all of two minutes.

'Not guilty,' I said, when the sheriff asked my plea, although the 'Not' came out so weak it sounded like I'd said, 'Guilty'. I was just doing what I was told. I pictured Pinstripe Suit. He hadn't asked if I thought I was guilty or not. He'd told me: all you need to do is confirm your identity and plead 'not guilty'.

Guilty. Guilty. Guilty.

The sheriff said she was committing me for trial. February, probably. I sat there, scared to breathe.

February? Seven months?

'You can go now,' she said, a tiny woman with short grey hair. She'd called me Ross. Ross Nathan Blake, same as the charge letter. Mum had settled on Nathan by the time I was four weeks old – 'You just seemed more of a Nathan than a Ross,' she would say. I'd hated it at school – hated having to explain to new teachers in front of the class that I was Nathan, that I never used Ross. I can't believe something so pathetic used to bother me.

Scotty was sitting on the doorstep when we got back, red and white from sunburn, a burgundy baseball cap hiding his big woolly head. If anyone looked like a farmer, it was Scotty – big, open face; big, friendly features; brown eyes; bushy, arched eyebrows like how a kid would draw them.

'How was Mull?'

'Sunny,' he said. 'Check out my tan lines.' He pulled up the sleeve of his T-shirt.

I shielded my eyes from the dazzling whiteness of his shoulder. 'Nice.'

'It's turning brown.'

'That is nowhere close to brown. That is pure pink.' Man, was it good to see him. The tight coil of my neck loosened – by, like, a trillionth of a Pascal. 'Why are you wearing hot pants, Scotty?'

'Just cos you huvnae got the legs for them. Lassies love rugby shorts. I'll be beating them off with a stick. "Form an orderly queue."' He elbowed my arm.

We walked round to his house. A massive invisible ball hung in the air between us but we both pretended it wasn't there. We played games on his tablet, played basketball in his garage, taking turns at shooting. It was 32–4 to Scotty and he let me get a basket – didn't try to defend it. My mind wasn't there. He looked at me. I was cold as ice, like in the Foreigner song.

'You all right?' he said. I nodded, looking at the hoop. He didn't push it, didn't ask anything else; understood I wasn't ready. Thank God for mates.

He made us cheese and pickle toasties for lunch and talked about getting a summer job. He was thinking of applying for a plumbing apprenticeship. Go for it, I said. When his mum reversed through the gate, I looked at him, left through the back door. I couldn't face his mum – didn't need to tell Scotty why.

Cutting down the wee lane to the side of the cinema, a smiling face jumped out at me from the street vendor's stall. Grey eyes, shining out from the front page of the *Evening News*. I stopped dead.

RIP My Beautiful Angel: exclusive interview with tragic teen's mum. The solidness of the text struck me between the eyes and the words choked me. I glanced up at the vendor. He didn't have many teeth, and the ones he had were the colour of black tea. In Chemistry, we once got a tooth and left it in a glass of Coke and the next morning it had gone all rank and discoloured. The vendor fished out change for a customer from the cloth pocket of his belly bag. The thin man in the dark grey suit waved his hand in impatience.

I handed over my pound.

I couldn't help locking eyes with the face in the centre of the page for a moment. Underneath: *continued on page 2*. I flicked over. Another picture: the boy, in white shirt and green tie, holding up a violin and bow, his sleeves rolled up. I closed the paper, scanned the edges of the front page. *Announcements, page 36*, it said, at the bottom right-hand corner. I flipped over to the back page, leafed in from the end until I found page 36.

Had to find out about the funeral, force myself to go and watch, face up to what I'd done. I read the words, but my brain couldn't make the connection that this was the boy on the road. The service was to be in Drumleith on Monday. Three days' time.

Is it right for me to go?

Is it wrong for me to go?

Shouldn't I be there to pay my respects when he's laid to rest?

I'd never seen a burial. The only funeral I'd been to was my granddad's, and it was a cremation. The whole idea of going up in flames didn't seem right to me. Feed the worms, that was what I planned to do, one day.

I didn't suppose Simon Paterson had planned to feed the worms at the age of thirteen.

Chapter Four

Cara

11 July, Drumleith

It was just us there. Mum, Dad and me – we all gave each other our own private time with him to talk to him and say goodbye. Because it had been eleven days and because of his injuries, they'd embalmed him. The undertaker said to take as long as we liked, to say anything we wished we'd said, or to just be with him if we couldn't say anything.

I went first. There was a chair beside the open coffin, at the far side. I stood at the near side, took a deep breath, and stared at him – this white, lifeless thing that looked like my brother but didn't look like my brother. Not really. Because Si was so lively and spirited. I'd never seen him still before. Of course I hadn't. He hadn't ever been dead before.

He wore a white T-shirt and his thin navy-blue jumper that really suited him, and his favourite jeans – he'd saved up for them and had worn them almost every Friday, Saturday and Sunday in the month he'd had them. I'd picked out the jeans and jumper; Mum had picked out pants and socks. We'd folded them into an M&S bag and given them to the undertaker.

A tear plopped off the end of my nose and onto his jumper. I wiped it off. I leaned forwards and kissed his forehead. Stone cold, waxy.

'I love you, little brother,' I said, and a great big hand reached in and snatched my heart. I tried to say, 'Goodbye' – my mouth formed the shape – but it caught in my throat. I backed out of the room, my hand over my mouth. Everything blurred and my soul welled.

Dad went in next. Mum and I sat in silence and held hands in the waiting room. Dad was only five minutes. The door opened, and I'd never seen him so pale. Mum got up and they hugged. Dad broke down, racked with convulsions. He held the door for Mum and closed it behind her. He paced four steps to the right, four steps to the left, four to the right, four to the left. He focused on the carpet and chewed his lower lip as he walked. I counted 228 sets of four steps, always leading with his right foot, always swivelling clockwise.

For some reason my old PE teacher came into my mind, teaching us the Canadian Barn Dance for our Scottish country-dance module. All those steps and turns.

Dad lifted his heavy head and glanced at me, the muscle at the back of his jaw pulsing, and looked back down. He came to a halt and leaned his forehead against the door.

I held it together, then got up and went to the loo. I rested my head in my hands and rubbed my cheeks; sucked in air through my nose, blew out through my mouth. When I came out, Mum was there.

She later said it was the absolute worst moment of her life, saying goodbye to her son. She wouldn't wish that on her worst enemy, she said. Mum doesn't have any enemies.

The hearse rolled into view, and that's when I went to pieces. Hearses are for old people.

We sat in the limousine – Mum in the middle, me on the left, Dad on the right. None of us spoke. Families lined the street, in suits and smart jackets. I dabbed at my eyes. Mum took in a huge juddery breath and blew her nose. I squeezed her clammy hand. Outside, it was sunshine, long grasses and blue sky, with storm clouds brewing. A red tractor picked up a golden bale and spun black plastic around it with an attachment, the plastic glinting white in the sun. It was like a spider wrapping a fly. The tractor speeded towards another bale. Rounding the bend into Drumleith, a stream of people in black and grey stretched up the high street, and clusters of kids in our black, white and green school uniform – mostly S1s, just started S2.

The undertaker pulled up outside the church and a camera flashed. The media. That was the deal – one coffin and hearse shot and they'd leave us alone. The minister took a step towards us, his mouth a line. The undertaker opened the door, and I took in a huge breath.

I squeezed Mum's hand again. 'We can do this.' My voice was drugged-sounding. We climbed out and the minister placed a hand on Mum's arm. Dad had his arm clamped round her shoulder.

I surveyed the church. We dragged ourselves inside, a muted black bubble around us.

The place was packed. I caught a couple of people's eyes – friends of Mum and Dad's from when we lived at Bellevue Park, and my schoolfriends – but then I focused on getting to the front.

What Si would have called the 'gooch' tones of Vulfpeck reverberated around the arched church. I closed my eyes and he was there, stretched out on the sofa clutching a cushion, smiling a cheeky smile at me like he was up to something and I was in on the secret – like he was amused he was playing funk in a church.

I gripped Mum's hand during the service, propped her up, stared at the programme, at the picture of Si. My lovely Sibo – I'd called him Sibo since I could remember. The dates of his birth and death slammed me in the eyes and I couldn't let them in. There's supposed to be eighty years or something between the first and last dates, not consecutive decades. Mum blew her nose and I squeezed my eyes tight.

The minister described Si as a 'gifted young musician' and a 'bright young spark full of talent and promise' and said Christ Jesus had prepared a place for him in God's holy city of heaven and that Si had been saved unto everlasting life. I'd argued for a humanist service since none of us are religious, but Mum and Dad decided it would be easier to do it this way. Auntie Carol got up – I don't know how – and told the story about Si falling asleep mid-sentence, face-planting into his baked potato when he was three. And another story about him refusing to leave a snail he'd stepped on until I'd glued a bit of eggshell to fix its shell then painted over it with Peach Sunrise nail varnish, and he'd ceremoniously placed it on the juiciest leaf he could find. A pause stretched when the words didn't come, and she took a few tight breaths and blew her nose. She talked about the 'kind, funny' boy who lit up our lives, and the whole place was so quiet I could hear the beating of my heart in my ears. Auntie Carol came to sit back down, and Mum reached out and pulled her in for a collapsed, half-seated hug, both of them gasping and sobbing. Their grief echoed around the vaulted stone ceiling.

The organ started up and all I could hear was sobbing from everywhere – the whole church a hysterical mess. A hand, rubbing my back. Shell – wedged in beside my cousins.

We stood at the front of a massive queue of people leaving the church. It was like a medieval torture, for me and for them. They said the same things, over and over. One guy – some workmate of Dad's – launched into a story about when his gran died and I wanted to scream at him: 'He was my little brother. Don't you get it? There's no comparison.'

Mr Thomas came up and put his arm round me and didn't say a thing. I just hugged him back and sobbed. He gave me what I really needed: a proper hug, with no words.

'Thank you,' I said.

Si's friends sort of understood, too. Lewis, Nish and Ciaran. And his swimming-club mates floated past in a unit, semi-hysterical – they were in too much of a state to say anything coherent.

Last out, Shell pulled me into a bear hug that was more like a headlock, then her mum, too – three of us knitted together into a single sobbing mass.

Like the last eleven days, the rest was a surreal blur. Walking along the path to a newly dug hole in the earth – how did we manage to walk?

That wasn't my brother they lowered into the ground. It wasn't. He was gone. He was in my heart, right there, the same as ever. And at the same time, he was gone. Whatever he was, that box was just his body.

The world was empty without him. Bare, barren, cold, dark. But mostly quiet.

I stood by my brother's graveside and didn't hear a word that was said.

A dog barked in the woods and the air felt heavy. Everyone left except family. Gran and Gramps had shrunk, and Papa had lost the power to walk in the last eleven days – Uncle Mick pushed him in a chair. My cousins hung back, out of place in their dark suits.

Then it was Mum, Dad and me. We stood over the coffin to say our final goodbyes.

Dad stood there, grey and hunched like the Grim Reaper, but also helpless and vulnerable-looking – a terrified child that had never been there before and didn't know what to do. Mum held on to both of us to stay upright.

Broken, that's what they were.

I crouched down. 'I love you for ever, Sibo.' My voice wobbled. I kissed my fingers and reached towards his coffin.

I looked up to the hill and a breeze shivered through the trees. Was somebody there, shoulders slumped, sitting on the ground? I blinked, and there was nothing, but an imprint remained in my vision, a figure and trees white against a black sky. Mum and Dad hobbled out to the front of the church – a few steps and I'd caught them. We rounded the corner and the heavens emptied.

A handful of people were still there, sheltering under umbrellas.

I managed to hold conversations, but it wasn't my truth. It was a means to get through those seconds, those minutes, those hours, that mounted up, insurmountable, before me, unbearable but to be borne.

That was my truth.

Chapter Five

Nathan

11 July, Edinburgh
Three days became no days. I finally got to sleep about 4 a.m. and woke at seven, feeling sick. Mum offered to make scrambled eggs – anything I wanted – but all I could stomach was tea. It was the first time I'd sat with them at breakfast since the last day of term. Mum kissed me on the cheek, Damo left to play football, and she headed off to work.

I checked page 36 again. *July 11.* I checked my watch. *Mon 11.*

I wandered through the Meadows to Lauriston Place, out from the bright day to the cool dark of the Blood Donor Centre – my second donation but this time was different. Last time was a laugh, all lined up outside the blood bus when it came to our school, Ms Flanagan, our head of year, saying we were the good guys; Zeno showing off his one-armed press-ups on the pavement then passing out on the bed inside the bus when he saw the bag fill – according to AJ anyway. This time I was on my own and it felt like a pilgrimage: the need was mine, to lose my blood, have it taken out of me, give it away; to feel a fraction – a tiny fraction – less killer, and a fraction more saviour.

I watched as the blood left my body, travelled along a tube, filled a bag. O negative – the universal donor. Simon Paterson must have had a blood group. I wondered which one; if it was the same as mine; wanted to tell them to pump it straight into him, give him a couple of shocks, bring him back to life. He'd get up, a bit dazed, pick up his smashed phone, look about, and continue across the street. I gulped down the thought with a carton of orange juice and a Tunnock's Tea Cake.

Upstairs on the bus, I found a window seat. We headed out past Cameron Toll, Arthur's Seat a big lion to my left, and crossed beneath the city bypass – an artery, streaming with blood cells and platelets.

Town became country. Gold-green fields stretched into rolling hills, old furrows leading like steps to blocks of forest. Sheep and cows dotted the land and dark green barns squatted like sentries.

20 DRUMLEITH Please drive carefully. I pressed against the window, saw a hearse up ahead, hordes of people in black lining the street. My chest seized and my hand gripped my inhaler.

I pinged the bell, darted along a side street towards the back of the church. Halfway up, the hill turned from scrub into woodland. I collapsed at the edge of the wood on the pine needle-covered ground and took a load of puffs of my inhaler. All around were firs, spruces, Scots pines, tall and spindly where they were packed close together. Something from primary school came to me: Mr Davidson, my P6 teacher, showing us how to tell the difference between pine, larch and spruce by their needles. I could see his face, hear his voice. *Spruces are single, pines are in pairs, larches are lots.*

The face of Mr Davidson morphed into *his* face through the windscreen, his eyes cartoon-wide, the pupils big and black. I waited, breathed, let him in, didn't try to fight it this time; couldn't keep pushing him away. His nose was fine, sculpted; his cheekbones and jaw still boyish. Sounds crowded in from near, then far: birds calling, cars, motorbikes accelerating, drilling and at least three different lawnmowers. They drifted past me like passing clouds.

Eventually they came, bearing the coffin, a never-ending trail of mourners. The church coughed them out onto the path, in twos and ones: a lead-footed procession. The schoolkids stuck together in clumps of black, white and green – they must have been asked to wear uniform, even though it was the summer holidays. I watched them from the hillside where I sat, hands clasped in front of me, knees resting inside my elbows. The solemn tones of the minister's voice carried up to me, but not the words. I couldn't make out the mourners' faces – thank God.

Six figures lowered the coffin into the ground. A couple of people stepped forward and threw on flowers.

A dog, barking, close. I flinched and shrank back into the ground.

'Freddy, wheesht!' came the male voice of the owner. 'Freddy, no!'

It was a terrier, barking and barking. *Stop barking. Please stop. Shut up would you.*

A ripple went through the mourners, a handful of faces

turned towards the hill, towards me. The owner walked past, dog now on lead.

Thank fuck they're gone. My chest was a knot.

I watched the final blurred huddle of a man, a woman, a girl – the family, presumably. I couldn't watch any longer.

I lay back, closed my eyes, imagined it was me in the coffin.

Alone, in the cold, cold earth.

I was motionless. Except for my chest, my breath, continuing, without my conscious will.

I sat up. The man and woman turned and walked away, every step heavy looking. The girl – green jacket and blonde hair – squatted down once more, then stood and looked up at the woods, right at me, it seemed. I looked back at her, but she turned and followed the couple – her parents, I assumed. She paused once more, taking one more look back at the grave, then disappeared out of sight beyond the red sandstone corner of the church.

His sister? Did she see me?

Bouquets of flowers formed a mound at one end of the grave.

I stood up. Now it was just him in the ground and me in the woods. The distance from the sliced soil to the hill felt like nothing.

'I'm so sorry, mate,' I said, my voice cracking. I exhaled slowly, towards the sky, gazed up. I sank back again into the earth, watched the sky, the puffy clouds sauntering, carefree. The pine needle piercing my neck felt good, almost. Punishment.

Would he still be alive if I'd been going slower?

Why didn't I get the bus?

Squirrels scampered high up in the trees. A small, round bird with greenish wings rustled its way out from under a bush. The volume of birds crescendoed until they were calling at me, accusing. I lay there, ignoring the ping of my old phone – hadn't heard that in a while. I reached into my pocket and switched it off.

The sky turned grey, then deeper grey; the air thickened. With a rumble, the storm clouds burst. I let the water soak through my clothes. I was drenched in seconds. It pummelled my skin, then it was gone, clear, erased by a magic wand.

I stood up, my clothes heavy, the air now light, the scents of the wood come to life.

Ouch! Bramble bush. Thorns. Bending over, I caught a metallic whiff. A crimson rivulet trickled down my ankle, pooling on my sock. I rolled up my trousers, marched through more bramble bushes and patches of nettle. Cuts, scrapes and stings crisscrossed my legs. I stared at the latticework of scratches, traced one of the lines with my forefinger, surprised at the release flooding my chest. Cleansing; right.

I jolted awake as the bus juddered to a stop at South Clerk Street. I legged it down the stairs and out onto the street almost before the brakes had stopped hissing.

I opened the side door to the house, took off my shoes, pulled up my socks and rolled down my trousers so there was no sign of blood. If anyone on the bus had noticed, I hadn't noticed them.

The inside door flew open.

'Nathan, I've been worried sick.'

'Sorry, Mum.'

'Where were you? Look at you. You're drenched.'

Even Damian looked freaked out. My little brother, scared I'd done something else stupid.

'Where were you?' she repeated. 'Nathan?'

'I had to go,' I muttered.

'To his funeral? You went to the boy's funeral?'

On the sideboard sat the *Evening News*. Mimi rubbed her body against my leg and purred, her tail wrapping round my calf. It stung a little.

'Yes.'

Mum had no more words for me – just a quaking hug. A scared hug, with her head on my shoulder, not the comforting, all-embracing sort of hug she'd give me as a kid when she was bigger than me and had the power to melt my worries in her arms. Damo kicked the doorframe and darted away, his elbow hiding his face.

Any good the thorns had done was gone. What was I doing to Mum and Damo?

'Sorry, Mum, I just . . . I had to go,' I said, pulling away and looking at her.

'It's all right,' she said, in a whisper. 'I understand.' She pulled me back into her, ruffled my hair. 'It's OK.'

I didn't tell her: *No, it's not. It's never going to be OK.*

Chapter Six

Cara

11 July, Drumleith

My room was smaller and darker, the air thinner. I leaned against Si's doorframe and looked around his room, at all the signs of him – his big-cats poster, the phone hub he'd made in Techy, the orca he'd done in Art. His iPad sat square on his desk, plugged into its charger. I picked it up – 908756. His Geography project on water quality was open, and some kaleidoscopic art – orange, red, apple green and olive – he loved clashing colours. His swimming goggles stared out, forlorn, from the corner of his chair. I picked up his electric fiddle, unplugged it from his amp, hugged it, then put it back down on the stand he'd rigged up.

I pulled out my phone and read all his messages to me and mine to him, over and over until my eyes throbbed. I couldn't watch any video clips – not yet.

One-eyed Croc was still at the side of his sock drawer. I took him out and sat on Si's bed.

Silence pressed in around us.

Chapter Seven

Nathan

September, Edinburgh

Damian came in from football and slammed the door so hard it shook the house and bounced open again. Then he was in my room, shoving me in the chest, his face in mine, his so red and angry it didn't look like him. He was crying so hard he could barely breathe.

'I hate you,' he shouted. 'You've wrecked my life.' He shoved me and I fell back onto my bed.

I gave it five minutes then knocked softly on his door and went in. I spoke quietly. 'What happened?'

'Leave me alone!'

'But what happened?' I studied his face. No cuts, no bruises. 'I'm sorry, OK.' A wave of something heavy washed over me, and I saw little Damian in his T-rex onesie, crawling about the house after me, little Damian on his balance bike, teeny legs drumming to keep up with me, little Damian, halo of curls lit up by the sun, smiling at me.

'I said, leave me alone! They're right – you are a wanker. You're acting like you've done nothing wrong. Get out!'

Jesus.

'I'm sorry, wee bro.' I walked out, clicked the door behind me, went back into my room, slid down my closed door and sat with my legs out.

I got up on the thirtieth of September and my very first thought was: *three months.*

Three months since.

That's one season.

Would my life be measured in chunks of time – from the thirtieth of the month – from now on?

I opened the curtains. Daylight. A blackbird swooped down and plucked a scarlet berry from the rowan tree.

I had to get out. Started walking to Benny's Bites but found myself stalling at the bus stop heading south, out of town.

Déjà vu. Town became country. The rolling hills were a patchwork of green, gold, brown and purple. Country smells – manure and crops – wafted down the bus as the engine eased a note lower into what sounded like top gear.

The bus swung left in Tweedshaugh. Did I have the guts to go to Drumleith, to punish myself, to face up to the fact that he was rotting in a grave while I'd been swanning about all summer? To apologize to him, face to face, instead of hiding in the woods on a hillside? To force myself to acknowledge that he'd been in the ground all this time, and I'd still been breathing? I did not. Was that why I'd boarded that particular bus? I had no idea. I ran down the stairs and got off. It felt good to move my body. It had been stuck in a semi-comatose state – in my bedroom, with the curtains closed but the window wide open – for weeks. It was like my muscles were waking up and yawning and going, *Oh, yeah, is this what we're meant to be doing?*

I pushed the door and went into a café at the end of the High Street. I sat down and asked if they had Monster Energy or Red Bull but the waitress said they only did teas, coffees, hot chocolate and fancy Fentimans soft drinks. I ordered a cherry cola and a pot of Earl Grey. The waitress read back my order and looked at me like I was nuts.

What was I doing? This was the town where he went to school. I shivered, looking around at the dark wood seats. Maybe he'd been here. Maybe he'd sat in this very chair. His eyes flashed at me.

I pictured him – this bloody, blue zombie – walking in the door, sitting down opposite me.

Zombie boy: Why were you looking at your phone?
Me: What were you doing in town?
Zombie boy: I'm the dead one. Answer my question.
Me: I . . . I wasn't.
Zombie boy: [Waits, then laughs.] We both know you were.
Me: [Silence.]
Zombie boy: [Shakes head.] OK then, why are you blaming me?
Me: I'm not.
Zombie boy: You are. You keep asking, Simon Paterson, what were you doing?
Me: What were *you doing?*

Zombie boy: Seriously?
Me: [Shrugs.]
Zombie boy: I was crossing the road at a pedestrian crossing when some fucking idiot comes roaring from nowhere and, boom, I'm dead.
Me: Sorry.
Zombie boy: Sorry?
Me: What d'you want me to say?
Zombie boy: I want to know exactly how it happened.
Me: You could have been paying attention, instead of listening to your tunes.
Zombie boy: You are *joking.*
Me: You wandered across the road.
Zombie boy: I wandered across the road when the green man came on. Kind of essential detail. You'd make a good lawyer.
Me: Nobody else was crossing. You didn't wait—
Zombie boy: [Visibly vexed.] I waited for the green man.
Me: You did? [Frowns.]

But the apparition or whatever it was, was gone. Only his gaze – his eyes – lingered, like sunlight burned onto film. I looked about. The waitress – Moaning Myrtle – brought my tea and cherry cola. She placed them on the table like she was terrified the saucer and glass would smash on impact. She stood there and gave me this weird, twitchy look, then said in this tiny voice, 'Enjoy your drinks' – she emphasised the 's'. How long had she been watching me stare at the chair opposite me, being grilled by an invisible zombie?

I pinched the paper square attached by a string to my teabag, and dunked it in and out of the water, and breathed in, to force back the choking that had sprung to my chest, my nose, my eyes. I rubbed my hands over my face and thought of Mum – her voice when I called her at the police station; her face when I came back late after the funeral.

A bell tinkled and a girl walked in. Straight blonde hair. Cute. She had a fresh, natural look. Something about her open features and easy posture made her nice to look at – the sort of girl you'd be chuffed to take home to meet your mum – if you were in a position to be taking a girl home to meet your mum, that is. Her skin glowed. She looked sporty, too – her solid-blue jeans hugged her thighs, and she wore a cropped grey jacket.

She scanned the room and came to sit at the window seat next to my table. She dropped her head and breathed out, her shoulders sagging, then caught my eye, straightened up and smiled – a warm smile, not flirty or anything. She took off her jacket and slung her faded jade bag on the cushion. I liked her belt – lemon yellow with a surfy white flower imprint. A tiny silver fishbone necklace sat in the dip between her collarbones, and a yellow disc dangled below her chest. Her whole look was confident, fit and quirky, if a little tired.

She glanced up again and her eyes were big and open and grey-green – almost familiar – and her complexion was smooth and milky, with peach cheeks. A dimple formed on the left one.

I felt a kilo lighter, just looking at her – someone who knew nothing about me.

'Hi,' she said.

Chapter Eight

Cara

30 September, Tweedshaugh

The café smelled of summer holidays – air freshener that reminded me of coconut suntan lotion, although a tan was a laughable notion to Miss Whitey McWhite here. Paler than a moonlit boneyard and almost as interesting, I liked to think.

I found a seat by the window. Sunlight spilled on the wooden table, dripped down the table legs, warmed my skin.

Three months. *Three months*. How could that be?

I'd been in Physics and I must have been looking blank, staring into space, because Mr K's voice and face had come into focus, right there, asking if I was all right, his whole being an embodiment of sympathy. It was like little black squares getting smaller then sharpening into an image, then crystallizing into full-colour saturation. Sound arrived at the same time as the visuals, and I was back in the classroom. I'd blinked a couple of times, a small part of me fascinated that the world that had made no sense seconds earlier – that hadn't even registered in my consciousness – was now there. I half laughed at the irony of it, sitting in a Nat. 5 Physics class – I'd picked it because one of the modules was Space, and we weren't allowed to fill up our timetables with frees. Mr Kyriakopoulos – everyone, himself included, called him Mr K – had taught Si. Did I want to go home, he'd suggested? I'd walked out of school and down the road, noticing birds singing for the first time since June.

At home, Mum and Dad sat stiff at the kitchen table with the police liaison officer, going over the details of the accident, the driver and the case against him. Who was he, this bastard who'd killed my brother? I didn't want to know. Something dark and hateful formed inside my chest and I pushed it away. I couldn't face it: my misery threshold was at capacity, maxed out. Bitterness wouldn't bring back Si. Plus today, something about the birds and the spells of sun shining between clouds lifted my poor little soul a smidge. I'd take a smidge. I changed and headed back out. I passed the shopfronts and paused by a window. Inside, two diners holding soup spoons leaned in and said something to each other, then glanced out through the window at me. I crossed the road and stepped on the bus to Tweedshaugh.

Grief coiled round me, sometimes tightening until I could barely breathe; occasionally loosening its grip for a moment. You had to seize those moments and breathe. It was still there, snaking round me, but it was slackening to rest and digest. I had learned to accept the lull before my soul was squeezed and suffocated once more.

Of the scattering of square tables, mine was the only one with a cushioned bench against the wall. The rest had plain, hard chairs, the same dark wood as the tables. I sat side-on to the wall, rested my coat and bag on the bench. A giant, cheap-looking clock in the shape of a coffee cup announced it was five to three. There were no hour or minute markings, no numbers; just a cupcake at the quarter hours. The whole place was trying too hard to be retro. The oversized ceiling light had three bands – chocolate, orange, baby-pink – and each table had a rubbery salt-and-pepper-mill combo in orange and lime. Still, it was an improvement on before – all stale tartan carpets, chintzy cups and saucers and a tired smell. The new owners had rebranded it Em*pour*ium. I liked the font.

The café was empty except for one guy at the next table. A little older than me, messy hair, nice dress sense. Handsome, well-defined face. Solid, amazingly straight, perfectly tapered eyebrows – some girls would give anything for eyebrows like that. Nice, open features, though there was a trace of something in them. Tiredness? No, anxiety. Yes, he seemed troubled – I prided myself on the accuracy of my amateur psychoanalysis.

He caught my eye, smiled slightly. To him, I was just some girl and for that, I was thankful. A few minutes, I told myself; a few minutes' respite.

'Hi,' I said, and picked up the menu.

'Hi,' he said. His voice was deep. His eyelashes were long and dark, his eyes ocean-blue, his medium-short hair a mid to dark brown. Left parting – ever since starting in the salon, I couldn't help noticing hair. Must be like a dentist every time they meet someone, silently gauging your teeth – the wonky, crowded ones, the stained ones. I glanced at his mouth. Nice teeth: square and solid. He fixed on my eyes, started a slow, spreading smile.

The waitress – purple hair tied back in a ponytail – appeared at my table.

'A latte and a slice of tiffin, please,' I said. She noted down the order and shuffled off. *Lord, girl, believe in yourself.*

The coffee machine grumbled. I inhaled the scent of roasted hazelnuts and closed my eyes, enjoying the red-orange swirls that danced inside my head, a kaleidoscope of colour. I opened my eyes, aware of the gaze of the boy. I looked right at him. Was that a trace of mischief in his eyes?

'I'm Cara,' I said. 'So, what brings you to Tweedshaugh?'

He cleared his throat. 'Ach, just fancied getting out of Edinburgh for a few hours. Bit quieter out here.'

'It's busier at the weekend.' *How dire is my chat?* 'This place'll be heaving tomorrow. I've got a Saturday job at a hairdresser's – people stare in the window when they're queuing for the butcher's.'

'I bet they do.'

Is he flirting with me? Is he?

'Well?' I said.

'Well, what?'

'I'm Cara. And you would be?'

'What, if I could be anybody?' He considered. 'Batman's pretty cool. I could be him?'

'Then you wouldn't be here talking to me.'

He bobbed his head to the side. 'Good point.'

'You still haven't told me your name.' I closed my eyes, raised my chin and angled my face away from him.

He laughed. 'OK, you win. I'm Norbert.'

I sighed through my nose. 'You are not Norbert.'

'I'm Bruce,' said in the worst Australian accent imaginable.

'You are definitely *not* Bruce.'

'I'm Nathan.'

I studied his face like it was hanging up in a gallery, raised a brow.

'OK, Nathan,' I said. I turned the name around in my head and nodded. Yes, I liked it. 'But seriously, why would you want to be someone else? No matter how rubbish things got, I'd still want to be me.' It was true. Despite everything, I wouldn't want to stop being me.

He looked down at his cup, poured the last of his tea, kept his gaze low, something toying with his face. 'That's a good thing,' he said. He blinked his dark lashes, then the serious face broke into another smile. 'But living in a cave and having a butler to run about after me?' He looked diagonally up and appeared to ponder this. 'Yeah, reckon I could just about get used to that.'

'So, day off?' I said.

'Yeah.' He shifted in his seat. 'I've been working in a bar a couple of days a week, but it was only meant to be a summer job.'

'Which bar?'

'The Banshee, in town? Market Street.'

I rubbed my thumb over my pendant – a smooth, glass lemon slice on a leather cord that hung almost to my waist. He kept looking at it. 'You may continue.'

He was taking my grilling well. 'I finished sixth year in April. Well, with exams and a couple of days I went back in for – charities day, prizegiving – it was June, really—'

Seventeen, eighteen, then – a year above me. 'School, please?'

'Teviot's. Jeez, you should be a— I dunno, somebody who asks a lot of questions for a living.'

I nodded, to say again: you may continue.

'OK, so I haven't really worked out what I'm doing yet. I was thinking of taking a year out. Travelling, maybe – get jobs here and there – and apply for uni next year. Think I'll be hanging about here for a while, anyway.'

'Where d'you fancy going?' I asked.

'I don't know. I'm just . . . I'm not sure.'

His hunched shoulders and pinched eyebrows told me to change the subject. He picked at the side of his nail.

'Mercury's going to transit the sun tomorrow from eleven forty-two a.m. to seven-twelve p.m.,' I said, keeping my voice jaunty, holding onto this moment of relief from the soul constricting. 'It only happens thirteen or fourteen times a century.'

'Where in the sky do you look?'

'You look at that big bright thing that gives us light,' I said.

'Oh, yeah, duh. I meant Mercury, but you did say it would be transiting the sun.'

He stared into my eyes, like he could see right into my soul. Shell would have ripped me to shreds for thinking something so mushy. Actually – I would have ripped me to shreds. I shivered, still holding his gaze. His own eyes were deep and dark like a well. I rubbed the side of my neck.

'Except you don't look at the sun, obviously,' I said, my voice sounding like somebody else's. My ear popped. *Weird.* 'But I do have welder's goggles.'

The waitress brought my latte and tiffin on a cream-metal tray, together with a knife wrapped in a lime paper napkin.

I cut a triangle off the corner of the tiffin.

'Best tiffin in town,' I said.

'It certainly looks . . . most enjoyable,' he said.

Those eyebrows – seriously? So lush and strokable-looking. Must stop staring at them.

I glanced over at the waitress. She pretended she wasn't reading something on her phone.

'Where's my manners? I can cut you a piece?'

'Nah, it's OK,' he said. 'That thing is clearly giving you a lot of satisfaction.'

'It is indeed quite the most satisfying piece of tiffin to be had.' I choked on a chunk of digestive.

He laughed so hard he hinged at the waist.

'Sorry,' he said, sitting tall in his chair and sighing. 'Ah, it's good to laugh.' He rolled his shoulders and neck and rotated his wrists. 'So, what about you?'

'I've just started sixth year,' I said. He looked at his watch and scrunched up one side of his face. 'Half day on a Friday.'

'Of course,' he said, nodding.

'I'm thinking Psychology and French at uni. Glasgow or St Andrews.'

He pushed out his lower lip and nodded. 'Wow.'

I smiled – couldn't help it.

'What are you doing now, right now?' he said, his voice a little quieter, his eyes a little more serious.

'I would appear to be . . . talking to some guy in a café.'

Message to self: stop being such a tit.

'What you doing after now?' he said.

Wow. Keen.

'I don't have any immediate plans,' I said. I brought my hands to my cheeks to conceal the explosion of pink. 'Why?'

Two middle-aged women came in. Their laughter could only be described as cackling. They sat down two tables away, just in from the window, and ordered cappuccinos and cake.

'What are *you* doing now. I mean, after now?' I said.

He grinned. 'Taking a hot, brainy S6 girl to a gig?'

'Ooh, presumptuous!' *Hot? He thinks I'm hot!* My heart did a victory dance. 'What gig?'

'Chastity Brown. Amazing voice. She's the real deal.'

'Never heard of her.'

'Well?' he said. 'Are you game?'

'Hell, you only live once, eh?' A wrench tightened around my heart and Si's waxy face in the coffin lurked at the edges of my mind. I pushed them away. 'What, you just happen to have bought a spare ticket in case you meet some random girl in a café earlier that day?'

'Nah, I've got a backstage pass and I have a hunch I can get you in.'

'A backstage pass? Check you!'

'I know the tour manager – I'm always in his music shop buying strings and plectrums and stuff.'

'You play the guitar?'

'Bass.'

'I love bass. D'you play in a band?' I asked. I caught myself twirling my hair around one finger. *Wtf?*

He hesitated, like a chink of light had escaped through a gap in his shield. 'Well, sort of. I mean, like, I was in a band at school with my mate Callum and a couple of other guys, but it was a bit grungy. We still get together and play sometimes, but we're not really going anywhere at the minute. And our drummer's buggered off. My little brother plays a bit but, nah – he's too annoying.'

My eyebrows decided to vault Everest, and my gut dropped to the floor. *Little brother.*

He frowned. 'You got any brothers and sisters?'

A thump to the gut – I felt winded, but shook my head

quickly. 'No, just me,' I said, all sunny. 'Just my mum and my dad and me – my stepdad, really, but I just call him Dad.'

Sorry, Sibo. It's only a few minutes of inane flirting.

He smiled and the tension drained out of him.

'So, you're looking for a drummer?' I said, all chipper and chirpy. Even if I was being an outrageous flirt, and even if it was all nonsense, how good did it feel, just to be normal and silly for a few minutes?

Never again will I take this for granted.

'Aye, well, I suppose we are.'

'A drumbeat's kinda useful.'

'If he can keep time.'

'He?' I glared, with a capital G. I lifted my cushion, as though to hit him with it.

A look of panic fluttered then left his face. "If . . . *she* can keep time? Sorry.'

His phone beeped. He apologized, read it, his expression clouding.

'I'm sorry,' he said. 'I have to go. It's been – well – really nice meeting you. I'll see you outside Queen's Hall at seven-thirty. You'll be there?'

'I'll be there.' Whoever Chastity Brown was, I didn't care. But to be out, anywhere, with him, instead of at home with Mum and Dad, drowning in misery – it was a no-brainer.

'Text me your number?' He scribbled his on a corner of napkin, tore it off and handed it to me.

I sneaked a look at his bum as he walked out. Washed-out blue-black Levi's, red label, lovely bum. He rapped my window and I smiled, waved, then gave him the V sign – I wasn't sure why. He laughed and strode off out of sight.

An absurd gratitude washed over me. Thank you, I mouthed to the disappearing figure. For letting me breathe. I looked at his name and number on the lime tissue. He'd written Nathan in capitals, a small tear at the top of the N. I typed it straight into my phone.

'Girl drummers rock.' I hit send.

My phone buzzed almost instantly with an eyebrow-raised smiley. *Cheeky git.*

I sent an angry-devil smiley.

He sent a laughing smiley. Then: 'Whatever you say, o wise one. see you 7.30' and a crown emoji.

I sent a gif of a beagle nodding. Who doesn't love a nodding dog?

A bunch of S2 boys walked past, japing around. A stab in my heart. I looked back down at the final swirl of coffee in my cup.

Chapter Nine

Nathan

30 September, Edinburgh

'That's not all,' Mum said, after perhaps a whole minute had passed. God, she looked wrecked: grey-white roots showing in her wavy hair – 'greying mouse' she called it. The front chunk was pulled back into a hair slide on the right, to look neat for all those X-ray patients – Mum was a radiographer. 'Damian's been getting – well –' she glanced at him then back to me – 'abuse.' She said the last word like it was a foul taste.

'Abuse?' I picked a bit of dried Weetabix off the table with my thumbnail.

Damian took out his phone, his nails bitten right back. He was all arms and legs. His head was buzzed on the sides, dark curls on top, and he had down on his upper lip, plus a few obligatory spots. 'Effing scum,' he mumbled, 'do the decent thing and shoot yourselves . . . always knew your family were' – he paused and looked up at Mum, then lowered his voice – 'cunts'. Mum hid her face in her hands.

'Brainless cretins.' I shook my head. Mimi padded between us, in that almost silent way cats do. We all watched her, and she stared back. She stopped by her bowl and miaowed, demanding her kibble.

Why now? I could see it, though: some idiot, bored, latching on to old news about Damian's big brother.

'It's not fair,' I said. Mum gave me a slight nod and leaned across to switch on the kettle. Just reaching over the counter seemed like such an effort. She was one of those mums that does Clubbercise and spin classes with her pals – not the last three months, though. She was running on empty.

'They can call me what they like but they've no right to drag you and Mum into it,' I said.

Damian gave me a black look, eyes drilling into me.

'They're just wasters,' I said.

'Thanks, big bro,' he said, shouldering the doorframe as he escaped the room. His nose looked like an Angry Birds beak. Me and him used to have such a laugh playing Angry Birds. He'd be laughing that hard he'd fall off the sofa.

I lay on my bed and thought about her, the girl from the café in Tweedshaugh. Cara – funny, clever, cute. Her grey-green eyes, her smile.

I rang Stevie at Sweeter Sounds and asked if I could bring a guest. No sweat, he said. I ended the call and pictured Cara, all impressed that I'd managed to get her a backstage pass. But a wail from Mum's room cut through my thoughts.

I knocked quietly. And again. 'Mum, you all right?'

'I'm fine. Just – leave me be for a minute,' she said.

A chill shivered through me.

I went down to the kitchen and prepared her a small plate with Earl Grey in her blue and yellow mug, with exactly the right amount of milk, and a caramel digestive. I knocked once and slid it inside then pulled the door behind me. In the silence that followed, I made out a muffled sob. My own eyes misted over. *I'm sorry, Mum.*

I leaned back against the wall and let out a slow, silent breath.

Cara.

I can't leave Mum, I just can't.

'really really sorry,' I texted. 'my mum's really struggling at the minute, i'm going to have to forget chastity. so sorry to miss it. let's go to something else soon?x'

She texted right back. 'Sorry to hear about your mum. Hope she's OK.x'

'she's just having a tough time at the minute.' It wasn't a lie, exactly.

She texted back a hug emoji.

I smiled. *She's too nice.*

I shouldn't even be thinking about a girl just now.

A squeaking from downstairs. *Not again.* I legged it down, three stairs at a time, and ran into the kitchen. 'What you got, Mimi?' A teeny wee shrew with a cute pointy nose darted across the floor, scuttling behind the rubber plant. Mimi clawed at the space between the wall and the pot. 'No! Bad cat.' She wasn't even planning on eating it; just leaving it twitching in the middle of the floor. I scooped her up and put her down in the hall, blocking the gap with my foot as I closed the door. She clawed at the other side.

I chased the terrified wee mite right round the edge of the room before I managed to get it. I held it in my hand – at least the crappy, woollen gloves Dad had sent one year actually had a use – and these black, beady eyes looked back into mine. 'You're just too cute, aren't you?'

A muted, pleading miaowing persisted from the hall.

I took the shrew outside, round the corner and let it out in a hedgy, tree-y bit. 'Off you go. Away and find your family.' It scarpered, escaping my rubbish chat. Mimi snubbed me when I let her back into the kitchen – I'd wrecked her fun, after all.

'Is anyone going to tell me what this is all about?' I asked.

For the first time all dinnertime, Damian looked at me. It was a cold and distant look, the way you'd survey a stranger you instinctively didn't like.

Mum blew her nose, nodded at Damian to ask if he wanted to tell me. He kept his mouth shut.

'OK,' she said, sighing. 'Damian . . .' She cleared her throat and started again. 'Some boys at football . . .' she paused.

'Yes?' I prompted.

'Some boys at football *urinated* on Damian's bag.'

'They what?' I said. 'No way.' My throat constricted and a bitter taste filled my mouth. How could anybody do that to my little brother?

'Yes way,' said Damian, his voice husky.

'They pissed on your kitbag? Did you see them?'

'They pissed *in* my kitbag in the changing room,' he said, 'all over my stuff.'

'His clothes, his phone.' Mum shook her head, her body deflating.

'Your phone?'

Damo nodded. 'My phone.'

'That's horrific.' I gulped down the queasiness in my stomach. 'I can't believe anyone would do that. D'you know who did it?'

Damo stuck his lip out, shrugged. He had an idea, obviously.

'Bastards!' I said. 'Absolute bastards.'

'Nathan, swearing isn't helping,' said Mum, whisking away my half-drunk tea.

She piled dishes into the dishwasher, clattering and banging.

'So, what are you going to do?' I whispered.

'What would you do, Golden Balls?'

I sighed. 'I am not Golden Balls.'

'She thinks you are.' Damo gestured towards Mum.

'She does not.'

He shrugged and skulked off to his room.

Mum sidled up to me. 'How are you doing, love?'

I looked at her.

'Talk to me,' she said. 'You used to tell me everything.'

'About what?' I managed, after a moment.

She sighed, folding the tea towel in her hands. 'Come on, Nath. Why won't you talk to me? None of us is coping. There's no user guide for *this*.' She laughed a sarcastic, almost angry laugh that was so unlike her. 'Help me out here.' I stared at her tired-looking, paper-dry skin. 'How are you feeling? What are you thinking? What can I do to help you? Talk to me, Nathan! Please!' Mum never raised her voice – not really.

'I'm sorry, Mum.' I felt like I was back at the police station, phoning her, hearing her pain. 'How are you doing at work?'

She screeched and went after Damian.

*

Tuesday night: band practice. *Why did I think it was a good idea to come back tonight?* I walked the eight blocks down and two along to Cal's. Brace, brace. Opened the garage door. Cal and his dad hadn't done a bad job of soundproofing the place. The noise hit me the second I twisted the handle, and it was back to usual. Seemed like a week since I'd been there, not four months.

Then, sandwiched in there, unmissable: a moment of silence that passed like an unspoken conspiracy between us.

'Good to see you,' said Cal, putting his guitar down and slapping me on the back. Matt and Donny stopped playing and greeted me, too.

Gus didn't even look up when I walked in, kept going over his solo, getting more and more annoyed that he couldn't get the right sound; wouldn't look at me. Matt was cool. We broke into 'Read My Mind', my fingers finding C, slapping the strings. Why did Gus always have to turn himself up so much? I used to love Tuesday nights, love band practice – the rhythm, the vibe. I shouldn't have come, but I needed to get out. Mum needed me out too, I could tell.

Gus whined out his guitar solo, holding the last notes, tapping his effects pedal. What was his problem?

'So, how's things?' he said. It took me a second to realize the question was directed at me.

'Yeah, fine,' I said, with a shrug.

'Fine?' he said. 'Everything's *fine*?'

I stared at him, not sure what to say or do. His chest puffed out and his face flushed.

'Let's just play something, Gus,' said Matt.

'Nah, fuck it,' said Gus, turning to Matt. 'How can he just

saunter in here like nothing's happened? He *killed a kid.*' There was a crackle-pop as he pulled out the lead and flung it to the floor. His eyes blazed and he turned back to me, jabbing the air. 'You're acting like – like you've cracked your phone screen or something.' He marched out, slammed the door.

'How d'you think it feels?' I shouted after him. I was clammy, jumpy, my heart pounding. The room swayed, then I scanned the faces of my other bandmates.

Donny lifted his palms, shrugging. Donny the drummer. Here, even though he'd quit the band.

Matt started back up, playing the synth intro. The drumbeat started, then Cal came in on vocals. The bass started up, without me realizing I was playing. My fingers knew what they were doing, even if my head didn't.

God, what a relief it had been to speak to Cara. No baggage. No history. Just easy chat.

I had a headache all the next day. I got up when the sun was going down. Mum made macaroni cheese for tea. Damian glared at me. Damian preferred bolognese. It was a never-ending battle between us: who got their favourite pasta. I wished she'd made bolognese.

'How come you get to sit about in your room all day feeling sorry for yourself?' An unexpected swipe to my gut. He shoved back his chair, which rocked then clattered against the wall. 'It's not fair.' He looked at Mum. That cold, dark wave was back, washing over me. I closed my eyes a second, breathed in through my nose. 'How come he never has to hoover or put out the bins or empty the dishwasher? He doesn't even feed the cat. She'd be dead if it wasn't for me.' He was yelling now. 'Just cos you're all cooped up, hiding away from the world, kidding on everything's fine. Mum and me don't get to do that. Mum has to go to work. I have to go to school. You get to swan about at home like a shite festering in its own juice.'

'Damian!'

'Well, he does! Two poxy half-shifts a week doesn't even count. We've all got to tiptoe about and not upset him, cos he's *suffering*.' He did air quotes for 'suffering'. 'And why're we supposed to feel sorry for you, anyway? If you hadn't been fucking about on your phone when you were meant to be looking out the windscreen, none of this would have happened.'

'Whoa. Steady on, little bro.' A stitch stabbed under my heart.

Mum jumped up, held Damo back, and I twisted away from his punch, but not before he'd given me a dead arm. A giant sob erupted from Mum, and she slid down the wall, face in hands.

Damo stepped back and ran upstairs. I kneeled down and held Mum.

'I'm sorry,' I said. 'You shouldn't have to deal with this.'

I fetched a box of tissues – like that was going to help – poured her a glass of Pinot Grigio and pulled her up to sit at the table. 'I'm sorry,' I said again. 'I'll speak to Damian. Maybe just as well I got an extra shift tonight.'

She nodded, tried to smile, but her face crumpled into another sob. 'He's struggling,' she said. 'We all are.'

I reached forward, rubbed her hand. 'I know.'

I offered to ring Chrissie or Suzanne, Mum's besties, to ask them over.

'It's OK, love.' She looked me in the eye, paused there, like the moment was suspended in time. 'Damian's got a point. I know it's only been three months but you're not really . . .' Her voice tailed off. 'What's the plan, Nathan? I don't think sitting about's healthy. Can I take you to see someone?'

'I—'

I tried – I really did – but nothing came. No words.

She sighed. 'Never mind, we'll talk about it another time. Don't worry about me, love, I'll be all right. I'll snuggle up on the sofa with *Strictly* and a bowl of popcorn. You never know, Damian might humour me and watch it, too – keep his mum company.'

Ouch.

I knocked quietly on Damo's door.

'Sod off,' he said.

Gladly, I thought.

'Mum could use some company,' I said, opening it a crack.

'What, so you go round causing mayhem and I have to clear up the mess?'

Nothing in me reacted. 'Damo?'

He didn't answer.

I peered round the door. 'Your essay on Douglas Teviot and slavery – it was good. Really, really good.' He'd left it on the kitchen table, all messy notes and arrows, after typing it into his iPad. With time to kill, I'd started reading.

He shrugged, as though to say, *really?*

'Get your grades and then you can do whatever you want. Ignore the idiots.'

He stared at me, turned down his mouth at the edges, dropped his gaze.

Thank God I had an excuse to head out to work. I walked past the bus stop and kept walking, even though a fine drizzle painted the sky a luminous orange-grey. The evening sun nudged round

Castle Hill, and a musty, autumn smell crept through Princes Street Gardens. The chill in the air felt good.

I saw the sleeping bag as I turned Joe's corner. I pulled the Snickers and Scotch egg out of my bag. 'How you doing, Joe?' I said. He gave the egg to his dog. Snoopy was obsessed with Scotch eggs.

'Ah, OK, OK,' he said in his thick accent. 'Thank you – a true friend,' and he saluted me. I saluted him back.

'Keep dreaming of that trip to the Bahamas,' I said. 'One day, Joe!'

'I'm there already,' he shouted back, and did a cheers gesture. I cheersed him back and he grinned.

When I pulled the door, I was hit by the unmistakable smell of the pub: beer and bleach.

'Hi, Natasha, Monica,' I said, giving each a nod. 'Mark.'

'Nathan, my man.' Mark slapped me on the back. 'How's it hanging?'

'Aye, not bad. You?'

'Ach, nae complaints eh.'

We talked about the Barcelona-Juventus match. As you do.

'Did you see that goal, man?' said Mark. 'The way he curved the ball in from way out left and you thought it was going out but it floated in. Schweeeeeeeet.' He shook his head, closed his eyes. 'That goal was genius, man.'

'He's got the magic touch, all right,' I said.

Nobody at work knew. I'd had the job two months – Mum had pretty much shoved me out the house and told me to come back with a job. It'll do you good, she'd said.

She was right. Pulling pints for strangers was like therapy. I'd have paid them to let me do it.

Chapter Ten

Cara

October, Portobello Beach

Cara Eva Milne will not be stood up again, I thought, the impatience souring and swilling like bile from my gut.

The filthy little toerag. How rude. How bloody rude.

A tap on my shoulder and I whirled, the thrill firing down to my toes and back up. Here he was, taller standing up, better looking than I remembered, his chestnut hair falling over the edge of his eyebrow, inches from my own. My chest, my neck, my face fizzed.

'Hi,' I said, cursing the breathy giggle that had escaped. *Get a grip.*

It wasn't a hot day, but it was one of those days when the wind and the waves and the people make the whole place pulse with life. The sky was a shifting wash of putty-grey and duck-egg blue, drifting on a dreamy southwesterly.

We walked along Portobello Promenade, all awkward smiles, and I broke away, sidestepped along the wall and jumped down onto the sand. We took off our shoes and socks. I glanced at his bare feet and a blush burst out, engulfing my ears. I'd never felt so self-conscious.

It was ridiculous. Just feet.

His were ivory, long, tapered, beautiful, with pale brown hairs emerging from his toes. The lines of his tendons reached up the front and the arches, well, *arched*, so . . . archily. I realized my gaze had lingered too long and looked up, shy, at his face. His eyes held a trace of a smile. Why did it feel so darned sexy to be together, wrapped in fifty layers, with bare feet?

I wriggled my toes into the sand, ashamed at my plaster-white boxy feet and chipped purple nail varnish – a shocking slackening of my usual standards. Until the end of June, I'd done my mani-pedi regime every Sunday night. *Note to self: sort your toenails out when you get home.*

I skipped off towards the shoreline, knowing he'd follow. An invitation, if you like. He caught me up, and we grinned at each other. I paddled into the water, and no, I didn't shriek. He picked his way between the coils of seaweed.

'Jesus!' he said. 'It's Baltic!'

I gave him an eye roll for effect. 'Wuss.'

'Aye, I'm not sure I'm cut out to be a polar explorer,' he said. 'Give me tropical waters any day.' He grinned again, his mouth a bit squinty. *Cute.*

'You're not planning on swimming, then?'

'Ach, maybe not today,' he said. 'But I'll happily sit here and watch you if nipple-stiffening, testicle-shrinking water's your bag.'

I gaped. 'Nathan! You're so . . . *naughty*!'

'Naughty but nishe?'

'Omigod, was that supposed to be that ancient James Bond guy? That was terrible – even worse than – what was it – Bruce. You really need to stop doing accents.'

He pushed out his lower lip and simpered.

'Deeply,' – fake sob – 'wounded,' he said, clutching his heart and blinking back pretend tears.

'A wuss *and* a diva,' I said. 'Did your mum not teach you how to court young ladies?'

He pretended to look about for young ladies.

'Very funny,' I said.

'My mum just said to be myself, be nice, and be truthful,' he said, taking both my hands and rubbing his thumbs over the backs of them. We both stared at our hands. The touch felt static and unexpected – some sort of charge sizzled through my groin. 'So, I'll tell you this: I'm really, really glad I met you. I feel totally relaxed around you. It's not me, it's you. You're like a magic pill or something. There you go.'

Ooh, yeah, ooh, yeah! I am a magic pill, no less!

I looked up, into his eyes. 'I think you're—'

'Devilishly handsome? Deeply riveting?' He pushed his eyebrows into some parody of a charming gent.

I gritted my teeth at one side, as though to say: *how do I break this to you?*

'Moderately acceptable?' he said.

I nodded to the side, pulled my mouth and eyebrows into a mock expression of doubt.

'A complete nob-end loser?' he said. 'A dim-witted dork? In the harsh light of day, a total minger?'

I laughed out loud and he pulled me close to his chest.

'Well, apart from the terrible, *terrible* accents.' I shook my head in exaggerated exasperation, 'I suppose, maybe, you're not so bad.'

He looked at me.

'Maybe even, quite nice?' I grinned, all toothy. 'As in, this is – actually – quite – fun?'

'You're nuts,' he said.

'Too many boring people?' I said, still grinning all toothily.

'Yeah, nuts is good,' he said. 'You're definitely not boring.' He gave a sheepish smile, his hand warm in the small of my back. 'So, I'm really sorry about cancelling Chastity,' he said. 'I was looking forward to it.'

'It's all right.'

'Something came up and my mum needed me to stay home and—'

I touched his arm. 'Really, it's OK. You're here now, aren't you?'

He looked down at his feet and back up. 'I do appear to be. Hey, I've got a confession. I totally forgot to look out for Mercury – you know, going across the sun.'

'Inexcusable. Instant detention.' I did my best stern-schoolmistress look, then squeezed Nathan's hand.

He squeezed back and stopped to face me. He tucked a strand of hair behind my ear. The touch made me tingle – a brush of his finger against the tip of my ear. My knees actually gave way for a moment.

OMG, why am I acting like some giddy brainless jelly bimbo?

'Tig!' I said. 'You're it!' And I sprinted along the beach towards the pier, coat flapping.

He chased me – course he did – and I dodged at the last minute.

I kept dodging him until he caught me. He locked me in, his hands clamped behind my back.

'Hey, that's cheating!' I screeched, and wriggled free. I let him grab me again, and we both laughed. God, it felt like being kids again, but with a whole other level of – I dunno – anticipation. I hadn't felt this giddy in forever.

He held me close to his chest, touched my cheek and cradled my head, my jaw in his hands, his fingers under my ears. He smelled good. Woody, spicy. I fixed my eyes on his. Full of mischief, they were. He stroked my mouth with his thumb, traced the outline of my lips, stared at them, his own falling open. He leaned in. I closed my eyes, the darkness amplifying the sensations.

My nerve endings flared.

When he pulled free, he rested his forehead on mine, sought out my eyes, looking from one to the other, back to the first. His eyes glistened. His pupils were pools. *You're beautiful. You're absolutely beautiful*, I thought. It was a rubbish thing to think, but I seemed to have temporarily lost control of all sanity.

So, how did we cement the moment? We queued up for an ice cream, then bought buckets and spades and candyfloss from some dodgy-looking guy and built what Nathan insisted was 'the best sandcastle ever', complete with moat. We sat on the sand and watched the tide rise, wave by wave, until it filled the moat then flooded the castle.

'I really like you.' He paused and looked at me. 'Like . . . like, I feel like I know you. I know that sounds super-cheesy.' He laughed and looked away, across the Firth of Forth to Fife, but there was a look on his face – the look of a scared little boy. There was something unsettling in it; something that made me uneasy, for a moment that stalled mid-air and was gone. *Get over yourself, Cara.*

Nathan stuck a shell on the top of the castle then pulled me by the hand. He didn't seem to want to sit still.

I should tell him about Si.

Should I tell him about Si?

Not now – don't want to ruin the moment.

We bussed it into town and climbed Arthur's Seat together. He grabbed my swinging hand, clutched it, didn't let go. His hand was warm and strong. I gave it a squeeze, and a squeeze returned, like the echo heartbeat. I glanced away to hide my eyes. A ridiculous, appreciative awe of this perfect boy washed over me, after everything that had happened. He pulled me in, his hand finding the arch in my back, mine finding his heart, through his shirt. I could feel the solid beat, reassuring, caged in by ribs. I traced the stubble on his jaw, smiled back at him. We kissed.

We held hands at the top, breaking apart for moments of narrow path. Simultaneously, we picked up stones to put on the cairn at the top. I saw the upturned flick of his mouth and the crease of his eye. I closed my eyes, pulled him tight to my side, made a wish. I would have taken the absolute mick out of Shell for this – for being so pathetic and lovestruck.

'Penny for your thoughts?' I said, breaking the spell of the wind cresting over the summit, of the gulls that circled and squawked.

He pulled me close, kissed me by way of an answer.

'You are an absolute gift,' he said.

Chapter Eleven

Nathan

October, Edinburgh

I walked her to her bus stop after Arthur's Seat. She rested her head against my shoulder, her two hands holding my left hand while we waited for the bus. She sat at the back and smiled and waved until she disappeared out of sight.

I went home and looked at my face in the bathroom mirror. What did she see? My reflection burst into a grin. I stepped onto the scales. 70.6 kg. I wasn't ten kilos lighter; I wasn't suspended from a clutch of helium balloons. It was a sleight of mind. It was the aerating, levitating power of Cara. I went into my room and listened to Snarky Puppy.

'What's she like?'

It was Damian, hands in pockets, in his usual black joggers, white T-shirt and black socks. He leaned back against my wardrobe, one leg bent at the knee, his socked foot flat against the wardrobe door.

Normally I'd have told him to sod off.

'Is she fit?'

I caught his eye, decided to answer straight for once.

'She's beautiful.'

'What's she doing with you, then?'

'Exactly.'

We grinned, then I jabbed him in the ribs before he got me. He reached out the door for Mum's foam roller and I grabbed a pillow and we whacked each other. He crouched, readied himself and pounced at me, landing together on my beanbags and laughing.

'Oh, my God, is that a tache?' I stared at his upper lip. My little brother.

His beamer was answer enough.

'What, you want me to show you how to shave?' I said and shouldered him.

That's what dads are for – ours was a crap excuse for one, ever since he'd buggered off when I was five. I still remembered coming home from Primary One and asking where Daddy was.

Damian shrugged.

'Or are you planning on going full beard?'

He grinned his goofy grin.

I fetched him a razor. 'Don't want it back,' I said.

'Thanks.'

I heard him drumming through the wall and felt like someone had tied me into a straitjacket so tight I couldn't breathe.

'Starlight'.

I knocked on Damian's door, went in.

'Please stop playing that,' I said.

He didn't hear me, but I wasn't in the mood for shouting. I tapped him on the shoulder. He shrugged, an unspoken *what?*

'Please stop playing that.'

'What? But you love Muse,' he said.

'I'm not in the mood for it.'

'Not in the mood for it? What you talking about?'

'I just don't want to listen to it, OK?'

'But you're the one who suggested it – I've nearly cracked it.'

'I don't like it any more.'

'How can you suddenly stop liking your favourite band? You're all over the shop.'

'I still like them. It's just that one.'

'"Starlight"? But you said yourself it's brilliant.'

I sighed, looked at him, said nothing. He frowned, confusion taking over from irritation.

'It was playing when it happened,' I said.

My words were what my English teacher, Mrs Wright, would have called passive and intransitive. I couldn't bring myself to voice the translation inside my head: *It was playing when I hit him.* Or, a step further: *I was listening to it when I hit him.* Or further, edging closer to shame and truth and accountability: *I was turning it up when I stopped concentrating on the road and crashed into him and killed him stone-dead.*

He watched me. Then it clicked.

'You were listening to "Starlight" when it happened?'

My jaw was a great wrench, seized and set.

I nodded.

'Oh. Jeez. OK.' He puffed out his cheeks and did a slow nod, and gave me an apologetic shrug, like now it all made sense.

'Damian?'

He raised his eyebrows in acknowledgement.

'Thank you – for, you know, putting up with all this shit. I'm sorry to have caused you so much grief.'

He pressed his mouth into a grim smile and nodded his acceptance.

'Sounds good, by the way,' I said. 'You're a good drummer.'

The door clicked as I pulled it closed behind me.

She stood under the streetlight in a dusty-pink jacket, like an angel. *Shit*. I so meant to be first there.

'So, are we in the mood to be shit-scared and totally freaked, my good lady?' I said.

'Yeah, whatever,' she said.

'You'll be shrieking like the rest of them,' I said. 'Mind you, so will I.'

She laughed and linked her hand through my elbow. I leaned in and kissed her hair – soft, like a cloud.

For some reason we'd decided an Edinburgh Ghost Tour was the ideal starting place for our next date, fuck knows why. So here we were.

A disembodied voice cut through the orange street lighting and the traffic sounds, and announced itself as our tour guide. It was the year 1746, apparently. A group of folk materialized – mostly tourists, you could tell from snatches of conversation and their appearance and clothes. A figure in a black cloak and white face paint wafted into view. He was good. Cara's arm felt warm against my ribcage.

A line passed down my spine and a screech sounded, and I yelped back in fright. A bent-over woman cackled, pulling her clawed hand away from my back, all white make-up and crazy, big hair – the other half of the act. Cara peeled with laughter, until the woman reached out a bony hand and rested the long nails on Cara's scalp. Cara shrank back and froze, looking wide-eyed at me, laughter in her eyes.

'Oh, my God, I nearly peed myself,' she whispered, once the witchy woman had retreated to pick on someone else.

They led us down a close and under an arch into Edinburgh's city under the city. It was pitch-black and damp smelling, and we had to feel our way, single file, along the cold stone wall. A wail and murmurs of multiple voices and a ghostly dog yapping and a baby's cry seemed to roll around us from the gutters and the ceilings and the walls. A wave of icy air curled over us, and the tour guide spoke of thirty-nine women and children boarded up in this room until death came for each of them.

'This is proper scary,' said Cara, in my ear, gripping my coat.

After the tour, we wandered up the High Street, stopped at the Heart of Midlothian outside St Giles' Cathedral. The mosaic-cobblestone heart glistened with a few globs of spit.

'D'you think we should?' asked Cara.

'I don't recall my mum telling me spitting was a good idea when courting young ladies.'

'But it's good luck! Then again, spitting's disgusting,' she said with a grimace, beginning to walk on, then stopping again. 'Actually, it's worth it for the luck. I'm going to do it. Promise not to look.'

'OK.' I looked up towards the castle, and heard her do a quiet, ladylike spit. The skyline was black against the amber grey of streetlight reflected on cloud, with a trace of urine and beer in the still air.

'Bring on the luck,' she said. She grabbed my hand.

'Keep going,' and I spun round and spat too, mine joining the multiple glistening globules.

We managed to get a window seat upstairs at Deacon Brodie's. Cara ordered a bottle of Kopparberg Pear. I got a pint of IPA. She told me about her friend, Shell, talked about places they hung out in Tweedshaugh – mostly each other's houses, it sounded like – and her plans for uni. She loved Psychology and English. And French. And of course she was interested in astronomy, so was half wondering about trying to incorporate that, too. Sounded like she'd pretty much have her pick of courses – her grades were good.

I couldn't quite get over that this glowing, brainy girl was here, with me.

'Are you still planning on the year out?' she asked. The question caught me off-guard. My chest tightened.

'I'm not really sure,' I said. What else could I say? 'Maybe next year – March or April – I might go somewhere for two or three months. South America, maybe? I've got to save up first.' The grip on my chest loosened and I relaxed a bit. 'I've been meaning to look into all those trips like Raleigh International or those volunteering-overseas ones.'

She breathed in then let out a shuddery breath, then laughed, embarrassed. 'Sorry, I don't know where that came from,' she said, all merry eyes and smile. 'That sounds fab. You should totally do it.'

'But—'

'Don't not go because of me,' she said quickly. 'You've got your life to live.'

I nodded.

'Anyway, what's two or three months?' she said.

I pulled her in for a hug, her head resting against my shoulder. I picked up her lemon pendant and felt its smoothness. Reaching my other arm round to her shoulder, I held her tight and closed my eyes, pushing back the tears. I had to tell her the truth: I was on bail and was going to be tried at the High Court in February for causing death by dangerous driving.

How d'you slip that into the conversation with the finest person you've ever met?

Chapter Twelve

Cara

October, Ratho

I switched off the ignition and looked at the building that nestled into the rock. It looked like some giant had come along and carved a lump out of the quarry with a single swipe of his digger hand, then pressed in the glassy block, like a piece of Lego. Edinburgh International Climbing Arena.

Si loved it. Used to go with his best mate, Lewis.

I'd never fancied it before, but now something drew me to try it. I wanted to experience all the things he liked, know everything there was to know. Some instinct prevented me from telling Mum and Dad where I was going – I said I was meeting Shell. It felt vaguely shameful being clandestine about it. Shell offered to come with me, but totally got it when I said I needed to go on my own.

The instructor got me all harnessed up and put me on the

easiest route. I shivered. It wasn't just nerves; it was freezing in there. I shimmied that wall like a spider.

'Well done. Now hold on to your knot – your knot – yes, both hands on the knot, lean back, and walk down the wall.'

He put me on a Level 4 on the main wall. He showed me how to unlock the carabiner and clip on to the auto-belay. I looked up. The wall was a massive iceberg towering before me, but not in a daunting way. I focused on the footholds, pushed myself up, reached for a handhold, pulled. I hooked my right leg to my right hand, squeezed my toes over the bowl of the hold, pushed myself up with my right leg and my left arm.

'You're a natural,' shouted the instructor.

My heart burned with adrenaline and a mix of euphoria and misery. I reached for the last handhold, pulled myself up. I paused at the top, looked all the way down. *Wow.*

My opportunity to climb with Si was buried with him. Yet for a moment I felt connected with him, close to him, in a weird but intimate way. My lovely baby brother that it had been my job to keep safe, always.

'Are you there, Sibo? Are you?' I said, under my breath. *I need you to be there.* My chest racked and my eyes clouded.

The auto-belay hummed as it lowered me, amid the noise and shouts that echoed around the hall. To me, it was an angel humming her approval, a gentle, treble hum. Crazy, I know.

The ground appeared and I collapsed into the arms of the instructor, whose face morphed from a big open expression of encouragement to one of alarm and confusion at my hysterical state. He took me upstairs to the café for a coffee and furrowed his eyebrows.

'What happened up there, Clara?' He'd called me Clara since

I got there – I should have corrected him, but I'd let it go too long. 'You were flying, bags of confidence, no problems, and then you went to pieces.'

I felt like I was at primary school with a favourite teacher. I looked into the instructor's eyes and explained my brother had loved to climb there and he'd been killed at the start of the summer, crossing the road. I didn't know this guy and he was nearer Dad's age than mine, but he pulled me in for a hug and let me cry.

'Thank you,' I said.

'Will you come back, d'you think?'

I looked through the big glass screen at the massive arena, at all the climbers dotted around the walls.

'I think so,' I said. 'Yes.'

He nodded.

'Hopefully this won't happen every time,' I said.

He smiled. 'That's a girl.' It was like meeting some benevolent uncle I didn't know I had.

I did go back. I went back the very next week. I told Mum and Dad this time. I had the jitters as I sat them down to tell them. I don't know what I was expecting. They were fine about it. Guess sometimes you've cried all you can cry, and there's nothing left in you to react.

It was the same instructor, Dave. He grinned, every bit the proud dad, and led me over to a stretch of wall with a small overhang two-thirds of the way up.

'I looked up Simon's account,' he said. 'He would have climbed this exact stretch of wall the last time he was here – a Level Five. I don't know if that helps any.' He put a hand on my upper arm, gave it a squeeze.

'Thank you.' My eyes misted, but a moment of peace settled around me.

I looped the knot over and under in a figure of eight, and then fed it back through the harness and doubled it up, copying Dave's every move.

Climbing that wall, I felt Si's presence in the air, so real it was tangible.

'You're here!' I whispered. 'Thank you!' The peace circled around – joy, too – and I really felt Sibo with me; we were climbing that wall together, reaching out our arms together, grabbing that handhold together.

'You launched yourself up that wall like you were on steroids,' Dave said, as I unclipped and climbed out of my harness.

My heart pounded. Actually, I felt great.

And a tiny bit guilty.

Guilt, the bereavement counsellor Alison had said, is one of the most common emotions people feel when they've 'lost' a family member, and the most unhelpful. 'Are you being reasonable?' she said I had to ask myself. 'Is this guilt reasonable?' *No. No, it's not.*

The high stayed with me all day. I'd always slightly mistrusted adrenaline junkies. And here I was, a convert to what I'd always thought of as an adrenaline-junkie sport. It was the freeing aspect, I decided, as I sat in the traffic at Hermiston Gait. Was it because Si was dead? Did that amplify the freeing, connecting thing? The word 'dead' stuck in my throat. *Really must tell Nathan.* And yet. Being with him was a break from the misery. Would he act differently once he knew? Could I bear him looking at me with that look everyone else had when they spoke to me?

I will tell him, when I'm ready.

I planned to go again the following week, but when it came round, couldn't muster the energy. Didn't wash my hair, or put on any make-up. I crawled out, caught the bus, went to the Baggity Maw. We used to go there after school sometimes on a Wednesday, if Mum and Dad weren't due home from work until six. Si always got mac and cheese. I always got a baked potato.

I ordered gingerbread with butter and a latte. I heard the jangle of the bell on the door as I left, with no recollection of eating the gingerbread, drinking the coffee or paying the bill. I'd heard the term 'autopilot' before, without really understanding what it meant.

Now I understood.

Chapter Thirteen

Nathan

October, Edinburgh

Cara sat down at Damian's drum kit and let rip. *Oh. My. God.* I listened, watched, hypnotized.

'You kept that quiet,' I said, after she stopped and placed the drumsticks together on the snare, like a knife and fork after a meal. She turned and shrugged, a half-smile forming. This girl was beyond perfect. Foxy, brainy, a thinker, and shit-hot on the drums – shit, she was as good as Dave Grohl.

OK, she wasn't as good as Dave Grohl.

'You're not bad,' I said. 'For a girl.' I dodged the small plastic box coming my way. I picked it up. 'Earplugs. Nice. So, you planned this?'

'I'll get you back. I will,' she said, hands on hips, but she was loving it.

'OK, you're brilliant at the drums.' You could just see

it from the feel she had, lost in the rhythm. 'How long you been playing?'

'Two years.'

'Seriously?' Two years? I'd been playing bass six and she was better than me. Drums take forever to master. 'Why didn't you say?'

'I dunno,' she said. 'Sounded a bit, like, self-trumpety or something.'

'Self-trumpety?'

'Self-trumpety,' she said. 'Definitely.'

I shook my head and laughed.

Those lips. Those cherry lips. Man, girls were sent to drive boys insane, I was sure of it. She tried to do a mean look, but she didn't pull it off. All she succeeded in doing was driving me mad.

And the rest of her. I didn't normally get a chance to look, but, well. Gotta grab a quick glance while you can.

To think I'd almost not met her in the café in Tweedshaugh, almost stayed in town and gone to Benny's Bites instead. I didn't know what had prompted me to get the bus to Tweedshaugh that day. Thirtieth of September. It was just so easy with her. What would she say when the time came to tell her about the accident; about the boy? I got one of those weird, full-body shivers that jolts you awake when you're falling asleep – when your leg pings out in reflex, to break a fall.

'He won't mind us being in here – your brother?' Cara asked, tapping out a rhythm with her nails on the hi-hat, her face unusually serious-looking.

I shook my head. 'You're only trying out his drum kit.'

We went through to my room and sat on my bed. Cara told me about her Saturday job at the hairdresser's.

'I answer the phone, shampoo clients' hair, make tea and

coffee, fetch their coats and sweep up. That's pretty much it. But the girls are a good laugh,' she said. 'And Danny, but he's basically one of the girls, too.'

Mostly, we talked about what music we liked, what films.

She couldn't understand how I wasn't into reading.

'But reading's like breathing,' she said.

I shrugged. 'Music's more my thing.'

She grabbed the massage ball I'd nicked from Mum and rolled it round her thighs. *Jesus.* I had to look away.

I showed her my GarageBand tinkerings on my iPad – thought she'd take the mick but she was all wide-eyed. She leaned in and her hair smelled of sweet apples – a sunny orchard. I closed my eyes a moment to feel the warmth.

'You do songwriting?' she said.

'Not exactly songwriting,' I said. There were no vocals; just layers of bass, synth, drums and other stuff.

'No, it is exactly songwriting,' she said, a really genuine smile lighting up her face. 'Own it! Don't play it down. I love creative people.' She gave me a big, warm, happy hug.

'God, you're easy to please,' I said. 'If I'd known, I would've whipped it out earlier.'

She punched me in the arm. I pretended it didn't hurt.

'Dick,' she said.

'If you insist,' I said, reaching, slapstick style, for my fly. We creased up.

'You *reprehensible reprobate.*' She enunciated every syllable in some ridiculous accent.

She played about with the tempo on the track, tried some different percussion effects.

'Strip club,' she said, putting on a really crap beat.

'Now you're talking,' I said. We both laughed. We were always laughing – that was the best thing.

I still couldn't get over the feel she had for the drums. 'You really are an impressive thing, aren't you?' I said. I did an 'I'm not worthy' worshipping thing with my hands and a bow of my head. She waved dismissively. 'And modest, too.'

She blinked angelically and laughed.

'There must be some flaw I can find.'

'Come and hunt for it, then.'

Instant stirrings. That's all I can tell you. I loved it when she did the whole coy thing. I kissed her deep.

My phone rang. *Mum*. Nothing like your mum ringing you to kill the vibe.

Cara pulled her hair into a ponytail.

'God, you're such a babe,' I said, pulling her towards me again. We kissed, for ages – so long the ice-cream van came past twice on its rounds, its tinny music shifting pitch as it passed.

Cara's phone pinged with notifications. *Bloody phones, killing my buzz.*

'How come you aren't on social media anyway?' she said. 'Mr Mysterious.' She rubbed the arch of my foot with the arch of hers.

'Ach, Instagram schminstagram,' I said and shrugged. 'It's just not my bag.'

She tilted her head to the side, smiled, showed me her Insta account, scrolled down to a picture of her with her mum and stepdad.

'An only child, eh?' I said. 'No fighting over the remote, then.'

She threaded her hands together and seemed to hesitate, then clicked off Instagram and went to the toilet.

*

We sat together on the sofa, flicked through some films, watched a bit of *Rob Roy*. But Mum and Damian would both be home soon, and no way was I ready for Mum to know about Cara yet, let alone meet her, or for her to meet them.

'Let's go out for something to eat,' she announced, her chin set. 'Where should we go?'

I tapped my nose.

We held hands all the way, milling through the Meadows and down Candlemaker Row. She paused and touched a pea-green scarf hanging on a rail at the doorway of a shop, then spotted a knitted hot water bottle in the window.

'Cute,' she said.

I stopped outside the tiny Italian in the Grassmarket, as if I'd done this a thousand times.

'*Voilà!*' I said with a sweep of my arm when we got there, even though I was thinking maybe it should have been '*Voici*' – and even though we were at an Italian restaurant, not a French one. 'What, you thought I was taking you to Burger King?'

'This is a bit posh!' she said. She chose a table by the window.

'Wine or beer?' I asked.

'Bottle of Peroni, please.'

She ordered mussels in white wine, and I went for a steak – hell, why not go all out?

The whole time, sitting there, watching her talk, smile, eat, I was thinking: *Is this real? You're amazing. You're beautiful. You're funny. You're hot. Look at you. You're an angel.*

How long before I fuck it up?

Chapter Fourteen

Cara

October, Drumleith

I lay on my bed, stared at the ceiling. I wanted to talk to Si, to call him up – a proper visitation, like in films. I wanted to see him, study his face, warn him to go back to the thirtieth of June and not get the bus into Edinburgh that day – tell him to do anything else, anything at all. But all I could see was Nathan, smiling, flirting, his mouth, his eyes. I closed my eyes, but I couldn't conjure up Si. Not even a hint. Just Nathan, smelling divine, reaching out and stroking my chin, my neck, his face open in a laugh at something I've said. And me, burning, outside and in.

My sweet little brother I'd known thirteen years, five months and twenty-eight days. And a boy I'd only just met. What was wrong with me?

But Nathan wouldn't leave. He hung around, sneaked up behind me, smiled, laughed, and I couldn't help it. Thinking about him made me feel alive instead of ripped apart. I didn't want to shut him out; he was the only good thing happening.

It was like he was anchoring himself into my soul, and I wanted him there – something stable and secure, to keep me from drifting into oblivion. I clung onto him, as I lay on my bed. He was there, taking my hand in his, kissing my fingertips, saying, *I'm here. I'm going nowhere. We'll get you through this.* Even though I hadn't told him yet. Just something about him – his familiarity, his easy presence, like I'd known him all my life – filled me with the certainty: this wasn't just any old fling. And I ached for this boy I barely knew. Was this what love at first sight felt like?

Wasn't it OK, for a few moments, to let him in; to not be mourning every second of every day?

And was there anything immoral, dishonest, about waiting a little longer before telling him about Si? Wasn't that OK, too? He'd understand, surely? But would it kill our relationship? Would he look at me with that look, speak with that voice people put on when they talk to me? Or would he get it, like Shell?

Only one way to find out.

'Is this a nerdy thing to do?' I asked. 'Probably,' I said, answering my own question. I had a habit of doing that. I would debate the meaning of life with myself for a century before growing bored of my own endless questions, or so my friends said. 'Time to embrace your inner nerd, Nath!' He just smiled.

After a pause, I continued my monologue. 'It's cool to be a little bit nerd.'

Two of the research fellows, Xiao and Sergey, were working late, and the security guy waved Nath and me through.

The sandstone building smelled like primary school. The Observatory – my favourite building in Edinburgh.

Xiao looked up when I paused at her door. 'Cara! How are you?' I'd done a bunch of volunteering shifts for my Duke of Ed. and she was one of the main people who'd found things for me to do. She was working on a programme on brown dwarfs and their atmospheres – showed me some images on her screen.

Nathan pinched my bum as I led him up the spiral staircase.

'Cheeky git!' I turned and made to tickle him but got tickled instead.

'This how you keep your glutes so tight?' he said.

It was just the two of us inside the copper dome that rotated on wheels. Our breath formed wisps in the air. Magnificent. Baltic.

I showed him the thirty-six-inch telescope, then led him onto the roof, pointed out stars, constellations, asterisms and nebulae; how many light years away they were.

'That one there that's a bit like a W, that's Cassiopeia. Then if you draw a line across you've got Polaris and then the Plough. We talk about Polaris – the North Star – like it's a single star but it's actually three stars close together – well, only like four-hundred billion kilometres apart, or something. I love that it's steady; everything else circles around it. If you stand here for a bit and blur your eyes you can see it happening.' We watched in silence a moment, and Nathan reached for my hand. 'At least that's how it seems to us, since it's above our North Pole. You could say it's all an illusion. S'pose it's all about perspective.'

He squeezed my hand. 'Cos it's us that's spinning?'

I nodded, then dropped his hand and pirouetted on the spot, nearly falling over at the end, stumbling into him.

'So elegantly done,' he said.

'Why, thanks!' I said and elbowed him in the ribs.

'Isn't that how ships used to navigate at night?' he said, looking back up at Polaris.

'Exactly. It's a lifesaver, a lighthouse in the sky.' I blinked up at it, made a silent prayer for Si.

'What if it's a really cloudy night – like, the thickest cloud you've ever seen?'

'Problemo! Who knows where that ship might end up?' I said.

I showed Nathan the viewfinder of one of the rooftop telescopes and he peered into the eyepiece.

'See that creamy-beige ball of tiramisu?' I said. 'That's Jupiter.' My favourite planet, on account of its crazy winds, turbulent atmosphere, powerful magnetic field and multiple moons.

'Wow,' he said, the lights of the city sparkling around us. His hand brushed mine, sparking something in me. I returned my focus to the sky; tried to ignore the explosions.

'Looking into the night sky is looking into the past,' I said, in a slow, posh voice, with a theatrical sweep of my arm. I'd heard it somewhere. 'How cool is that?'

'Pretty cool.'

I wandered over to the rooftop lecture room Xiao had unlocked for me. I riffled about in the 'box of tricks', as they called it, and returned to Nathan with a lump of metal. I pressed it into his palm. More explosions as skin touched skin.

'A meteorite. Four-and-a-half billion years old – same age as the solar system.'

He stared at it.

'Asleep yet?' I asked.

'Wide awake,' he said. 'It's amazing – heavy.'

'Mind-boggling, isn't it?'

'It is. It really is.' He nodded, looking earnest. He didn't seem to be faking. 'Everything's . . . so . . . big and we're so. . . small.' I smiled as he paused. 'OK, a two-year-old could do better than that. It's . . . it's incredible.'

Secretly I rejoiced that music was his thing and he seemed to be into this, too – or at least he was interested enough in us to humour me.

'But, y'know,' he took my hand and started playing with my fingers, 'it's kind of difficult for a red-blooded male to concentrate when the teacher's so damn hot.'

We kissed then, our breath joining in clouds that dissipated into the darkness. Time stilled. I melted, melded, into his soul, and we were one, until a distant ambulance cry soared across the city. I pulled away.

'You want to meet my parents?' I said. 'They want to meet you.'

His hesitation registered in my gut.

Why wouldn't he want to meet them?

'I guess,' he said, looking down. 'And I can introduce you to my mum and my brother some time. No mad rush, though, is there?'

'No. I don't suppose there is.' A coldness passed through me.

'I'll definitely meet your folks soon,' Nathan said. But it seemed more like he was saying what he thought I wanted to hear than that he meant it.

I thought he liked me. Like, really liked me. I frowned.

He lifted my chin.

'Hey,' he said.

'Yeah, sure, whatever,' I said, recoiling from his touch.

'Look, I really want to meet them, OK?'

'It's fine.'

'It doesn't have to be some big formal meeting or anything, does it?'

'God, course not.' I shivered.

'Good.'

'Glad that's settled then.' A bat darted past my face and a smell of fireworks carried up from somewhere.

'Do you know how fine you are to me, Mary MacGregor?' It was a line from the film *Rob Roy* that he'd kept saying since we watched it together at his house.

I didn't give the response he was looking for: *You know how fine you are to me, Robert MacGregor?*

'You haven't told your mum about me, have you?'

Nathan went quiet. He dropped his gaze.

He took my hands in his, studying them like they were a sculpture or something, running his thumb over the skin on the back of my hand.

'I'm going to tell her when I get home. It's . . . I promise it's nothing whatsoever to do with you. I just haven't got round to telling her.'

'You haven't *got round* to telling her?' I snatched back my hands and frowned, focusing all my attention on not crying. It had been nearly four weeks, but it felt big, special.

'I didn't mean it to sound like that. I just . . . haven't . . . told her yet. I've barely seen her. That's all.'

'Hmm.' *Bit bloody weird.*

'I'll tell her when I get home – promise,' he said. He hugged me. 'I do really, really like you, you know that. You're my first proper girlfriend. I've never brought a girl home to meet my mum before.'

'A random girl.' I plucked an invisible girl out of the air. I couldn't quell the surge of irritation I felt instead of euphoria. He was making a proper balls of this, that was for sure. 'I thought I quite liked you, too, but I'm a bit thrown by why you're being so secretive about us. Like you're embarrassed or something.'

'Yeah, like clearly I'd be embarrassed to be going out with a beautiful, intelligent, witty, *hot*, philosophical, totally amazing in every way, totally individual, totally unique, kooky, cool superbabe.'

'Keep going,' I said, aiming for the light banter we'd settled into, pretending I wasn't still feeling super-pissed off and paranoid.

'Who also happens to be a shit-hot drummer.'

'And?'

'And whose knowledge of the stars and planets makes me look like a toddler.'

'Yeah?'

'Cara, you are a hundred per cent the best thing that's ever happened to me. It's not you, I promise. We've had stuff going on at home. Shit to deal with. You can meet my mum and my brother any time you like.'

'You never mention your dad.'

'Don't have one worth talking about.'

'Sorry.'

''S all right. He buggered off and left us when we were wee. Sends me a Christmas card and a birthday card, and randomly, an Easter egg with a soft toy every year. This year's duck made a mark on the wall, I chucked it that hard.' His chest and arms tensed. 'Like, I'm fucking eighteen, not two, Dad.'

I un-balled his fist, stroked his hand, pulled him to start walking down the stairs and out to the car park. 'Sorry, I shouldn't have said.'

I couldn't imagine having no dad, even though mine wasn't actually my own father. He'd been Dad since I could remember, and he'd always treated me exactly the same as Si – my half-brother, if you wanted to get technical about it – his actual son. My own father had died when I was two. I had the vaguest impression of a memory of his face, smiling at me, but it was probably just from the photo I kept in a small pine frame on my chest of drawers. But one thing was clear: I knew who I was, and I was determined – 'deter-minded', I used to think it was – to own my space on this little blue planet. By the time Mum married Dad a year after Si was born, I was so insistent on telling anyone who'd listen, *I'm Cara Eva Milne and I'm four and three-quarters*, there was never any discussion of changing my name to match theirs.

Something unsettled me in my sleep that night. I dreamt I brought Nathan back to meet my parents, and he was super-keen, and everything was perfect, and everyone was laughing and joking and I was so happy to see Mum look happy, then Mum's face dropped and dream-me looked back to see Nathan was a clown, like in a horror film, and he leaned in and said, 'I do really, really like you, you know,' and then he was Si, smiling.

I struggled through my shift at the salon, saved by the vacuous nature of the conversation. Holidays obviously, celebrities and Netflix. *Now 78* played: Bruno Mars, Adele, Jessie J, Rihanna. CeeLo Green, Katy Perry, P!nk. The acrid smell of serum spray caught me in the back of the throat – I could taste it in the air. Valentina and her client laughed and chatted behind me, and I caught snippets about the client's puppy, a miniature dachshund, and how it had weed all over the piano and had a thing for Co-op carrot cake.

Valentina blathered on about some embarrassing dance video on TikTok and I massaged shampoo into the next client, Ginny's, scalp. I liked her – easy to chat away to. But she wouldn't meet my eye today and whipped out a book before I'd even started combing out her hair.

I held out the first client's navy wool coat and she turned round, put in her right arm, then her left, hitched it onto her shoulders. Her little girl had sat in an armchair in reception, drawing the whole time. She clutched a toy horse. She jumped up, took her mum's hand. 'Didn't you have a brother that got killded?' she said.

The client, Sarah, covered her own mouth with one hand and her daughter's with the other. 'I'm so sorry,' she said, her face white. 'Maddie, it's not nice to say things like that.' Maddie looked up at her mum and dissolved into tears.

Opposite of what the mum said, I felt the warmth of the little girl. I squatted down so we were eye to eye. 'Hey, I like your horse. What's its name?'

'She's called Horse.' Said with a slight lisp.

I smiled. 'Horse. I like that! I like your name, too. You're Maddie, aren't you?'

She nodded.

'What've you been drawing?'

Her head dipped, then she tilted her book so I could see. She peeked at me through her hair. 'Flowers.'

'You like yellow? I love yellow. Hey, Maddie, you're right.'

I took a breath. 'I did have a brother who I loved very much. And he did get killed, and that makes me feel sad, but I like to talk about him, because he was happy. So you've done nothing wrong, nothing at all. I like that you're able to ask me about it.' I lowered my voice to a whisper. 'Sometimes kids can be cleverer than grown-ups at understanding things.'

I stood up, smiled at her mum, who mouthed 'Thank you.' She took Maddie's hand again.

I knelt back down. 'I'll tell you about him, if you like, next time you come in. Or we can talk about Horse, or your puppy, or anything you like!'

'Can we talk about fairies?'

'Of course we can! When I was your age, I used to love a fairy called Apple Blossom. Have you got a favourite fairy?'

She rubbed her cheek, pulled her mouth into an expression of grave concentration. 'I like all of them,' she said, all earnest. 'But most of all I love Scarlett. She lives in a boat made from an acorn shell, and she sleeps on a bed made out of moss, and her best friend's Ebony, and she likes to eat . . . What does she like to eat, Mummy?'

'Come on, pumpkin, you can tell Cara all about her when you come back.'

I put out my hand to shake Maddie's. 'Deal,' I said. She looked confused, then tipped her head to one side and put her tiny warm hand on mine.

'Is it like potatoes?' she asked. 'One potato, two potato, three potato, four.'

'Kinda,' I said, and bumped her potato fist. 'Except you have to say "Deal", too. And it means I'll not forget to ask you all about Scarlett next time I see you.'

'Deal!' she said.

I got the bus then walked the six minutes home.

When I turned into our road, I slowed, pausing as I approached our house. Pixie bounded up to greet me, tail wagging like mad, and nudged me with a wet nose. I squatted and dropped my bag to hug her.

A hunched shape sat by the kitchen window. The shape was Mum, slumped over some paperwork on the table, clutching a mug and gripping Sibo's worn, soft plush elephant. I swept in and she hugged me as usual. Mum was petite like me – tiny, in fact – but she still gave the biggest hugs of anyone in the universe, I was convinced of it. From the pinkness of her eyes, her pinched-looking skin, her drained face, I could tell she'd been crying all morning. Maybe she should get away on holiday or something. A week in the sun. Change of scenery.

I glanced at the sheets of paper in front of her, my chest tightening. She read the unspoken question in my eyes, in my hesitation, and gestured for me to sit down.

'It's the details of the case,' she said. 'Come and have a look, love.'

I sighed, pinched the bridge of my nose. I couldn't – just couldn't. Not just now. 'Can I look another time?' I asked. 'You look like you could use a break, Mum.' I put my hand on her shoulder, gave it a squeeze.

She breathed out, closing her eyes, then opened them again, like she was putting all her energy into brightening, for me. 'I can't wait to meet your Nathan, sweetheart,' she said, all major-effort-lively. 'He sounds lovely.' And she gave me a nudge, lifting her eyebrows in a suggestive way.

OK. *Let's roll with this.* Who cared if we were both pretending and both knew it. 'Mum!'

'You really like him, don't you?'

I nodded, concentrating on controlling the quaver in my voice. 'Yes, I do.'

'I'm sure he's lovely. You're a clever, clever girl, and you're a good judge of character. And you're so blooming fussy he must be *gorgeous*.'

'Mum!'

She shrugged.

'Does he know about Si?'

It was a jab in my conscience, transporting me to somewhere unsettling, not the comfort of my own kitchen.

'I haven't told him yet,' I said.

Mum looked at me, stock-still, nodded.

'I dunno, Mum, it's just, I dunno.' I leaned against the back of her chair and ran my thumb over the ends of my fingernails. 'I was going to tell him – I mean, I will tell him, obviously – but meeting him has been the only tiny little window of, you know, escape from it all. Everywhere you go, everyone knows. And I know it sounds selfish, but I suppose it's been nice, when I'm with him, to be normal, even just for a few minutes.' I paused. 'Like a little oasis of normality or something.'

In an ocean of shit.

'You don't have a selfish bone in your body, sweetheart.' Mum's head dropped, and her shoulders started to go, and she sniffed, then sucked in a sharp breath. A guttural moan sounded from some primal place deep inside her.

I knew what she was thinking: *Neither did your brother.*

'I can't—' She gulped and choked. 'I just want the pain to end.' And she racked with chest-heaving gasps.

'Stop!' I said. 'You're scaring me.'

I kneeled down and hugged her, and rocked back and forth with her, and rubbed her back. 'Shhh,' I said, until the sobbing softened and slowed, and eventually stopped. We stayed like that until my legs went numb.

'C'mon,' I said, standing up, jogging my leg up and down to get the life back into it. 'I'll hang up the washing. 'Nother cup of coffee?'

By four, I needed a breather – needed to get out alone – craved the cool air, great gulps of it. My own grief was bad enough, but Mum's, too – it was too much. I'd expected grief to be brutal, but I hadn't expected it to be quite so relentless; quite so exhausting. Every bone ached, every molecule of my being drained of energy. Mum snored evenly, slumped in her chair, dribble pooling from the side of her open mouth. I draped a blanket over her back – the soft yellow-and-grey beehive one that was folded on top of the dresser.

I tied a purple ribbon in Pixie's poodle hair. Pixie loved having her hair done. I lifted her lead off the hook at the front door and she jumped up and started snuffling, super-keen. 'Aw, you absolute superstar, you!' I said and nuzzled her furry snout.

Dad was in the drive, rubbing wax into his car and buffing it with a cloth. He scrubbed away, round and round, at the same bit, not satisfied. I laid a hand on his back and he flinched. 'Carabelle,' he said, looking up. He hugged me with one arm and sighed hard.

I walked to the park by the caravan site. The scaly bark of the Scots pine – not cold, not warm – felt reassuringly solid and steady, somehow. I walked on and sat against the trunk of the big beech, hugging my hot water bottle to my chest under my puffer jacket. It was a present from Nathan, its knitted Nordic cover a red-and-white snowflake and reindeer design – he'd copped me stopping and admiring it in the shop window. Even though it was only four degrees, I needed to be outside; needed the light and the space. I focused on deepening my breath.

The roots gripped the soil like bony fingers. I leaned forwards. A bronze beetle clambered around the grass, in and out of view, its back winking in the weakening sunlight. *Shouldn't you be sleeping, little beetle?* Above me, branches swayed and shadows shifted. A northerly breeze carried down from the Arctic, fresh and raw. As the sun began to set, the wind sank like a sigh.

The sky was a painting. A lilac skyscape, the light seeping out of it. There was a glow to the north-west – the city lights of Edinburgh and Tweedshaugh, illuminating the blanket of cloud. To the east was the golden glimmer of Gala, and to the south, an inky darkness bled into the mauve. And up there, sparkling behind the clouds, was Sibo.

I swallowed the salty tang of tears.

'U ok hun?' and a kiss-blowing smiley. It was Shell.

'Yeah, you?' – with a kiss-blowing smiley back.

'wanna chinese + netflix binge at mine?xx'

'On my way!xx'

'give it half an hour hun'

'You not in?x'

My phone didn't buzz back. It rang.

'I'm on my way back from the BGH.'

'What?' My chest constricted. 'You've been in hospital?'

'I kind of crashed.' Her voice sounded a bit sheepish and her mum's voice muttered in the background. The October wind whipped up some leaves and a damp, fungal smell and I shivered and hugged myself.

'But you don't drive,' I said, feeling like I'd left my body a moment.

'Omigod, sorry, I didn't mean . . . Crashed, as in I kind of went a bit too hypo a bit too long.'

Ah. Shell was diabetic. My shoulders relaxed a bit. 'Shell!'

'I know, I know!' she said, half giggling, half apologetic. Her mum's voice again, in the background.

'You OK now?' I said, relief flooding over me, the warmth of my blood tingling in my fingertips.

'Fine. Promise.'

'OK, see you in half an hour. I'll let myself in?'

'Yeah, do. See you in a bit, hon!'

Chapter Fifteen

Nathan

October, Edinburgh

Mum was chuffed to bits when I told her about Cara. I kept my word – told her as soon as I got home from the Observatory. She sort of visibly relaxed, like her body was a coiled-up spring and the news that I had a girlfriend had built-in spring-slackening properties.

'I knew there was something you weren't telling me,' she said. Guess she'd been worried it was something bad.

'She sounds nice,' she said, her voice weary but less strained-sounding.

'She is.'

I texted Cara. 'mum can't wait to meet you.x'

She texted back a thumbs up and a blushing smiley and a row of kisses.

But a few days had passed, and Mum didn't look so chirpy now.

The way she looked at me across the breakfast table, the way she eyed me and breathed out slowly, the way her shoulders sagged, I knew she had something brewing. God, she looked wrecked.

Maybe it was Damo. He'd flunked his first set of assessed coursework for his Nat. 5s, and Mum had been called in for a meeting with his head of year. As if she didn't have enough to stress about. Maybe she wanted me to have a brotherly talk with him. I doubted it; nobody trusted me with anything any more, and he wouldn't listen to me anyway. Mind you, could I blame her? I wasn't exactly in a position to be handing out life advice to my brother – my brother, who once looked up to me and now seemed to hate my guts, most of the time.

Poor Mum. She'd aged thirty years. It was like *Back to the Future II* – sitting down opposite an older version of her. I looked at her across the table, raised my eyebrows in question.

'Twinkletoes!' I shouted at the ceiling. 'You up?' And to Mum: 'Hasn't he got a match this morning?'

She put down her teacup and stood up. 'She goes to Tweedshaugh High, you said?'

'She does.'

'The same school as Simon Paterson?' A question settled in her eyes.

'You don't even know half the people in your own year, let alone some first year from a different town.'

She released a deep sigh, her neck slumping.

'I just hope you know what you're doing,' she said, and kissed me on the cheek.

The doorbell rang. Mum glanced in the hall mirror, gaped, but her eyes fizzed with expectation. 'I'll run and sort out my hair and put my face on. Look at the state of me!' She disappeared off up the stairs.

My chest swelled. Cara – here for me. There she was on the doorstep, looking shy and sweet. The way the sun shone on her hair made her look lit up. An angel.

Tell her now. Right now.

'Come on in. My mum's desperate to meet you. She'll be down in a sec.'

Mum'll be here in a minute. I'll tell her once Mum's gone.

Cara looked around the hall, at old pictures of me and Damian.

'Aw, adorable!' she said. She smiled at the photo, then glanced down, her chest deflating a moment, then bobbed up again, like a buoy. 'You're like two little cherubs!'

Mum skipped down the stairs. 'Cara! I'm Diane. So pleased to meet you.'

'I'm pleased to meet you, too.'

Mum gave me a wink. I felt a surge of pride that I'd brought home such a perfect girlfriend.

'Come on through.' Mum led her into the kitchen. 'Nathan tells me you're from Tweedshaugh – such a lovely town!'

And they were off, Cara all natural and bubbly, Mum all different and girly, me looking from one to the other across the table like watching Wimbledon. I got the French Fancies out of the cupboard and arranged them on a plate the way Mum usually did, and made a cafetière of coffee for Cara and a pot of Earl Grey for Mum and me.

'Thank you, love,' said Mum. 'Here's me too busy nattering.' She fetched a jug for the milk, and teaspoons. I thumbs-upped at Cara and she squeezed her shoulders up, and on her face was a beaming smile.

*

I walked Cara to the bus stop and waited with her – she only got the car when her mum wasn't working.

'D'you never borrow your mum's car?' she asked me.

'I don't drive.'

'Oh.'

We decided to walk to the next stop, and then another and another until we were out at Cameron Toll. A bus had whistled past but who cared? We kissed goodbye and I waved her off – she sat halfway back on the top deck and breathed onto the window then started to draw something in the white circle as the bus pulled off – a smiley face? I could almost hear the squeakiness of her finger drawing on the steamed-up glass.

I texted Scotty in case he was in, but he was working.

Mum was all giddy, still, when I got back – she kept saying how Cara was 'such a lovely girl'.

But then she went sort of quiet. No more 'giddy Mum'. I groaned inwardly – it was obvious what was coming next.

'Nathan, have you told her?'

I looked at the tear in the lino.

'It's an awful thing for you to have to tell her, but you seem pretty serious about her. Yes, it'll be a blow for sure, but once she's got over the shock she might be able to help you, you know, deal with it all. Your nightmares haven't been bothering you so much since you met her.'

Dread snaked round my torso.

'I get what you're saying, Mum. Course I need to tell her. It's just . . . what am I supposed to say? Like, "Oh, by the way, I sort of killed a boy – hope that's OK with you." And she'll be like, "Hey, don't worry, it's fine." I keep meaning to find the moment, but it's not the sort of thing you can just drop into a conversation.'

'You'll just have to say, "Cara, there's something I have to tell you," and come right out and say it, before you get talking about other things.'

Mum sighed, poured some tea and handed me my cup. 'I know – you've been putting it off because you like her.' She pulled a tray out of the oven with six mini roll-your-own croissants. That buttery smell.

'Mum—'

'You're scared she'll run a mile and you'll lose her.' She touched my forearm. 'You're going to have to get past this. You're going to have to get past this with anyone you want a serious relationship with, Nathan. You know that.'

I nodded. 'Thanks for reminding me.'

'Come on, love. Let's not turn this into a fight.' She took my face in her hands, pushed my hair away from my eye. 'Such beautiful eyes – that's what the midwife said.'

I rolled them. 'Mum!' She'd only told me this story a thousand times.

She smiled, chastened. 'You're more yourself lately,' and she gestured, with both hands, at all of me. 'That's all.'

I hugged her.

'It's been such a relief to spend time with someone who doesn't know and isn't judging me.' *And pretend that it might be possible to be even a teeny smidge happy.* 'It's like there's one world – just me and Cara – and then there's everything else.'

'I know, love.'

Mum smiled, that sad smile that broke my heart. That sad smile that said, *I would take your pain if I could, Nathan.*

'She likes you.'

My poor little beating heart soared a second.

'Just let me do it in my own time, OK? I will tell her – I promise.'

Chapter Sixteen

Cara

October, Drumleith

I stared at my bookcase. I loved books. Every story gave me a fragment of truth, like one piece of a trillion-piece jigsaw that held the secret to the universe. I hadn't been able to read since it happened. I'd opened books, scanned pages, but the black shapes threw up no meaning. A new conundrum for which I hadn't figured out the code.

I was having a low day – couldn't gather myself into anything close to being able to face school. Laura from the office answered my call.

'Take as much time as you need, Cara. It's absolutely fine.'

A cloak of tiredness shrouded me, so heavy.

The sockets of my eyes throbbed, a weight pressing into them. My jaw ached.

The postman's uneven footsteps crunched louder as he

hurried up the gravel; the letterbox hinge creaked and post whumped onto the hall mat – with it, an envelope addressed to me from Auntie Carol, with the final few photos for the album. It was one of the bereavement counsellor's suggestions – making an album, putting together a memory box, writing a letter to Si, writing a poem.

I blew my nose after sticking in the final picture – him pulling a silly face, standing behind me in the sun. I closed the book, looked up, saw nothing but blurs. I pulled it to my chest, let out a great, heaving sigh, which morphed into another sob, and put it on the bookshelf.

I tiptoed into his bedroom and looked out the window at the view he would have looked at. I sat on his bed, breathed the air he would have breathed, saw what he would have seen. Three darts stuck out of the dartboard on the back of his door – seven, fourteen and treble twenty. I looked at pictures he'd drawn, things he'd written – school jotters, silly little notes, funny giraffe doodles. I touched the pictures, touched his handwriting. I even got under the covers and gazed at the ceiling. Maybe he was at the end of some wormhole at the outside of the universe, somewhere in spacetime, chatting with Mozart and Martin Luther King Jr and Marilyn Monroe. Maybe I was there with him. I closed my eyes, inhaled: a smell of Si, his hair gel. *Are you there, Sibo?* If I was trying to get close to him, it didn't work. It just felt like I was laced into a corset with someone pulling the cords tighter and tighter, intensifying the pain.

Shell came round after school and we sat on my bed, doing each other's hair and sorting through my collection of nail varnish. I went for Dove, a light grey, and Midnight Dazzle for my toes.

Shell chose Coral Crush. I thought it was a bit bubblegum poppy, even though I'd bought it. But Shell could get away with it.

We sat on my bed, leaned against my Maya Angelou poster and looked through the photo album. I laughed and cried as I told the story of every picture. Shell sobbed, too, a box of hankies and a bowl of popcorn between us, a mug each of hot chocolate already drunk, the white and pink of melted marshmallows lining the insides.

'That was the time we went to the zoo and he screamed and screamed because he couldn't bear seeing the big cats and sun bears look so sad.'

'Aw, sweet pea, c'mere.' Shell pulled me in closer, wiping away a tear with the heel of her other hand.

'That was when we went to Pizza Express for his birthday and he was just about hyperventilating with excitement when his ice-cream sundae came and it was almost as big as him.'

Shell and I did some deep breathing together, until we were both laugh-crying.

I turned the page of the album to a picture of Si, pasta sauce all round his mouth, clutching a plastic fork, and, underneath it, one of him on his first day of Primary One, in his brand-new school uniform, staring into the camera, his eyes big and round, his shorts reaching halfway down his shins. A memory flashed so clearly: me, in P5, crying because some of the girls were being mean to me, and Si looking into my eyes and asking, *'But if you don't like them, why do you mind if they don't like you?'* And me, looking back into the eyes of my tiny five-year-old brother, realizing he was right, and feeling instantly that all was fixed.

'Aw, Shell,' I sobbed, leaning my head back, the poster

rustling. Here was this boy, four years younger than me, yet possessed of a wisdom and clarity of thought I had never encountered in another soul. His perspective on things never ceased to illuminate something for me.

'Thank you,' I whispered to him through a veil of tears – for being Si. Unique. Funny. Kind. For the legacy of his mind and soul. For his joyful presence that was now a bleak slice in my bookcase. For his vitality that filled my world. That lovely face that made me smile and cry. His absence was physical, acute – a bottomless pit, a vacuum that followed me around. A heavy heart was a cliché, but that's exactly how mine felt in my body – heavy, so heavy; too painful to look into, the pain dazzling. His absence stilled the house. That was what we were having to endure; the stillness of life without him, and it was too much to bear. But bear it I must.

I pushed the album onto the bookshelf, my fingers lingering on the spine. *Memories of Si*, I'd written, in gold lettering.

People talk about loss, but this wasn't loss. I hadn't lost my sunglasses or my scarf or my phone. He was a great, meaty hole through my family, right through the core. It was me who was lost – wholly lost – without him. Shell was doing a sterling job of stepping up, of being my steer, but, y'know.

'Come on, babe, let's get you out. Kopparberg Pear, or voddy and Coke, what's it to be?' Shell dabbed my face with cotton wool and did my make-up. She thrust skinny jeans and a black top at me, pulled me by the hand and marched me out of the house. 'We'll take the long way, eh?' she said. And we linked arms and walked along the side of the Drum Water, the sky a billboard of pink and blue in spongy slices, like marble cake.

We stood outside the Pink-Footed Goose with its brightly lit windows, the din of music and voices carrying out, and Shell looked at me, always a step ahead when it came to knowing how I was feeling.

'We going in, hon?' she said, her voice gentle.

I couldn't do it. I knew everyone in there, and their collective sympathy was suffocating, like trying to breathe at high altitude, I imagined – like the air was skimmed milk, not full fat. I needed a change. Somewhere where nobody knew me. Or almost nobody.

'Change of plan!' I said.

We got the bus into town, Shell and me, our arms still linked and our heads resting against each other. Shell was even smaller than me, but we were exactly the same height sitting down.

'So, come on, when am I going to meet him?' said Shell, flicking out her long, black hair. 'The *beautiful* Nathan.'

'Piss off,' I said. 'He *is* beautiful. But I shouldn't have bigged him up. You'll probably think he's a minger.'

'I will not think he's a minger. I'm sure he's a total babe. And he might even have a personality.'

'He does.'

'And hopefully he's nice, too. Nice but not dull. Nice *and* a babe.'

'Hopefully.' I let out a sigh.

Shell knitted her fingers through mine and held my hand. 'So. When *am I* going to meet him?'

'Soon.'

'Soon?'

'As in, when we get to the pub,' I said. 'He's working tonight. At least I think he is. He said he was.'

She clapped her hands and waggled her head about. 'Which pub?'

'The Banshee.'

'The Banshee old-man pub?'

'The very one.'

'He's working at The Banshee tonight, and he's expecting us?' said Shell.

'I think he's working at The Banshee tonight, and no, he's not expecting us.'

'Excellent. I like it. We sneak in unnoticed, watch him. Thrill him with our unexpected company.'

'Something like that.'

'I can check him out without it being obvious.'

'I wasn't thinking stalker scenario, or surveillance, but now that you mention it,' I said, sticking out my bottom lip and frowning, then grinning. 'Winning idea. And I can't be held responsible for your actions.'

'Exactly. You really like this guy, don't you?' Shell's faux-leather jacket groaned with the effort of excessive nudging.

'Shut up, Shell!'

'You so do! I am sooo up for this! He'd better be nice, or I might have to, I dunno, slice off his member.'

'His *member*?' We both creased up. 'You're giving me a stitch!'

The old boy two rows in front turned round and gave us a dirty look, and we descended into hysterics for a full five minutes. Shell kept trying to speak, but each time she steadied herself and opened her mouth, she cracked up again. The old boy got up and shuffled downstairs, muttering something.

Shell looked at me, and her nostrils started pulsing – her tiny diamond nose ring catching the streetlight like a miniature beacon – and she was off again.

'Stop it!' I said, clutching my tummy.

'I'm going to love him, I know it.'

'Hope so.'

'Don't you worry, sweet pea, Surreptitious Shell is on the case, and she is gonna suss him out.'

I covered my face and shook my head as if to say *What have I done?*

'Subtle is my middle name.' She grinned and jiggled her eyebrows.

'Why did I think this was a good idea?' I groaned.

'What, that one?' Shell nodded toward some toothless wee man who must have been one hundred years old, and raised a flirty eyebrow.

We erupted into giggles.

'I mean, I'm sure he's got a great personality—'

'Stop!' I said.

Shell silent-laughed like some mad mime artist. 'Him? The babe-issimo one there?'

'We've got to stop cackling.' I pulled Shell to a table near the door, out of view of the bar. 'I don't want him to think I've been watching him. I just have to go and order something, and make sure it's him that serves me.'

'Go for it.'

'Should I?'

'Go! You big wuss!'

'Aghh!'

'Cara, this is your boyfriend, that you came here to introduce me to.'

'Come with me.'

'The poor guy. Bad enough springing him at work without warning, but you want to just show up at the bar with your best friend?'

'You have summed up the situation perfectly.'

Shell sighed. 'All right, then. It's your life.'

I looked up. He was there. Standing in front of us.

'I'm Nathan,' he said, holding out his hand to shake Shell's.

'Shell,' said Shell.

'Nice to meet you. Chelle, as in, Michelle?'

'Shell as in a shell that you find at the beach.'

'Oh, OK. That's nice,' he said. 'Unusual.' And to me: 'And to what do I owe this pleasure? You spying on me?'

'No. I just . . .' I felt Shell's eyes on me.

'We just felt like a wee drink and a natter,' said Shell.

'What can I get you?' said Nathan. He was all in black. Black jeans, black shirt. Obviously the staff dress-code. Smart, though. I liked black. He had a bit of stubble – looked more edgy unshaven.

'Vodka and Coke please,' I said.

'And a pint of cider for me, please,' said Shell.

'As you wish, ladies,' he said, doing a butler bow with one hand behind his back and a deferential nod.

'So?' I leaned into Shell, watching as he headed to the bar. OK, I was watching his bum.

'Cara, he's a babe. He fancies the pants off you, it's so obvious.'

'You reckon?'

'Hundred per cent.'

'How d'you know?'

'Uh, only the way he looked at you; the way he lit up when

he saw you. When he was standing over there, he was, like, *whatever*. When he came over here and saw you, it was like, I don't know. You know what I mean. You're better than me with words.'

'D'you think he's nice?'

'He's *beautiful*.'

'Stop taking the piss.'

Shell laughed. 'I'm only teasing, hon. You know that. He's an absolute keeper.' She paused. 'Newsflash: That boy is be-sot-ted!' – she bobbed her shoulders, arms and head around as she said it.

'Whatever. Thanks, m'love.' I leaned into Shell. 'You're ace.'

'Cos I tell you want you want to hear?'

I did a coy smile and a cartoon wink, and we descended into another burst of giggles.

Chapter Seventeen

Nathan

November, Edinburgh

I got out the smoky BBQ fajita kit and reheated some leftover chicken, till it exploded all over the inside of the microwave. Cara sat there, all polite, her eyes dancing, but said nothing, resisting the urge to take the piss. It was drier than chalk, but she was nice about it anyway. I'd never given a toss before about cooking, but the shame of being exposed as crap at something so basic came over me like a rash. I vowed to start watching *Masterchef*. Practise in secret, then wow her with my culinary talents. I wanted to be somebody impressive, to be worthy. Nobody had ever made me feel like that.

I played her some of my favourite tunes, introduced her to some early Prince. She played me some stuff on her phone too – a couple of singers I hadn't heard of. Mostly, they were all right. Then she played this Danish girl Alaudidae – great voice and nice simple snare, kind of hypnotic. Cara liked it cos it wasn't 'busy'. I added it to my playlist.

She pulled out Scrabble from the living room. I reached into the bag and pulled out U, T, N.

I could've put BOG on the triple word score and got eighteen. But it was too tempting: NOB. Still, fifteen. Not bad.

Cara giggled. 'You are such a . . .'

'Lovely chap?'

'I was thinking something shorter. Something more along the lines of three letters . . . Like, maybe something beginning with N and ending with, I dunno, *ob*?'

We laughed, but it was actually slightly embarrassing. My words all came out of the primary-school book of vocabulary. BOOK. TIGER. NORTH. FINE. HOUSE. CLIP. My best, and I was rightly chuffed, was NOMADS. A double letter score and a double word score. Twenty-two points. Even though I actually got more for TAX.

Cara had all these way too brainy things like PI, combined with PA, IT and ATOM, and words I would never have thought of, like GAUGE, REALM and VAPOUR.

She played 'The Lion Sleeps Tonight'.

'*Weeee-ee-ee-ee-ee-amumbaway*,' we sang.

She played Ultravox. '*Oh, Viennaaaaaaaaaa*,' she sang.

'Anything from this millennium?' I asked.

She played Dolly Parton.

I stood up. 'Right, that's it. I'm sorry – it's been nice and all – but I have standards to withhold.'

'Uphold, ya donkey,' she said.

'Uphold, yeah. Standards to uphold. Have to draw the line. That's it. It's over.' I turned my head and showed her the hand.

'What are you talking about? Dolly Parton's a genius.'

'Dolly Parton is not a genius. Dolly Parton is a donkey.'

'Takes one to know one?' She brayed. Then she straightened up, all assertive, and shook her finger in front of my nose. 'Uh-uh.' She put her hands on her hips. 'She most certainly is not.'

'OK, perhaps that's a little uncharitable *tae oor* Dolly.'

'Genius,' she said.

'Why, thank you,' I said, and preened.

She started dancing, as in dirty dancing.

I reached for her bum.

She batted me away. 'Repeat after me: Dolly Parton is a *genius*.'

I stroked her hand, watched her body respond, before she pulled it away.

'Dolly Parton is a . . .' she said.

'Halfwit?'

'You're the halfwit.'

'Bampot? Totally ancient diva spanner-attack that sounds like a goat?'

Her jaw dropped open in mock shock. When she motioned to whack me, I ducked.

I reached for the clarinet mouthpiece and rolled its smooth coolness over her skin – I'd been made to do clarinet lessons for a term when I was ten before they realized I was a lost cause. I stroked her hand again. Her neck arched.

'OK, you got me,' I breathed into her neck. 'Dolly Parton *is* a genius.' I kissed her earlobe. 'At crosswords,' I added, half under my breath. I leaned in, kissed the curve of her neck at the back, felt her arch further into me, a small groan. I moved round her neck, planting kisses all the way round the side until I was kissing the skin under her chin. She tipped her head back and my mouth pushed into her. Grabbing me by the hips, she pulled her body tight against mine, her hands on my jeans, a bum cheek in each hand, pulling me close.

Dolly sang a surprisingly good cover of 'In the Ghetto'.

Claythorpe. That's where I'd take her. With a name like that, you'd expect to find it nestled in middle England somewhere, not next to Coldingham on the St Abbs coast. I loved Claythorpe – always had, ever since Mum had first taken us as little kids.

Cara typed it into her satnav and off we went. We stopped and stocked up on picnic stuff – crisps, strawberries, a baguette, sausage rolls, salted caramel fudge KitKats, a packet of Haribo Tangfastics. The sausage rolls were me, obviously, as were the KitKats and Haribos.

'You got the munchies or what?' she said.

'Severe case of munchitis,' said I.

We parked up and grabbed our stuff out the boot. She'd even brought a tartan blanket to sit on – more her mum's taste than hers, I reckoned. Cara went for cool geometric patterns or Scandi folk-art in bright colours – lime, or tomato red, or yellow – like a cutesy fox print or something. I nodded towards the steps leading down to the beach – couldn't take her hand because I had plastic bags of shopping and she had the blanket wedged under one arm and a multicoloured cloth bag with a big smiley face on it draped over her other shoulder.

There weren't many folk about. We stopped at the top of the steps and looked out across the North Sea.

Cara breathed in the sea air. 'It's beautiful,' she said. She smiled a big, happy smile, then leaned over and kissed me.

I rearranged the shopping bags in one hand, pulled the blanket from under her armpit and shoved it under my own, grabbed her free hand and we swung our arms as we walked down the steps to the beach. Cara half walked, half skipped by my side. 'You're so natural,' I said. 'I love that.'

She squeezed my hand, gave me another smile, then broke away, like she had at Portobello, her hair flipping in the wind. I stopped and watched her – couldn't get enough of her.

She turned left at the bottom and turned round. 'What?' she said. She knew what. She knew how crazy I was about her. I don't think she knew quite how beautiful she was, though; quite how much she made me feel.

'I love you!' I said. 'I love you, I love you, I love you.' My heart soared with it, a bird on a thermal.

She threw down her bag. 'I love you, too,' she said, blinking up at me, her grey-green eyes bright, the green flecks luminous. 'I love you, I love you, I love you, too.'

I dropped my bags too, and the blanket. She'd opened the door of my cage and freed me. I lifted higher and higher, weightless.

She hugged me really tight, for ages, and it was the best feeling of my entire life.

We picked everything up, and Cara found a spot at the back of the beach, just below the machair. She threw open the picnic blanket and laid it down, nice and straight. The front flipped over, so I dumped the shopping on the two corners, grabbed her round the waist and sat down, pulling her back with me. We sat there, her in front of me, my arms clasped round her tummy, her hands on top of mine.

'D'you think we're here for a reason?' she said.

'What, as in fate?'

She leaned her head back, rested it between my neck and shoulder. 'Not necessarily fate, no,' she said. 'Like, we all have some purpose to fulfil.'

'I don't know,' I said, ignoring the chill that seeped through me. 'Maybe.'

'Like, I don't mean it's all *destiny* and *fate* –' she put on an operatic voice and swept her arm out theatrically – 'and it's already been pre-decided by some higher force or something. Maybe we get to choose our own purpose. I just mean we've all beaten the odds to be here – all those sperms desperate to be first into the egg – and surely there's got to be some point. Don't you think?' She turned round and looked at me.

I tried to put on a profound, pensive look and gazed out to sea, as though I was looking for the answers to the universe. 'I think you're right. There's got to be some reason for us being here. But . . . all this talk of eggs and sperm's kind of getting me sidetracked.'

'Nathan!' She grabbed the baguette out the bag and whacked me over the head. In slow motion, the baguette, standing up proud, flopped in its paper sleeve. We both laughed.

'I hope I don't have that problem,' I said. 'In fact, I can report everything is perfectly alert in the baguette department.'

'Nathan!' She whacked me again. The poor baguette broke in half in the bag.

'Ouch!' I said and winced, still laughing. 'OK. I am, as you said before, a reprehensible reprobate. Guilty as charged. But, yeah, it would be nice to think we're here for a reason.'

'Don't . . .' She pinned my arms to my sides.

'Don't what? You thought I was going to say I can think of an eminently acceptable reason for being right here, right now, with you, Miss Moneypenny?' I did my best James Bond look, one eyebrow levitating. 'Wow, you read my reprobatic mind before I'd even thought that. Now that you mention it . . .' I cartoon-made to go for a tit stroke and she batted my hand away. All very predictable, but fun.

'Reprobatic?'

'If it's not a word, it should be. We should write to those dictionary folk and start a campaign to get it in there. But yes, maybe we do have a purpose.' I paused. 'I haven't worked out what mine is yet, but I guess it's early days.' I paused again. 'Gotta be careful cos, y'know, I've got my Neanderthal reputation to uphold – but, yeah, if we're really asking what we want to do with our lives, I need to do some saving.'

'You need to?' She looked at me, her eyebrows forming a peak, clearly surprised, or thinking it was an odd thing to say, or a bit of both. She played with sand, pouring a palmful from one hand to the other, over and over until it was gone, then scooping up more and starting again, all the time looking down at the sand in her hands. Despite all the banter, she looked dead serious.

'I hope – I really hope – we all have a purpose,' she said, after a while. 'Otherwise, it's all a bit pointless, a big waste of time.'

I looked at the cliffs. 'See those cliffs, how rugged, how sheer they are. There's something magical about them. I love those cliffs.'

She studied the cliffs a few moments, wiped her hands together until every grain of sand was gone, then looked at me, a big smile settling. 'Celebrations! You are not a Neanderthal!'

'Actually, Neanderthals were total brainy gods, so you're not wrong there.' I picked up the broken baguette in its bag and held it up in a threatening gesture. 'And now for revenge!' One piece of baguette and then another fell on to the blanket, but I continued to raise my hand proudly, even if my trusty sword was now a flaccid four inches of cooked dough.

Cara giggled and handed me one of the broken off pieces. I wiped it, then bit into it.

'You cannot ever escape sand in your sandwiches when you're at the beach,' I said.

'Profound statement of the day,' said Cara, grinning.

I took out my phone. 'Hey, Siri,' I said. Siri beeped. 'What's the meaning of life?'

Siri did his higher beep. 'All evidence suggests it is chocolate,' he said.

See when folk say they fall about laughing? Well, that's what we did. We fell about laughing. 'Who knew the folk at Silicon Valley had a sense of humour?' I said.

'Hold on, I want to ask him something,' said Cara. 'Hey Siri?' Beep! 'Why is my boyfriend such a nob?' Beep!

'I found this on the web for "why is my boyfriend such a nob?"' said Siri. 'Check it out.'

Cara read out the top link: 'Ten signs your boyfriend is a jerk.'

'Sorry for ruining the moment with crappy tech,' I said. 'Bye-bye Siri, back to bed with you, my friend.' I slipped my phone back in my pocket.

We took off our socks. She stroked from the front of my ankle right down to my toes. I groaned – I didn't even know I had nerve endings there directly linked to my nethers.

'You have beautiful feet,' she said.

'Random and blatantly inaccurate statement of the day,' I said.

We rolled up our jeans, went for a paddle.

She trotted off to the edge of the beach and squatted by a rock pool. I followed. She poked the water with a razor shell – I knew my shells – and I squatted too, on one knee. There wasn't much to see, except seaweed and algae. Then she lifted a tiny red crab out of the water and placed it at the edge of the pool. It scuttled away.

Meandering back across the beach, Cara picked up a tiny, white and grey periwinkle and laid it on her palm. 'It's so pretty!' She gave it to me. It had a perfect spiral, all pearly. 'Just imagine how tiny the little snail inside must have been, tootling about happily.'

I smiled. How nice to be in Cara's head. I put it in my pocket and kissed her hair. I hunted around and found a snail shell for her – pure white.

'Thank you!' She skipped in her Cara way and kissed my cheek, then bent down and picked up a brown-and-cream horn snail shell, like a unicorn's horn. 'For Shell.'

Back at our blanket, we shared the entire mega pack of Haribos.

'What's your favourite?' I asked.

'Cola bottles, obviously. Then the cherry ones.'

'Agreed,' I said. 'Then the other all jelly ones, then the ones that are half white foamy stuff last.'

'We are completely incompatible Haribo sharers,' she said. 'It would be much better if you liked all the rubbish ones.'

'There aren't any rubbish ones. Not like coffee creams or something.'

'Coffee creams are heaven.'

'Coffee creams are repulsive! Tell me you hate the fruit centres.'

'Orange and strawberry creams?' She grimaced.

'Fruit centres are crafted by angels! I think you might just be the perfect girl.'

She drove to this clearing in the woods – some place in the Borders I couldn't remember the name of. We gathered some dry sticks and set up a fire – Cara insisted on what she called the 'tepee method'. She lit it with a cool little Zippo lighter her dad had bought her.

She took out a wee penknife and whittled the end of a stick, then handed the penknife to me.

'From your dad, too?'

'Yep.'

'Your dad sounds cool,' I said, rolling the handle in my palm, then whittling my stick to a point, sweeping away from me the way Cara had. She handed me the bag of marshmallows she'd insisted on stopping at a corner shop for, and we jammed three each onto the end of our sticks, even though we'd already had sugar overload. They puffed up and went burnt on the outside and gooey on the inside.

Cara poked the fire with her stick, then threw it in. I chucked mine on, too.

We stared into the embers.

'Hashtag atmospheric,' she said.

I laughed.

She threw her arms wide. '*This* is the meaning of life.'

She took my hand, drew fireworks on my palm with her nails – *man* – and pulled me to lie down next to her as the sun dropped out of view behind a massive tree. She dragged her nails down my chest, then rolled on top of me and onto our sides and reached round and stroked her fingertips and nails down my back.

Jesus.

We lay on our backs, hands interlocked, and watched the stars, bats flitting before us like a dance performance.

'Isn't it comforting to think we'll all be stardust one day?' she said.

'Comforting?'

'I think so, yes. For me, it's not just about the things we can see,' she said, sounding almost shy. 'What about the spaces between the stars? What's there, that we can't see? It's not nothing, is it?' She paused, and squeezed both of my hands. I squeezed hers back.

We lay silent a while, gazing up together, before Cara started telling me all the stories of the constellations, the gods, the rivalries, the dramas.

'See that whole band over there, that's Andromeda. And next to her is Perseus, that bright star there – no, left a bit – yeah, that one, that's Mirfak.

The touch, the warmth of our hands plugged me right into her soul. I turned my head to the side and looked at her face, her cheek all smooth, her eyes still gazing skyward.

'So, anyway, Perseus was the son of Zeus and Danaë, and he slayed Medusa in her sleep—'

'The snake-headed one that turns everyone to stone?' I said, looking back up into space. It seemed colossal.

'Yeah, and he brought back her head to his king, and Pegasus and Chrysaor sort of materialized from her body. And every August, Perseus produces a meteor shower, and Catholics say it's the tears of the martyred Saint Lawrence, the patron saint of comedians and cooks, who the Romans roasted alive on a gridiron.'

'A gridiron?'

'An iron grid.'

'The guy was barbecued on a grill?'

'Pretty much, yeah.'

'Harsh.' I stroked her arm. 'How do you know all this stuff? Are you, like, the hot swot girl at school? I've never met anyone like you.'

She squeezed my hand again, and I looked back at the star-studded sky – at what she'd called 'all that history' – twinkling away, even in death.

'You're, like . . . the goddess of the universe, or something.'

She turned her eyes to mine, slapped me on the leg with the back of her hand, smiled, that beautiful smile turning her mouth up a touch at the edges, her eyes glittering. For a Cara smile – or the one I hoped was reserved for me – was an eye-smile. A dancing, cartwheeling eye-smile that reeled with fun and promise and warmth; that made me feel wanted and safe. I reached out, touched the two small smile lines on her right cheek – the side of her mouth that turned up a fraction. I took a mental photograph of her mouth, her eyes. Two shots that were my world – the only thing saving me from the nightmare.

Chapter Eighteen

Nathan

November, Eildon Hills

I bussed it to Tweedshaugh and Cara drove us out to the Eildons, behind Melrose. A nice hill walk and late pub lunch.

It was so beautiful. Browns and bracken, and an amber glow from the sun sitting low in the sky. Everything was bathed in this warm, peach light. And here I was, climbing a hill with Cara in her hiking boots. They were pretty worn – she'd obviously done this a lot more than I had.

'Got to find stuff to do, growing up in the Borders,' she said.

'Oh, yeah?' And I danced my eyebrows up and down like an old perve.

She giggled and thumped me.

Her parents lived in Drumleith – they'd moved there when she was eight, she said. They'd lived in Tweedshaugh before that.

I shivered. It was the word Drumleith that had snagged,

like a thread on a barb. I saw myself, standing on that hillside, watching the funeral, running back down through the nettles and brambles.

'You said you were from Tweedshaugh,' I said.

'Well, yeah, I am, but now we live in Drumleith.'

'How did I not know that? You said Tweedshaugh.' We'd been going six weeks – my longest ever girlfriend. I thought I knew everything about her.

'Maybe you just assumed, cos I said I was from Tweedshaugh and I go to school there and work there and hang out there, that I live there.'

My body tensed. From my one trip there on the bus, Drumleith didn't seem that big – one of those places everyone knows each other. What if he was one of her neighbours or something? I puffed on my inhaler.

'All this time I've pictured you in some house in Tweedshaugh.'

'Well, you'll just have to adjust your mental picture, won't you?' She looked at her watch. 'So, you still up for meeting the parents tomorrow?' She grinned.

Her parents. Hallelujah!

More like full-on hairy yikes, with a cherry on top.

'Yeah, totally,' I said, all breezy.

'Great. Mum's beside herself. Dad's looking forward to meeting you, too, but Mum's something else.'

I could imagine. 'I'm looking forward to meeting them, too.'

Oh, my God, tell her now.

A snatch of wind blew strands of hair across her mouth. She tucked them behind her ear and grabbed my hand.

We got to the top of the hill. Cara had a right solid pace on her – good legs. Sticky willow burrs stuck to her leggings, above the boot-line, where her calves curved out. I felt like a small kid, trying to keep up with an impatient parent.

'Bloody hell, you trying to show me up?' I said. I exaggerated the huffing and puffing but only a bit. Here was this super-fit goddess, and here was me, actually out of breath – pure mortifying. She broke away and ran up the last bit to the trig point. She leaned over it and traced the lines in the metal plaque that was embedded into the top. I caught up, reached my arms round her, leaned my head on hers, took her hands in mine.

'You're freezing,' I said.

The plaque showed all the surrounding hills, mapped out and named.

'This is Eildon Mid Hill,' she said, pointing at the sign, which said: 1,385 feet (422 metres). 'That one's Eildon Wester Hill.' She pointed at a smaller summit pretty much due south. 'That one –' she swung round to a third – 'has a big Bronze Age fort.'

She swung back round and I realized her eyes were wet.

'Cara,' I said. Her shoulders quaked. 'What's wrong?'

The silence drifted in the air like a breeze. She tried to speak, but the words were stolen before they formed.

'You OK?'

She shook her head.

'I'm not OK, Nath,' she said in a whisper. 'I'm not OK.'

'Tell me,' I said, the dread rising in me. 'If you're about to dump me, just say it.'

'No,' she said, shaking her head. 'That's not it.' Still she couldn't find the words.

Maybe she'd been hiding something, too. Something bad. That would be a relief.

So I took her hand, and we walked, slowly, like I was taking an old, infirm person along the street. We stopped at a nice big rock. I patted it, but she didn't sit.

'It's OK. Whatever it is, you can tell me.'

She gazed at me, her eyes filling again. She looked distraught, but also unsure.

'Listen, if you've met someone else—'

'Stop. I haven't met anyone. I haven't snogged anyone, cheated on you, nothing like that. I'm not dumping you.' She paused. 'I love you.'

OK, that's a start. She still loves me!

'So, what is it?' I reached out and held her shoulders. Can I do something? Is it about meeting your folks?'

'It's not that, Nath.' She hugged herself. 'It's my brother.'

'Your brother?' Dread rose inside me. 'You said it was just you and your mum and stepdad.'

'It is now,' she said, her eyebrows pinched, her eyes puffy. 'My beautiful little brother was killed four months ago. He was crossing the road when some fucking maniac bastard driving too fast appeared from nowhere and ran him over.'

Everything stopped.

The world swayed.

My nerves stretched, taut, sinews of pain and tension, the air a transparent film of electric wire. I reeled, punched in the guts, letting go of her shoulders.

'Oh, my God, that's awful,' I said, my voice faraway.

'Yeah.'

Everything heaved and I silent-retched. I swallowed down sick.

'Where did it happen?' I said, my voice croaky, flat.

'Edinburgh.'

'How old was he?'

'Thirteen.'

The orange seeped out of the sky and land. All was black.

'I'm so sorry.'

Understatement of the century.

I steadied myself against the rock.

His name's Simon, isn't it?

His name's Simon.

'What was your brother called?'

'Si. Simon.'

I nodded, then swallowed back more sick.

It was you.

It was you, beside the grave that day.

That girl was you.

I saw you.

I have no clear recollection of the rest of our walk, our conversation. I said all the right things, I guess. It was like my life stopped for a second time up there. I'd left myself up there. This body with legs walking was a robot.

I wasn't hungry but I swallowed down my baked potato, anyway. She had prawn mayo and cheese in hers – weird combo. I had cheese and beans, washed down with Coke. She sipped her sparkling water through a straw, with ice and a wedge of lemon bobbing around in her glass, her hair twisted into a clip at the back of her head.

She reached across the table and took my hands in hers.

'I brought you a wee present,' she said, pressing something into my hand. It was small and heavy, wrapped in dark blue matte paper with a thin, gold-foil ribbon tied in a bow, the ends curled into spirals. Mum used to get me to do that with the Christmas presents – curl the ends along a scissors blade.

I opened it. A nice little Leatherman multi-tool. My gut clawed my conscience with the wrongness of it – a gift, from her to me, today.

'Thank you,' I said, staring down at it.

'Don't you like it? You liked the penknife my dad got me, and I thought, you know, your dad—'

'It's perfect,' I said, examining all the bits. And it was. 'These pliers are . . . very nice pliers. You're so thoughtful, Cara.' But I just wanted to throw up and cry and never wake up.

Slices of hair hung down the sides of her face, and her eyes and nose were pink, like a baby rabbit.

You're beautiful. A giant, weary sadness welled up inside me, bubbling up, threatening to spill out – into tears or rage or something.

I studied every detail of her face – every freckle, the shape of her nose, her mouth, her eyebrows, her eyes, her hairline, the tiny hairs on her cheeks – committing every bit to memory, vowing never to forget that moment. *Thank you*, I told her, inside my head, *for everything*.

I couldn't get back in her car.

I just couldn't.

How could I?

'Come on, then,' she said, tugging my arm and unlocking the car. She opened the driver's door.

My feet were rooted to the spot, and my heart was in the grip of that giant fist – again.

I couldn't look at her.

I let go of her hand.

'Nathan?'

'I—' I started.

'I had to tell you before you meet my parents tomorrow, just so's you understand,' she said.

I nodded.

'It's not been the best time in our house, obviously.'

'No.'

'So. Come on then. I'll drive you home. Would you please get in the car?' She was starting to lose it. There was a waver – panic, fear, confusion – in her voice.

I paused.

Coward.

'No. I can't. I'm really sorry but it's . . . a lot to take in. I'm just going to go for a wander about the town and catch the X95.'

'O-K.'

Clearly, not OK.

'I'm sorry. I'm going to go.'

'You'll come tomorrow, though?'

'Oh yeah, that.' My voice was this distant thing again, and I didn't feel there at all. I looked to the side. 'Work rang, and—'

'What are you talking about? Mum and Dad are expecting you. We planned it. Together!'

I shifted my weight. 'I—'

'Mum's planned a lunch and everything. It's the only day everyone's off!' I'd never seen her raging.

'I'm—'

'You're sorry. You're going to go. You're going to go. So you keep saying.'

I opened my hands in surrender. 'I don't know what else to say.'

'You can't handle it.' Her face was all red and blotchy. 'What about me? I don't have a choice. I can't just walk away from it.'

'I really am sorry.' I moved to kiss her on the forehead, but she backed away, putting her hands up, so I turned and strode off into the fading afternoon light.

The car door slammed.

'I don't get it,' she shouted, coming after me, her voice slow and deliberate. 'One minute you're totally, like, loved-up, and then as soon as I mention my family you can't get away quick enough. What's your bloody problem?' She paused. 'I should have told you about my brother sooner, but I don't really see how it makes any difference to you meeting my parents.'

'I've been asked to work tomorrow – they're short-staffed. I should have told you earlier – sort of forgot. I'm—'

'Let me guess. You're *sorry*,' she said, the tears coming now, her face ready to explode. 'You're not right in the head.'

You're not wrong there.

'I can't believe you're doing this,' she said. 'You're a selfish bastard.'

Chapter Nineteen

Cara

November, Drumleith

'So, we're not meeting Nathan tomorrow?' Mum said, sagging a little.

I shook my head.

'I told him about Si, and he kind of lost the plot – said he had to work tomorrow but . . . I think he was lying.'

'It's a bit of a shock for him, sweetheart – a lot to take in.' Typical Mum – always looking for the best in people. She cut me a slice of gingerbread and sat down next to me, picking up my hand and sandwiching it between hers. 'Sounds like he can't cope with meeting us now that he knows about Si. Some people can't. They don't know what to say, how to behave.'

'Yeah, as if we've all been given a manual on how to behave.'

Mum squeezed my hand between her palms. 'They don't mean it badly.'

A growl erupted from my throat. 'But I didn't think Nath was that much of a coward.' I'd thought he'd be shocked, for sure, but I hadn't expected him to go all AWOL on me and do a whitey at the prospect of meeting Mum and Dad. I sighed at the ceiling. 'I don't understand.'

She shook her head, as if to say *it doesn't matter*.

'Sorry, Mum – I should have told him before now. I know you were desperate to meet him. Place looks great by the way.' I gestured around the room. She'd dusted all the picture frames and placed her ornaments just so. Almost like her old self.

I couldn't hold it back. I tried not to, but I couldn't stop, now that I was inside and Mum was here. I flung out my arms and wailed. 'One minute he seems so keen and serious. And then . . .'

'Give him time, Cara. Give him time. We'll meet him when he's ready.'

'Thanks Mum.' And we hugged. I felt Dad's hand, too, on my head.

'Hey, Princess,' he said. I reached up and wrapped my hand around his – his felt warm and hairy, like a furry animal.

'Nathan wasn't ready to meet us, Craig. Cara told him about Si, and he obviously needed some time.'

'Oh,' said Dad. I turned my head and saw him release a sigh, grey crescents under his closed eyes.

'You OK, love?' Mum whispered to Dad. He looked up and connected with her eyes, and I glanced from one to the other, something concealed in their silence.

Chapter Twenty

Nathan

November, Edinburgh

I sat bent forwards on the edge of my bed, my head in my hands. Hadn't slept for 30-odd hours – lay there like King Tut but sleep wouldn't come.

Her words bounced around my brain. 'My beautiful little brother.' Her beautiful little brother, his arm flung out on the tarmac, his face white and young-looking.

Your beautiful little brother.

'Some fucking maniac bastard.' *That's me. And you don't even know it.*

'I'm not dumping you. I love you.'

What was I supposed to do? I knew I had to tell her, but I just couldn't – not there, not then.

Guess I should have told Mum, but it's almost like I didn't want any love or sympathy; didn't deserve it. I'd wrecked my girlfriend's joy: didn't deserve a comforting hug from anyone.

My favourite thing in the world was to watch Cara's face break into laughter at something I'd said. To make her laugh – I was convinced it must be better than any drug. To make her smile, watch her body double up.

I couldn't believe she'd managed to hold it together these last few weeks and not tell me about her brother, but looking back, it all made sense. Guess she was just doing what I was doing: enjoying a few moments of uncomplicated fun without having to think about all the shit.

Imagine if it was my brother. How would I feel?

I imagined it. I sat on my floor and imagined looking up and seeing Damian's face wide open in a scream, seeing Damian's body slide down the bonnet, seeing Damian dead on the tarmac, his face turning blue. The horror of it being him bulldozed me flat – my goofy little brother who used to follow me around and copy everything I did; my gawky little brother who wasn't little any more and was just trying to stumble his way through the swamp; my little brother, who was the only person guaranteed to get all my jokes and understand every tiny rule of every game we'd made up over the years.

I heard him in his room, the bass drum, the snare. White Stripes. 'Seven Nation Army'. What I'd give to feel like that – like nothing could hold me back. Then the cymbals, muffled through the wall, but still there.

Thank God. Thank God it wasn't Damian.

And I imagined an eighteen-year-old just out of school, all happy and driving too fast, his head down, faffing about on his phone, smashing into my little brother, and a surge of anger ripped through my chest and rooted down through my hands and feet.

Thank fuck it wasn't Damian.

And I imagined being the seventeen-year-old sister of that dead body. I imagined being told your brother's never coming back. I imagined going to see his body, helping pick what clothes he'd want to be buried in. Standing in a huddle with my mum and dad – her mum and dad – looking down at the coffin, not being able to comprehend that it was my brother in there, and looking up at the hillside and seeing a guy – pale, with floppy hair – sitting in the woods.

And how I hated that driver. That fucking maniac bastard.

I punched my naff, pine wardrobe and collapsed back onto my bed. I wept for that boy on the tarmac, that big sister, the driver, alone behind the wheel.

Shit. I'd slept longer than I meant to. I legged it into work, didn't have time to shower.

I was only ten minutes late. And it's not like there were any customers in yet – not for another fifty minutes.

'But you can't just—' I said, trying to keep the desperation out of my voice.

'I can just. And I just have,' said Kevin. Kevin the boss. Kevin the wanker.

'But why? What did I do wrong?'

'Only just that you're consistently late, you make mistakes.' *Ouch.* 'Your presentation has deteriorated noticeably.' *Double ouch.* 'And you didn't tell us.'

'Didn't tell you what?'

'Why are you doing this to yourself? You know what you didn't tell me. We've known for weeks, Nathan – and here you are, late again. Do I need to spell it out?'

'But why does it matter? I don't see how that affects this.' And I gestured to the bar.

'Except that you're totally messed up in the head right now – of course you are – and you're not in the right place to be serving my customers. Sorry, Nathan, I have no choice.'

Brilliant.

I texted Scotty. Scotty always came to the rescue.

'sorree man, just started shift at millers. meet u 5.30. bugger k?'

Burger King.

'thx man, see you then' I texted back.

Shit. Not even Scotty could be relied upon these days. Having to earn money was rubbish.

'been sacked'

'shit man. u shouldve said. dont worry we'll sort something.'

'thx'

Five-thirty. Six hours to kill.

'Jeez, man, you been drinking?'

'I've had a couple.'

'Aye, a couple of triple vodkas, maybe.' Scotty pulled out the chair opposite me and sat down, elbows on the table.

'Yeah, so I got sacked from my shit job.'

'Man, that sucks. Did they say why?'

I shrugged, burped.

'You'll find something else, though—'

'It gets better, Scotty.'

'How d'you mean?'

'Cara told me her little brother was killed by a driver.' Scotty's big farmer's jaw fell open. Actually, by a "fucking maniac bastard" I think were her words.'

'No.'

'Yes.'

'Shit.'

'Yes.'

'You're not telling me . . . How old was her brother?'

'Thirteen.'

'The same—'

'Yup. She's his bloody sister isn't she.'

'Whoa.' He reeled back and round in his seat, like he was on a funfair ride. 'What are the chances? That's, like, seriously shit. I don't know what to say, man. That's like proper fucked-up, isn't it.'

'That would be the technical term for it. Big time.'

'Bloody hell.' He rubbed his forehead, scrunched up his eyes a second. 'You're cooked.'

'Yeah. So you can see why I wanted a couple of drinks.'

'Yeah. Totally.'

We wandered round to Rose Street. I steadied myself on a pay-and-display machine.

Scotty went to the bar while I stumbled into a corner bench. He knew the barman.

We stared at our pints. Scotty broke the silence.

'Guess that's it over, then. With her.'

'Guess so.'

'Didn't she, like, punch you or something?'

'She doesn't know.'

'Doesn't know what?'

'Doesn't know I'm the fucking maniac bastard.'

He slapped his hand over his mouth, his eyes bulging. 'Seriously? Oh, man. Oh, no.'

'Yeah. Exactly.'

'Aren't you gonna tell her?'

'Not sure I'll see her again. I can't, can I? Oh, sorry, gorgeous, but I'm the fucking maniac bastard that drove into your brother. Doesn't sound so good, does it?'

He sat back in his chair, rubbed his face. 'Not really, no. But she'll find out sooner or later, won't she? Wouldn't it be better coming from you? She'll be in court when it's your trial, won't she?'

'Yeah, guess so.' I pictured her at the High Court, all in black. I'd been trying not to think about that. I downed the last of my pint and put the glass back in the centre of the cardboard coaster, rotating it so the writing faced me.

'Nathan, I was thinking, maybe you should, you know, go and talk to someone or something.'

'Talk to someone?'

'You know, like a counsellor or somethin'.'

'A counsellor?'

He shrugged, flipped a cardboard coaster, catching it as it rolled over his fingertips.

'You're telling me to see a fucking counsellor?'

'Seemed to sort out my cousin. It was only a suggestion. It's all right – just ignore me.'

'You're saying I need therapy?' The room spun clockwise, Scotty's eyes orbiting round.

'No, not like *therapy*, no. You know – like folk go for bereavement counselling when they—'

'I'm not fucking bereaved, you fucking cretin.' My pulse whirred in my ears and the room pulsated.

'Calm down, man.' His head diverged into two heads – two Scottys, speaking together. 'You're being a right numpty.'

'You think I'm a mental case?'

'Man, calm down.'

'You think I'm a fucking mental case, you fucking bastard. You're meant to be my mate.' The air sucked me back and I reached out, beer spilling across the table, the cardboard coaster soggy under my hand.

'I was just trying to help.'

'Well, you can fuck off with your advice.' I balled my hands into fists, the right fist hovering into my field of vision.

'You need to sort yourself out. Look at the state of you.'

'What are you fucking talking about?'

'Nathan, all I said was—'

His two heads focused back into one. I punched him, square in the face. I punched my best mate and staggered to the door.

Everything was blurring at the edges.

I am not a fucking maniac bastard.

I am not a fucking maniac bastard.

'Well?' said Mum. 'Have you told her yet?'

I concentrated on not breathing out.

She came closer. 'You've been drinking.'

I said nothing.

'What have you done to your hand?'

I hid it behind me. Too late, obviously.

She reached for my hand. 'How did you do that?'

'I banged into a wall.'

Mum frowned.

'You need to get that dressed. Bandaged. I'll do it.'

'It's fine.' I snatched my hand away and leaned into the doorframe, pushing a ball of dust around the floor with the toe of my shoe.

'You can't keep putting it off. You're—'

Her voice tailed off when she realized I was shaking. Shaking with silent sobs.

'You're a good person, love.' She hugged me, trying to connect with my eyes. 'She'll be able to see that. If she loves you it won't matter to her. It was an accident.'

I shook my head. I kicked the door, making a hole. A proper hole. We both stared at it.

I swung round – still couldn't speak.

'You didn't mean to drive into that boy, Nathan. It was an awful, awful, tragic accident. It's not like it was malicious. It's horrific for the boy's family – those poor people – but if Cara really likes you – and I think she does – she'll get over it, just like one day you're going to have to.'

Her surname's Milne, Mum, but the rest of her family are Patersons.

I didn't think it out loud.

Chapter Twenty-One

Cara

November, Tweedshaugh

I remembered it like it was fresh and new each time, raw and undiluted in its awfulness.

Thirtieth of June: a date that would be forever etched in my memory. I had always thought of the first of July as the start of summer; the last days of June a preamble. Now the heady anticipation of the last day of June had morphed into something ugly, horrific. I couldn't even touch elderflower cordial any more – the smell of early summer.

I remembered Mum's shadowed face through the kitchen window when Shell and I had rolled up in the taxi. I remembered how heavy that walk up to the house had been, and how I'd vomited over Dad's dahlia. I remembered the way the door had opened – it had sort of crept open with heavy resignation. Everything had been heavy.

I remembered connecting with Mum's eyes.

I remembered her voice collapsing, the sobbing, the weeping, the heaving.

'Oh, baby,' I remembered her saying, over and over. 'Oh, baby.'

I remembered reaching to touch Dad's arm, his trace of a nod, his small voice. I remembered being shocked at how old he looked – old, scared, grey. I remembered staring at his quivering lip. I remembered the way he couldn't look at me. The man's son had just been killed, and I was thinking, *why won't you look at me?*

The very instant I'd thought that, I remembered his desperate, ice-blue eyes seeking out my own, locking slowly, painfully with mine, as his mouth turned down and burst open.

What a bloody nightmare.

That was then. This was now. Four-and-a-half months since our world turned black. Finally, I'd managed to pull it together enough to do this.

A picture of Si laughing shone out from the white screen, beamed from the projector. Above it: 'In Celebration of Simon Paterson.'

I stood up on stage.

Why had I thought I'd be able to go through with this? I breathed out slowly, found Mum and Dad over to the left, gripping each other. Dad nodded, his face grave.

I breathed in, closed my eyes a moment, then leaned into the microphone.

'My little brother . . .' I started, then faltered. The head-teacher, Miss MacPherson – MacFearsome, everyone called her – nodded encouragement. 'My little brother was the most thoughtful, kind, funny, deeply curious, intelligent, creative, probing and loving piece of matter I've ever known.'

Around the hall, sorrow was etched on every face. I had the attention of everyone in there, and even Dougie – never one to sit still – didn't break the silence.

'His body is decomposing into the soil. But his substance, his essence, his spirit will live for as long as each of us keeps it alive in our own minds.

'The body that housed Si will rot eventually to dust. Does that mean he will be erased, or blow away in a breeze? No. There may be no mass, no volume, no matter, but a human soul is more than matter. A human soul *is* immortal, in some ways.' I opened my arms wide, then knitted my hands together.

'Si wasn't religious, and neither am I. But look at that picture of him. He's not actually there, grinning out of the screen; it's a clever trick of light. But look at his face, and you can feel him here, in this room; you can get a sense of the boy that some of you have taught, some of you have shared a classroom with, some of you have sat round a desk with, sat beside in the canteen, walked past on Linksford Bridge, queued behind at Gregg's (he probably got the last pizza).' A smattering of laughter.

I sniffed, shivered.

'Si wanted to make this world a better place.' I swallowed, my throat dry. 'Everyone in this school should be proud of him. He had grand plans to volunteer at an elephant sanctuary in Thailand, he wanted to be CEO one day of Friends of the Earth or Amnesty International. He was a fierce believer in justice and compassion. If I'm making him sound all boring and worthy, I'm failing him. He was incredibly funny, as some of you will know. He was the clearest thinker ever. His mind was a one-off thing. Of course, he drove me berserk sometimes—' My voice tapered, and I sobbed and blew my nose. 'But I'd give anything—' My chest and neck constricted, and I couldn't get any more words out.

I caught his friend Ciaran's eye and breathed. He blinked back tears, gave me a nod. Leo sat next to Ciaran, the muscle in his jaw tensing – Leo that I'd half wondered if Si had a secret crush on.

'Sorry. I just wanted to tell you how lucky I am to be his sister and to have shared thirteen years, five months and twenty-eight days with him on planet Earth –' again, my voice wobbled – 'that's four thousand, nine-hundred and twenty-seven days of my life – every one of them a gift – that were lit up and lifted by the existence of this tiny, bawling, bald thing that grew into the loveliest and most extraordinary boy that ever walked the earth.'

I surveyed the hall – the red eyes, the hunched bodies, the hush; the teachers all smiling sadly at me. A warm blanket wrapped around me – all these eyes, all these hearts, sending me their strength, their care. 'I didn't mean to put everyone on a downer,' I said, smiling back at everyone through my tears. 'Si wouldn't want us to be miserable. Si would want us to get up, go out and live our best lives. Si showed me that life is to be lived and you can make an indelible mark on it, even if you don't get long. He'd want us all to get out there and live our lives as best we can.' I blinked up at the ceiling, took a breath, scanned the sea of faces. 'So, it's up to every single person in this room to do that, to honour the memory of my little brother, and also for yourselves.'

Shell sniffed and gave me the thumbs up.

I turned back to the microphone. 'I love you, Sibo, and I'll— I'll miss you forever,' I whisper-wept, breaking down in loud, ugly sobs. Mr Thomas walked me to the seat next to Shell, who was waiting, arms outstretched, eyes glistening.

The school had put together a video of photos, and a couple of clips from Si's residential, and snippets of people remembering some happy memory or funny anecdote. Si's form teacher, Ms Littlehope, got up and gave a tribute that was somehow touching and funny and sweet, and Miss MacPherson read out a poem and ended by saying Si was a huge asset and an even greater loss to our school community, but that his outstanding spirit and exceptional character would inspire a generation of compassionate, proactive, aspirational future adults, and that he would be eternally honoured and never forgotten by the school and the community.

Then Mum and Dad were ushered up on stage to launch the Simon Paterson Memorial Foundation, to fund and support 'an exceptional student in any subject or discipline', to undertake a trip and study to pursue 'an altruistic endeavour'. An anonymous funder was 'coughing up the cash' – the headteacher's words. They stood there, lost and vulnerable-looking, clamped together at the shoulder, then limped off to the side, Miss MacPherson guiding them with a hand on Mum's back.

The electric string quartet – a trio, minus their fiddle-player – played 'Canon in D', and Shell and I drowned in each other while the hall emptied, until we were the only ones left. The weight on my chest was too much to fight, and I surrendered, giving in to the full, dazzling, lung-squeezing pain of it.

Shell offered to come with me, but I needed to walk alone, to face my thoughts, and form them into a rhythm. I threw up into the verge of the lane leading down to the main road, remembering. Remembering Dad's desperate eyes. Remembering Mum's body – small, fraught, injured, a nestling fallen from the nest, pulling me to her. Remembering, remembering.

It'd been Hallowe'en a couple of weeks before. When guisers showed up at the door and asked, 'Trick or treat?'. I wanted to say 'Neither. No thanks. Piss off. Leave us alone.' At the same time, I wanted to hug them for not avoiding our house; not singling us out as the only one on the street to swerve.

Then it was Sibo's favourite night of the year: bonfire night, down in the field. I sat in my room and did drumming practice to drown out the sound of the fireworks. Once most of the banging was over, I crawled beneath Si's bed and cuddled up with Pixie, then got her a chew bar to entice her out.

Remember, remember the thirtieth of June, was all I could think. I'd rather remember the twenty-ninth of June, or any other day, even though I'm ashamed to say there was nothing special about the last day we had with Si. Nothing of note. Fish and chips from the Wednesday chip van. That was about it. I watched telly with him, grabbed the remote off him, argued about what to watch, with no knowledge it would be our last evening together.

If I hadn't been such a prize bitch and teased him about his teeth, would he have been at the orthodontist that day?

Was he was crossing the road to buy a birthday card for Dad, cos I asked him to?

Why do the Edinburgh schools finish up a different day from us?

Stop, Cara. Don't do this.

I walked. Away from school. Pupils everywhere, like ants.

Why him? Why not one of the other ants? How could they all just carry on without him?

I walked, along the riverside, over roots, to the aqueduct. I stopped at the top, watched the mass of water pass below.

I walked on, past Heldspath Castle, its walls three-feet thick, barely changed through centuries. Two dog walkers and a family walked by.

'Lovely day,' I said, with a nod and a smile. 'Nice and fresh.'

Four and a half months it had been.

Four and a half months of days, none of them lovely.

I walked, past bare trees, bracing themselves against the icy wind. I walked, alongside the swollen Tweed, flowing fast. I upped my pace, broke into a jog, to flow with it, feel its exact speed, share a tiny segment of its journey. The river was alive; it moved like I did, except it kept on flowing, all day, all night, every day, every night, for eternity. The resident heron stood on one leg, at one of his favourite spots, and a bunch of little kids and mums, hair wet, emerged from the riverside pool, smelling of chlorine. The church bell sounded once for the quarter hour, and a light drizzle started, bringing to mind Ms Strachan, my S1 Geography teacher, and her silly song for different types of precipitation.

Crossing the steel footbridge, an old man looked through me, past me, then I noticed the stick – the white stick. Tap, tap. Feeling, not seeing, his way through the world.

The pain was an ocean, vast and cold. An abyss, never-ending, infinite. Pain can never be imagined. Not fully. You can conjure the sadness, think of the sorrow, remember how you felt, but the intensity only spears its way into the picture when it's real.

This was a hideous, surreal horror show. But real and inescapable.

Chapter Twenty-Two

Cara

November, Drumleith

I spooned granola into my bowl, tipping on extra hazelnuts from the tray. That freshly roasted smell. The morning sun warming my legs through the kitchen window from ninety-three million miles away was giving me a tiny dose of cheer.

Yeah, he was a total shitbag for running off like that. But was it a dumpable offence? He obviously couldn't handle it there and then. Or maybe he was upset at the thought of losing his own brother. Maybe he was right. Maybe another day would be better – give him time to digest it. Maybe it was unreasonable to expect him to take it all in, in a oner. Maybe he was pissed off I hadn't told him earlier – angry with me, even.

Maybe, maybe, maybe. But he still ran off and left me, even when he knew how upset I was.

I felt Mum's presence at the doorway. I turned round.

'Would you like this, sweetheart? Si's belt.'

I could see it was Si's belt.

My heart panicked. My eyes welled.

'Thanks, Mum.' I held it round my black jeans. I quite liked a boy belt. 'I can't.'

'Take it,' Mum said. 'A small piece of him to keep you company.'

'You're right. Thanks, Mum.'

And I hugged Mum, so tight. I held the belt to my nose, breathing in the smell of leather and a hint of Si.

'I wonder what this other boy's doing,' Mum said, in a quiet voice. 'This Ross. I wonder if he feels bad. I wonder if he has any idea what he's done.'

'Probably not. 'Scuse the language, Mum, but this *Ross* –' the name tasted sour on my lips – 'is a total, complete, bastard. He's ruined our lives, and he's wandering around the streets, free to do what he likes. For now, anyway.'

'It's not fair, is it, sweetheart?'

'No. It's not.'

'I often wonder how his mother feels. Her son's alive and mine's not.' A heave erupted out of her.

'No justice in the world,' I said.

Mum pursed her lips. Shook her head.

'That's why I can't go anywhere near Edinburgh,' she said. 'I could walk right past him and not know. The thought of it makes me sick.'

'Me, too – I could have walked right past him.'

I looked at Mum's washed-out features. She'd always been so tidy. Never a hair out of place. She didn't wear much make-up, but the little she did wear was always immaculate. You wouldn't notice her make-up, but I noticed its absence. The lines, the circles under her eyes, the eyelids – normally unnoticeable. Now they folded, white and vulnerable without their rose eyeshadow. Mostly, though, it was her hair. Four and a half months, and still she hadn't got it cut. She religiously got her hair done monthly. The greys poked, unruly. Her clothes and all were fine – the usual neatness maintained.

'I need to cut your hair.' I didn't cut Mum's hair – she still went to Stella, who she'd been going to since before I was born.

Her chin wobbled.

'Yes, it's fair to say I'm not looking my best, am I?'

'Mum, you've had more to deal with than any mother ever should.'

Rain drummed its unrelenting rhythm on the windowpane.

'I know, sweetheart, I know. Thank you.' And she pulled a kitchen chair into the centre of the floor and fetched a towel to drape round her shoulders.

'D'you want me to wash it first?' I said.

'I'll wash it myself,' and she disappeared off out the room.

Relief, then shame at the relief, swept over me at not having to touch her unwashed hair, that smelt ever so slightly stale.

I found the parting, combed out her hair.

'So, sweetheart, you know the date's been set for the court case?'

'Yeah, you said.'

'February sixteenth.'

'OK.'

'We'll have to prepare ourselves to see the driver. God knows how I'll find the courage.'

'You will, Mum. You're stronger than you think.'

'We'll all have to. Will you come, love? Will you come with Dad and me?'

My hand stopped cutting before I realized I'd gone quiet, the air squeezed from my lungs.

'I hadn't really thought about it.' I really didn't want to think about it. Ever. I studied Mum's double crown and nape whorl. Of course Mum and Dad needed me there. I'd always thought of myself as someone who faced life head-on, didn't bury my head in the sand and avoid things. Courage – that's what I wanted to stand for, not cowardice.

I thought about it now: pushed through the layers that I'd built up in my mind to prevent me from having to go there. Imagined the courtroom, full of faces. Some boy racer in the dock. This hatred I felt for him, so strong and scary.

'You want me to be there?'

'Yes, love, that would be a big comfort. The three of us, together. For Si.'

The 'three' bit stung.

The Si bit stung more.

'Of course I'll be there, Mum.'

The gravel grumbled. I looked up to see a police car in our drive. The scissors slipped from my hand and my grip tightened around the top of the chair, even though she was nice, the liaison officer. PC Rhona we called her, instead of PC Savage, her surname. She was the opposite of savage.

She had the collision report. Mum invited her in.

Time to face up, stop avoiding it; stop leaving it all for Mum and Dad to deal with.

'There's nothing much in it that you don't already know,' said PC Rhona. 'From examining the tyre marks and vehicle, together with CCTV and dashcam footage, they've established that the veh— the car was travelling at thirty-four miles per hour just before impact.'

I leaned over to look at the file.

Three words leapt out from the page, in resolute Roman lettering: 'Ross Nathan Blake.'

Nathan Blake.

Nathan.

No.

Sound fell away and I was left with a silence that was spherical and absolute, the edge the blackness of infinity. I felt dizzy, spaced out.

'The driver's called Ross,' I said, trying to keep my voice steady. 'Ross – that's what you said.'

'Ross – yes, that's right,' said PC Rhona, exchanging a confused look with Mum.

I grabbed the report off PC Rhona, kept reading.

'What is it, Cara?' Mum asked, her voice small.

I turned the page, and my insides liquified. I was free-falling down, down.

The words pulsed.

It can't be.

It has to be.

That's why he ran.

I forced out my voice, this weird, disembodied voice in this weird, echoey chamber. 'Then why does it say he goes by his middle name, Nathan?'

Mum shrank back, her hand over her mouth, and reached her other hand out to the wall.

'People have all sorts of strange name anomalies,' said PC

Rhona, putting on her glasses and leaning in. 'It's not unusual.' She looked up, not understanding.

'It's not my Nathan,' I whispered, dropping the report and clutching at the air. Mum's hand was still clamped over her mouth. 'It's not my Nathan – he doesn't drive.' My voice came out pleading, desperate.

PC Rhona's chin dropped, and she looked at me, her own face draining of colour.

'Your Nathan?'

'Cara's new boyfriend . . . Cara's new boyfriend's . . . called Nathan,' Mum said, with forced calm.

I darted the five paces to the downstairs loo, threw up, spat and flushed. Mum came in after me, rubbed my back.

Mum followed me back out. PC Rhona stood there, her mouth set. She cradled her hat in her hands.

I braced myself. I wanted to scream but gripped on to my control. I spoke slowly and quietly, and clearly.

'How old is Ross the driver?'

'Eighteen,' said PC Rhona, looking stricken. 'How old's this Nathan?'

I paused, pulling everything inside together so pieces of me wouldn't crash to the floor. 'What's his date of birth?' My voice was reed-thin, barely a voice.

PC Rhona found it in the file, read out the date of birth and the address: *80 Janvier Terrace, Edinburgh*, and looked back up at me. Her alarmed eyes hovered on the horizon a moment, sliding a little.

The room blurred and imploded. I was the centre of a black hole, infinitely heavy, infinitely crushed.

'No!' I screamed and bolted up to my room. Mum and Pixie

chased after me, Mum grunting with each step, leaving PC Rhona stunned in the hall.

I dived onto my bed and wailed. Mum held me, resting her head on my back. Pixie whined and pushed her nose into my neck.

'I love you, baby girl,' said Mum.

I beat my duvet, like I was possessed. I had no control over it – my body was doing its own thing.

Mum shook her head, her own eyes streaming, and supported me, cupping her arms under mine. I flopped into her and she rocked me as we sobbed into each other. My sobs were so intense I gasped for air between them.

I dragged myself off the bed, hauled myself down the stairs and snatched the file off PC Rhona.

'Is there a picture?' I said. A different Nathan Blake, who happened to be born on the same day and live in the same house.

A puzzled expression played around her eyes for a second. 'Of the driver?' she said. 'Here.'

I stared at the image, at the eyes – dark pools of eyes. My hand was at my mouth. The hair was shorter, the eyes were wild and baggy, but it was him – my Nathan – the bastard who'd killed my brother. I looked into the eyes, pictured hands in front of the face, gripping a steering wheel – the same eyes Si would have seen through the windscreen. I thrust it back at PC Rhona and stumbled back up to my room. Mum sat on my bed with her bedraggled head in her hands.

Wait a minute – no way. Had he sought me out deliberately?

No.

No.

'I'll let myself out,' came PC Rhona's voice.

'Just a second, sweetheart,' Mum said to me. She lowered my upper body onto the bed and kissed my forehead, soft as fairy dust. I kicked out and collapsed back onto my covers.

Chapter Twenty-Three

Nathan

November, Pentland Hills
'Baaa.'

'Maaa.'

'Baaa-aa-aaa.'

'Mhe-he-he-he.'

It was a new level of mentalness, even for me. Talking to sheep.

I lay back on the heather, in the dip between the hills – Caerketton and Allermuir. The air was cool but a slant of sun shone right on my face. *Warm*. The Pentlands were the best place in the world – when you didn't want to speak to anyone. The sky was blue and the clouds were fluffy. Ships, sailing across the blue.

'I owe her an apology. An explanation. A something.'

'Me-heh-heh-heh-he.'

'She'll hate me for ever. But I have to tell her before she finds out.'

'Maaaaaa.'

'You're right. I just need to tell her, don't I? See when I ran off the other day without meeting your folks. Yeah, well sorry about that – just couldn't face meeting them. Because I'm the fucking maniac bastard. Yeah, you heard – it's me who drove into your brother.'

'Mhe-he-he-heh.'

'Any other pearls of wisdom? Sage advice? Tips for how to get through the next, like, however many years of my life?'

'Baaaa.'

'You again? OK, thanks for that.' *You've totally lost it this time, Blakey. Like, proper lost it.*

'Maaa.'

'Oi, less of your cheek, you. Me-he-he-heh.' A quad bike, buzzing below. I looked down at the fenced fieldy bits. 'You meant to be up here, by the way?'

'Baaaa.'

'Baaa to you, too. What, I should just text her, right now?'

'Baa.'

'Right. You're right.' I pulled my phone out my pocket. 'Look, I'm doing it.'

'hey, can we talk. up allermuir. meet later? x'

'Done it. I've texted her. Happy?'

'Me-eh-eh-eh.'

'Roger. Glad we got that sorted.'

I turned my head and picked up a little orb of sheep shit, rolling it around my fingers – after all, it's just grass. According to legend, I'd eaten one once, thinking it was a blueberry – a 'boobie'. I was three. It's one of those memory illusions that's probably based on zero per cent actual memory and one hundred per cent the memory of being told about it. It never failed to reduce Mum to tears – the right sort.

There was a blonde girl with a cream beanie in the walkers' car park, pacing. My stomach dropped and tiny invisible fists pummelled at my chest.

Ho-ly—

'Why didn't you tell me?' she screamed, marching up to me, her eyes red and puffy and filled with rage. 'Maybe just, possibly, that was a slightly fucking majorly important piece of information I might just need to know.'

I squeezed my eyes tight, breathed in, even though it felt like a fuck-off great HGV was sitting on my chest.

'You arsehole.' Her voice was lower now, the edge blunted. 'You big total arsehole bastard. Maybe you didn't mean to, but you killed my brother and you knew it that day at the Eildons and you didn't tell me. I hate you, I hate you, I absolutely hate you.' She shoved me, hard, in the middle of the chest, her face crumpling. She swiped at my face and wiped a bitter sob from her own. 'I hate you.'

Ice inched its way through my veins and into my heart, turning it solid. Solid things can't beat; can't feel anything. But this ice, this pain – it was too strong. I let it take hold; didn't put up a fight.

'I'm so, so, so, so sorry,' I said.

Pathetic.

'Why didn't you tell me?' Her eyes bored into mine, and the pain on her face was my pain – it seeped through my pores, into my tissues, my bone marrow, my heart, my soul.

'I was about to tell you. I wanted to tell you.' *Pathetic, snivelling fuck.*

'Why didn't you, then? You sat and held hands with me at lunch that day and you *didn't tell me.*' She growled the last three words. Then she was statue-still, like she was paused in time, or maybe it was my mind wanting to pause this final picture of my girlfriend.

'I was about to tell you that day that I'd hit a boy – killed a boy – then you told me about your brother. You said it was just you and your mum and dad; how was I to know you had a brother?'

I reached out to touch her, but she stepped back, like I was a threat.

'You told me you don't drive,' she screamed.

'I don't – not any more.'

She sobbed, and my soul smashed into shards.

'I'm so sorry,' I said, my voice breaking. 'I love you.'

'I hate you.'

She shoved me.

I couldn't hold everything in. It was too much, boiling, bubbling, churning inside.

'I love you for ever,' I said, my face wet. Miniature needles pricked all the way up my spine. My mind took one last snapshot of her – cream beanie, blotchy, heart-shaped face, olive scarf, grey jacket, blue jeans, mint wellies.

I turned round and legged it, and roared and wept as I ran.

Fucking coward.

'I hate you.' Her words chased me, bursting with sincerity, like the hate had risen in her and crystallized into something solid. A big cancerous lump of hate.

Chapter Twenty-Four

Cara

November, Swanston, Pentland Hills

The boy I loved – the boy I loved more than anyone, the boy I couldn't stop thinking about every second of every day, the only decent thing in my life since Si was killed – turned and ran, kicking up flecks of mud with each step.

I got back in the car and sobbed, my forehead resting against the bottom of the steering wheel. A different steering wheel, a different car, a different driver from the one who'd exploded our world and sent shrapnel into every part of our lives.

His voice came to me, that time at Claythorpe. 'I need to do some saving.' I remembered thinking it was an odd thing to say.

I stopped for fuel on the way back to Drumleith.

'Cheer up, love. Might never happen.' Some guy in black and orange workman's trousers.

I spun round.

'Excuse me?' I said, though it was more a bark than a question. Then I put my hand to my mouth and my eyes welled.

The guy stood there, staring.

I got back in the car and drove home, wondering what Si would make of all this. I sat behind a tractor for a couple of miles – I was in no hurry – before it turned right up Shiplaw. A badger lay at the side of the road, dead. I kept seeing them – dead animals. I'd never really noticed them before. Was it a new obsession, like when people start noticing 'For Sale' signs when they're looking for a house, or cars of a certain model? Dead animals for me, and hearses.

I stopped at the garden nursery and bought thirteen snowdrop bulbs, then went back to the till and bought another one – Si's final half-year was more than zero.

I parked a couple of streets short of the turning for our house and walked back along the pavement, up the path to the graveyard. An orange sun hung low in an invisible sling, illuminating the tops of the trees.

'I had to come and see you. Needed to talk to you.'

And I talked and talked to my little brother, buried in the damp earth.

I told him I'd been seeing a boy I really liked – a boy called Nathan, a year older than me, near enough. That he was funny, and thoughtful, and quiet, and kind. And that I hated him. And there was a big pause, and the silence and the wind and the air and the spirit of Si seemed to ask why I'd said that, why I hated this boy, Nathan. I glanced up at the hill, at the woods, and the weirdest déjà vu flashed up – a negative of a figure, sitting on the ground, on the day of Si's funeral, and I gasped.

Nathan. It was Nathan. Was it? Or was my mind playing

tricks – it hadn't exactly been a normal day, and my poor little soul had been through a bit of a battering.

I whispered my confession to Si.

'I hate him because he killed you, and I love you, little brother,' I said, wiping my nose on the back of my hand.

Si – or his spirit or the air or the universe or whatever you want to call it – said nothing. I stared at the headstone, tipped my head to the side, awaiting his verdict. I almost expected a big deep, phantom voice to clear the skies and announce, 'OK, earthling.' Like the tour guide on the ghost tour Nathan and I had been on.

How happy I'd been that night, sitting in the pub, holding Nathan's hand and leaning against his shoulder and looking into his eyes and hearing about his plans. So much for the good luck the spitting on the Heart of Midlothian was supposed to bring.

A bitter chill tried to work its way into my soul – it pressed in through my veins – and I pushed it away. *No! Begone!* I didn't want bitterness. Bitterness wasn't me.

I touched the grass. 'Do you forgive me?' I whispered. A whip of wind lifted a cracked, curled leaf in a loop and dropped it back to the ground. I sobbed. 'Sibo, can you forgive me?' I listened out for a sign and let out a long breath.

So cold. So tired. I pressed my fingers to my cheeks, and they were slivers of ice.

'I'm sorry,' I told Si. 'I didn't know it was him.'

The wooden handle of Dad's trowel felt nice in my palm. I dug little holes and planted the bulbs in front of the headstone – a bit haphazard rather than neatly spaced – then filled them in and pressed the earth down. And I sat, cross-legged, and traced the letters of Si's name, carved out of the granite, and felt the ground hold my weight and the blades of grass between my fingers, a nearly full moon looking down.

We were in English and Miss Fernandez was chairing a class discussion on a short story she'd asked us to read. Instead of an author's name it said 'Anonymous' so we all reckoned she'd written it and was trying it out on us. It had some sweary bits and a saucy bit, too, and there was violence and prostitution, so if she really had written it, I reckoned it was a wise move to deny all knowledge.

'Yes, Douglas?' she said, an upbeat note masking the weary tone.

'Who's the author, Miss?' asked Dougie. 'Do they like to go *for Nando's?*'

Miss Fernandez was a pro. She'd mastered the art of ignoring Dougie.

I wished Dougie would kick the back of my chair – he used to do it all the time. Since when had he ever spared me?

I dropped my head forward, hunching over my desk. A warm hand, rubbing my back. Shell.

'You all right, hon?' she asked.

I nodded, sniffed, paused, then shook my head. There was never any warning, when the pangs would come.

Miss Fernandez asked the class to write their top five impressions, good and bad, about character, plot, theme – anything – then write a page or two expanding on one. Then she was beside me, kneeling, her box braids falling over my desk, her kind face looking up into mine, her eyes shining. She gave me a sad smile and said Shell and I could go and get a coffee in the S6 common room. I shook my head.

'I love this story,' I said, in a low voice. I had lots to say about it – it had taken me out of my world and into its own. And even though it was undeniably sad, it had moved me, and that sadness felt comforting – like shared human experience or something; company in my pain.

I glanced over my shoulder. Silence all around. It was the same in all my classes, and in the corridors, too. Everyone was quiet and calm around Cara; not the usual sarky comments, banter and general silliness. If the school wanted to do a promo video of how well behaved all their seniors were, they only had to video me, surrounded by model students.

My form teacher, Mr Montague, messaged, asking if we could have a chat.

A chat? A *chat*? Chats weren't good. Everyone knew that.

I knocked on the open door and went in.

'Come on in, Cara, have a seat,' he said, all big smiles.

I sat back and watched him. The smile fell from his face, like it had been stuck on with an old Pritt stick. Mr Montague stood up and frowned and paced the length of the room slowly, rubbing his fingers up and down his chin, pushing his lower lip up each time.

'What's the problem, Mr Montague?' I asked – a slug could have worked out there was something bothering him.

He sat down, pulled his chair out to face me. A bare bulb glowed behind him, casting a shadow over his face, making him look like a ghoul. A friendly but tormented ghoul.

'Cara. You've always been a strong student. One of our top students, in fact.'

'It's been difficult, Mr Montague – really, really difficult.' I felt myself slump a little. 'It's my grades, isn't it?'

'You've dropped from As to Cs in all your subjects except English.' I balled like a hedgehog. His voice was low, gentle, kind. 'We want to support you in any and every way we can, Cara. Have you spoken to anyone, been to bereavement counselling? Maybe you need to take a couple of weeks completely off – a clean break, to focus on your well-being?'

I nodded, couldn't speak. Maybe he was right. I so wanted to keep going, to hold it all together, but my world was crumbling.

I stepped along the High Street, settling into a brisk rhythm, the regular clicking of my boot heels interrupted every so often by an old lady or an S1 or 2. Darn them all at lunchtime, queuing for Greggs. It would take five hours to get a cheese and onion pasty at this rate.

I had always been so committed to my work. To everything.

I sighed, long and juddery.

Nobody had told me how exhausting misery was.

Chapter Twenty-Five

Nathan

November, Bathgate

So yeah, I did a runner. I'm not proud of it. I exited her life. For her. For me, it was like that big fist had me again in its grip, going, *you really thought you could get away from me, you pathetic loser?* And it squeezed and squeezed, tighter and tighter.

I ran, through fields, woods, followed rivers, climbed barbed-wire fences, got an electric shock from an innocent looking wire, like an almighty kick up the arse. The cows, the sheep stared. A horse whinnied.

I ran, up a hill, scrambling up the scree slope, my fingernails black-red from blood and dirt. Black clouds shifted overhead. The air was a whip, relentless in its coldness. Then, a beam of sunshine punched through, as if the angels were bursting into song, with zero consideration for how I was feeling. I roared. *Nutter.*

I ran, along the edge of the M8, the traffic speeding past to its own deafening rhythm. The sky darkened. My legs ached.

It was night when I ran down the slip road to Bathgate. I couldn't believe I'd run twenty miles. It was like my body had taken over and all it knew was to run. I dodged over the roundabout at the bottom of the slip road, a driver gesticulating and swerving.

'Fuck you!' I shouted, giving him the finger.

Fuck everyone.

Straight on for ages, three rights and a left, and another right. There it was, right on the corner. 1 Baird Crescent.

Bing bong.

'Nathan, dear.' Gran tried to hide her alarm. Oh, Nathan, look at you, said her eyes. 'You don't need to ring the bell,' she scolded, touching my arm. 'For goodness' sake, come on in. I'll get you something to eat.'

It wasn't long before she got to the point: 'We really must ring your mum – she's worried sick.'

'Tell her I've gone to bed and I'm fine.'

'Don't you think she'll want to speak to you?'

I put my hand up. *Enough.*

Gran blinked fast and gave me a tight hug. She wasn't really a hugger. 'Oh, Nathan, darling. You're always welcome at your gran's. Always.' She held my face. Hers looked plucky and full of life. She had the same eyes and eyebrows as Mum, but Mum hadn't been looking so good lately.

I closed the guest-bedroom door and sank back on to the bed that was made up with the Star Wars covers I'd been obsessed with when I was eight – had she been expecting me?

I lay there and closed my eyes, breathed in a faint smell of

Vicks. Gran's face morphed into Mum's, except it was sort of grainy and pixelated, and it rotated and was two-dimensional, an illusion, and floated off like a sheet of tissue paper lifted by a breeze.

I opened my eyes, stared at the woodchip ceiling, like exploded popcorn, held it as long as I could without blinking. I crawled over the covers, reached out past the foot of the bed, picked up the framed photograph on the bookshelf – a striking man in military uniform and cap, smiling, his jawline square. He gazed right at me, right into the camera. Gran's American dad. The story of his death had become legendary in the family. Shot down in the Vietnam War, on his twenty-seventh birthday, the day his only daughter was born. I felt a ridiculous, illogical envy of the great grandfather I'd never met. To be the one who got killed, instead of killing someone. I put him back on the bookshelf, sat back on the bed.

Cara.

Cara.

Cara.

What a fucking mess.

I looked down and found I was fidgeting with my Leatherman, warm from my jeans pocket. I turned it over. The weight in my palm, the smoothness against my thumb and fingers, was like an old friend. I flicked up the knife and pressed the blade to my wrist. The sensation of sharpness surprised me. It registered somewhere deep. I imagined the chemical impulses messaging my brain, panic alerts. It felt . . . real. Right. Satisfying, somehow. I held it up, studied the point. I pushed it, harder this time, pulling the blade across the flesh of my forearm. It left a pink line. *Pathetic.*

I raised the blade, watched the way the streetlight caught the angled edge, making it bright white. I pushed, harder, the point making a dip in my skin. I twirled it round, pulled it across my forearm, but it jumped. *Blood!* I felt a surge of something. Release?

A tiny bead of scarlet sat on the tip.

I put on my headphones to drown out the sound of Gran's voice. Her voice was low, hushed, but I needed to cut her out.

I listened to Royal Blood – 'Figure It Out' – laughed at the irony. My blood was far from blue. Then Si's body flashed up in my mind. His body, his blood. I needed it to be my blood, not his.

That last snapshot of Cara – her blotchy face framed by her scarf and the collar of her oilskin jacket, her blonde hair – shiny under her cream beanie – popped into my head. Then the day I'd met her, in the café – her friendly face and sure posture, her glowing skin, her lemon pendant, her grey-green eyes and the dimple on her left cheek when she smiled. Then her hair flipping in the wind on the beach, her eyes shining, telling me, 'I love you, I love you, I love you, too.' The surge of pure joy. Then darkening into the red eyes and angry mouth shouting, 'I hate you, I hate you, I absolutely hate you.'

I sobbed, salt stinging my throat.

What had I done to her – the girl I loved? How could I have hurt her so much? She was right: what I'd done, it was unforgivable. There was no excuse; I should have told her earlier. And when her shoulders quaked at the top of Eildon Mid Hill and she'd told me, puffy-eyed, about her little brother, I should have said it there and then – fessed up like a man, instead of the loser wuss I was.

'Nathan! Nathan, love.' Gran, knocking at the bedroom door. 'Nathan, your mum wants to talk to you. She really wants to speak to you, dear, to hear you're OK.'

I pulled the covers over me, huddled under my duvet. Gran was in the room now, moving about. Her hand pulled gently at my shoulder.

'Nathan, love, please.' It was almost a whisper. 'Your mum's been through it too. She needs to hear your voice. She's coming over with Damian.'

I didn't budge. My eyes were closed anyway. I lay still as death.

'I think he's asleep, love,' I heard her say. 'I'll watch him until you get here.'

Had she seen the knife? Had I left any blood? It was dark, but you never know.

She sat there, and I lay all tensed up, unable to twitch a muscle, desperate to shuffle my hand under the covers to find the knife before she did. Thank goodness for the Star Wars covers. Dark sheets don't show bloodstains.

I knew it at that moment. There was only one solution. Only one way out of this mess.

Chapter Twenty-Six

Nathan

November, Bathgate

'So, how are you, man?' said Scotty.

'Fine,' I said.

'Fine?'

We sat in the kitchen at my gran's house. It was all a bit awkward, which was nuts. Me and Scotty had been easy-osey with each other since the first day of S1 when he'd plonked down next to me in form class.

'Could have fooled me,' he said.

I shrugged, focusing on the toaster.

'Hey, I got onto the next level,' he said – change of tack.

'You did?' I knew what he was talking about – *MadrushX4*, a game we played together. 'Show us.'

We went through to the living room, sat side by side on the sofa. We played for a bit, and I did some kickboxing with *T-Bron* – another game we used to play.

I caught Scotty looking at me, at my wrist. I pulled the cuffs down on my hoodie and gripped them in my palms.

He leaned towards me, fixed me in the eye, his brown eyes serious. *No messing*, they seemed to say. His bushy eyebrows furrowed. 'Man, enough of all this pretending everything's fine bullshit. Tell me what you want me to do,' he said. 'Anything – just tell me what you need. You need to see someone.'

I nodded.

'Sorry,' I said. 'About last time.'

'It's OK.'

I squirmed into the sofa, braced myself. Mum was the only one I'd ever talked to.

'Seriously, man, just tell me what you want me to do,' he said.

I stared at him.

'What?' I said.

'You look terrible.'

'I know.'

'You look, like, a hundred years old.'

'Been working on it.'

'Seriously, ring me. Text me. Any time, day or night. OK?'

I nodded.

'Promise?'

'Promise.'

'I know it's beyond horrific but we're going to get you through this, OK?'

Jesus.

'OK,' I said.

'All right. Sorted.' He slumped right back into the sofa, exhaled, looked up at the nasty swirls on the ceiling.

Chapter Twenty-Seven

Cara

December, Drumleith

'Yeah, that sort of splodge of stuff there, that's Andromeda,' I said. 'It's two-hundred-and-twenty-thousand light years wide and it's got a trillion stars. She's supposed to be the beautiful daughter of Cassiopeia, the queen.'

'Oh, dot, my, dot, God, you are such a geek. A galaxies and Greek myths geek. And such a babe, babe. A geek-babe. The world's babest geek.'

'Shut up, Shelly.'

'Do not call me Shell*ey*.'

'Shell-y as in Bill-y, not Shell-E-Y.'

'We are a Shell-y or Shell-*ey* free zone.'

'OK, then. Shut up, Michelle, ma belle.'

Shell zipped her lips with her hand, pushed her mouth into an exaggerated sad-face.

It was my seventeenth-birthday present from Mum and Dad. A totally amazing telescope. But it had been spring then summer, and y'know, no dark skies and the slight inconvenience of a death in the family. It had sat there, some ghostly spectre under its white sheet.

All I wanted to do was show Si. He'd thought it was cool when I'd un-sheeted it on my birthday.

I wanted to tip the telescope out of the window and hear it smash.

I reached out, touched the snail shell Nathan had given me that day at the beach. It sat there on the bookshelf, shiny white, so tiny and perfect.

I couldn't hold it in any longer, the tears flowing now, my chest juddering. That day, at Claythorpe, then at Cleuch Forest . . . Everything had felt so right. We'd had so much fun. And the last time I'd looked at Cassiopeia . . . The memory fizzed with an intensity like it was real again.

'Oh, hon.' Shell pulled me in tight and rubbed my back.

Mum had pressed £300 into my palm that morning, a few days after Mr Montague had sent me home. 'Go on, love. Book yourself a weekend away with Shell.'

I'd cried I was so happy.

'OK, Shell: caravan on the west coast or beach holiday in Majorca?'

'Majorca, obviously.'

'Thought you might say that.'

'Well, come on. Sun and beaches or pissing rain and midgies?'

I laughed. Majorca it was. Even if you don't get midges in December.

*

NATHAN IS A BASTARD, I carved into the sand at Puerto Pollensa with my toes. A five-line font. But even the sand in my toes conjured him up, smiling at me, chasing me along the beach, laughing when I whacked him over the head with the baguette, pressing the shell into my palm, pulling me into him, his breath ragged when we kissed.

His voice appeared in my head: *'Do you know how fine you are to me, Mary MacGregor?'* But it wasn't matched by a happy look, or the look of someone out to use me. All I saw was a deep, aching sadness. How could I have been so blind? Here was me with my psychology this and psychoanalysis that. I should have been able to spot it a mile off: the truth behind the eyes. The vulnerability had lifted off him when he'd told me about his dad.

No wonder he'd stared, blank, at the multi-tool I'd given him at lunch after our hike up the Eildons. He hadn't exactly gushed with gratitude.

His face again, at his house this time, meeting his mum, how chuffed he'd been – the pride radiating off him like a pulse. The way he'd arranged the French Fancies on the plate like he was desperate to please. Then he was taking the mick out of himself, talking about having to uphold his Neanderthal reputation – I loved his modesty and wit.

The picture in PC Rhona's file jumped out at me – the wild, baggy eyes – reminding me he deserved no compassion. Si would be alive if it wasn't for him. Where was my hate, my anger? It should have been piercing, spearing its way through me. *I'm sorry, Si. You deserve better.*

'Oh, Shell, it's like he's implanted himself into my soul or something.' I kicked at the 'D' but my leg was weak and my insides wilted.

Shell gave me a sideways look, picked up a stick and drew a giant willy and balls. Then she started stabbing the willy with the stick, like some psycho. I laughed so hard my sides hurt.

I was still giggling when we played mini-golf – I was *rubbish* – and when we ordered a mushroom and pineapple pizza to take away. We ate it watching the sun setting over the bay.

Later on, in our hotel room, I scribbled:

Cara Milne loves Nathan Blake
20020
2022
224
46%

I hadn't done it since I was thirteen. Adding up all the Ls, Os, Vs, Es and Ss in my and a boy's name, then adding each number with its neighbour and continuing each line until you got 100 or less – to get a percentage. Cos that's the only way to be sure about true love, obviously.

Cara Milne hates Nathan Blake
15120
6632
1295
31114
4225
647
1011
112
23%

I scored out 23 and underlined 112%.

Cara Eva Milne loves Ross Nathan Blake
21132
3245
569
1115
226
48%

Cara Eva Milne hates Ross Nathan Blake
16132
7745
14119
55210
10731
17104
8814
1695
71514
8665
141211
55332
10865
181411
99552
1814107
995517
18141068
99551614

1814106775
Infinity%

'I don't hate him. I miss him. I miss him so much.' I collapsed forwards, resting my head on my crossed arms. 'I want to hate him – I should hate him.'

'C'mon, love.' Shell's arms reached around me, pulled me up. She touched my cheek and turned my face towards her. She looked into my eyes, stroked her right thumb under my left eye, but it only made more tears come. 'You *will* meet someone else. Some day. You can't imagine it now, but it will get better. OK?'

'But I don't want anyone else. I want him.'

Shell sighed. 'You can't have him, Cara. You've got to stop thinking like that.'

'I know!' I wailed. 'But I can't help it.'

She waved a finger in my face.

I nodded and found myself laughing between sobs, like some madwoman.

'Sangria?' I said, and Shell gave a thumbs up. She grabbed her handbag and applied some lippy. I picked up my purse and we started walking, down the stairs, past the hotel bar and out into the warm night.

We paused outside a bar with a sunflower-yellow front and laminated pictures of cocktails with little umbrellas sticking out the top. Two palm trees in giant pots guarded the doorway.

Shell smiled. '*Litro?*'

'Tell Alejandro there,' I said, pulling her into the bar and nodding towards one of the waiters – slim, hair smoothed back, black trousers, white shirt. 'Just your type.'

'Ya big slapper!'

The Proclaimers came on. '500 Miles'. Honestly. Nuts. Had they followed us 1,000 miles from the Port of Leith to here? Shell screeched.

'*Dadela-da*,' she yelled, and I joined in, both of us waving our arms like maniacs. '*Dadela-da. Dadela-dadela-dadela-dadela-dadela-da-da. Dadela-da. Dadela-da. Dadela-dadela-dadela-dadela-dadela-da-da.*'

We sat down at a table that had a pineapple in the middle with multicoloured strips of plastic exploding out of it like a firework. Garlands of fake flowers in bright pink and yellow and white were wrapped round pillars and draped along the wall, and the UV light made everyone look super-tanned and amazing.

Shell put her arm round me, dabbed my eyes. 'What is it, babe?'

I looked at her, my shoulders shaking.

'Noooo,' she said, drawing out the vowel sound, 'Stop it!' She narrowed her eyes at me.

'Paddington gave Mr Brown a hard stare,' I said. I felt like a kid whose pockets have been found bulging with sweets from the pantry – caught thinking about Nathan *again*.

'What?'

'Shell gave Cara a hard stare.'

She laughed. Then recovered the hard stare. 'It's OK, gotta get it out. It's your call if you need to talk about him, hon.'

'I promised myself I wouldn't ruin our holiday talking about him or thinking about him.' But everywhere I went, he popped up in my head, all funny and charming and tender. Every time I closed my eyes, he was there. Every time I opened my eyes, he was there too, pulling me into his shoulder or tucking my hair behind my ear, his eyes pools. 'I really thought he was the one, Shell.

I honestly thought we were going to get married and have kids and live happily ever after and all that stuff. It didn't feel like a fairy tale, it was real.' A snot bubble escaped from my nose.

'Just as well he's not here to see *that*.'

The snot bubble sob morphed into a snot bubble laugh, then back into a sob. I wiped my nose. 'I thought this would make me stop liking him. But it's not working. I can't stop thinking about him. But he hasn't even texted once.' I hugged myself. 'He hasn't called – nothing.'

'He knows he's messed up as much as it's humanly possible—'

'He has kind of destroyed all of our lives,' I agreed.

'And there's nothing he can do to fix it. He's leaving you alone to be kind,' said Shell. She shook her head. 'And you're meant to be the brainy one.'

I felt Si's mini-elephant bookmark he'd made me in my purse, and a great sadness engulfed me. Behind the Nathan-stalking-my-psyche layer was Sibo, and that inescapable feeling of betraying my little brother.

'I think Si would have liked him,' I said, in a small voice. I let out a long, shaky breath. 'You know, the last holiday we had was in the Algarve and it was the whole family –' I sniff-gasped – 'the four of us.' I barely got the last words out.

Shell squeezed me tighter to her side. 'Oh, hon,' she said.

'And it hasn't really hit me until now that we'll never have a family holiday ever again.' I broke down in giant sobs, Shell rubbing my back and holding my hand.

'Babe.' Shell shook her head again, her own eyes welling, and squeezed her lips together. 'Your wee brother was so fab, Cara. You were the best big sister he could ever have asked for, and he loved you to bits.'

'I know he did. It's all a bit shit, is all.'

We downed a glass each of sangria, then I collapsed into her, Shell cradling my head on her shoulder, stroking my hair and making shushing sounds.

Walking arm in arm back to our hotel, I found Polaris, twinkling in the night sky. A celestial power station, emitting its own light and heat. *Sibo.* 'Isn't that how ships used to navigate at night?' Nathan had said, at the Observatory.

Sibo, lifesaver, lighthouse in the sky.

Chapter Twenty-Eight

Nathan

December, Bathgate

I scribbled the note – *Sorry*.

I climbed into the driver's seat. A wee sky-blue Clio, with the seat so far forward and the back so upright I didn't know how Gran managed to fit in. I felt weirdly calm. I pressed the ignition, revved the engine. It was the first time I'd driven since that day, but I felt no fear, no nothing.

I flipped down the visor. The brightness of the day was dazzling. The dull ache behind my eyes was back. I pressed the heels of my hands into my eyeballs, and dug my thumbs up into my eyebrows, into the bone. I could have drawn blood, and I wouldn't have noticed.

Poor Gran. She'd only nipped out to get some bread and milk. She'd been watching me constantly, the whole time I'd been there. She was a hawk, but I'd lulled her into thinking she was being silly and over-protective. She was only letting her guard down for as long as it took her to walk briskly to the dead end of the street, through the footpath shortcut, along two short blocks, into the tiny shop and back home, her oatmeal canvas bag slightly fatter on the way back. Plus, she thought I was still sleeping. It was fairly obvious she was timing her outings for when she thought there was zero chance I'd actually haul my sorry arse out of bed.

It was plenty long enough.

'Back in a minute,' she'd called. This, I reckoned, pretty much amounted to suicide watch. She didn't think I'd nick her car, though, did she?

I cruised off, heading for the coast. The beautiful cliffs of Claythorpe. They kept flashing up in my mind, silhouetted against a blue sky, kind of like an invitation; kind of like my subconscious was telling me where I wanted to be.

I drove, with no awareness of time passing. It was poky, Gran's wee Clio. I was used to Mum's old Focus. Green and yellow blurred the sides of my vision as the East Lothian countryside sped past.

I pulled in at a petrol station just outside Claythorpe. I fancied a mint-chocolate-chip Cornetto. Why the hell not, eh?

As the woman behind the till handed me my change, I suppressed the sudden urge to tell her: *'You have no idea you're the last person I'll ever speak to.'*

Turns out she wasn't, though, because half of Scotland had decided to go to the beach that day. OK, slight exaggeration. When I pulled in at the car park, it was empty except for six cars. Still, six cars too many.

Last time I was here, Cara had leaned over and kissed me and said it was perfect, and we'd held hands and swung our arms down the steps to the beach, and her face had lit up and her hair flipped in the breeze. 'What?' she'd said when she caught me watching her. God, she was beautiful.

The memory pierced.

I left the key in the ignition, shut the door and the biting salt and seaweed air licked at my nostrils. I peeled the wrapper off my ice cream, listened to the sound of the tearing paper. The car-park bin was jammed full, but I stuffed my wrapper in. The coldness of the ice cream worked its way down inside my body. Despite the sun, the coastal chill gave me a full-body shiver – actually, more convulsion than shiver. Normally I'd have been embarrassed – two girls a couple of years younger than me passed me, possibly giggling, possibly not. I didn't care. Nothing mattered any more.

I made my way up the path that followed the edge of the cliff. It seemed more exposed than I remembered from childhood trips to the seaside. It amazed me that more people didn't fall off and die. The people I passed said the same thing: 'Lovely day.'

'Beautiful,' I replied.

When I got to the top of the cliff, I felt calm, at peace with myself. I scanned the seascape, noting dots of ships on the horizon. I sat down at the edge, breathed in deeply, listened to my breath. I said I was calm, but my body didn't seem too convinced. Five-thousand beats a second, it felt like. *Be still, my beating heart.* I don't know why that line came to me, but it did. I didn't have a clue what it was from, but it felt like a truth, a message for me. I willed my heart, my breath, to slow and sink into a rhythm. *Eight in, eleven out.* I closed my eyes, watching magenta turn to scarlet, to orange-yellow, lighter lines dancing between swirling blotches. For the first time in my life, I felt the stillness and absorption of an absolute, profound calm.

We'll all be stardust one day.

I watched the sky, the passing clouds snatches of something, changing shape, a greyness behind them, unfathomable, though the clouds themselves seemed soft, so soft.

Out of nowhere, her words, ferocious: *I hate you, I hate you, I absolutely hate you.*

I looked down at my hands: the hands that had held the steering wheel of the car that had killed an innocent boy.

Chapter Twenty-Nine

Cara

December, Drumleith

A friend request from Scott Adair. Scott Adair? I clicked on his profile. *Oh! Nathan's friend Scotty.*

A DM popped in two minutes later.

> Hi Cara, Nathan's mate Scott here. Sorry to bother you, hope you don't mind me messaging. Just wondering if you've seen/heard from Nathan?

What?
I messaged him back.

> Hi Scott, hope you're well. I haven't heard from N. When did you last hear from/speak to him? Where is he?

A shiver ran across my shoulders and up my neck. I waited, the seconds ticking louder in my head as they mounted.

> He was staying at his gran's but has taken her car and disappeared. He's been ignoring me, who can blame him eh but I thought maybe he'd gone to see you. Don't mean to alarm you, just wondered if he was with you or if he'd been in touch.

The chill was an instant full-body thing: skull to tips of fingers and toes. If I wasn't panicking before, I was now. Nothing like the words 'Don't mean to alarm you' to alarm someone.

I've been through enough. You can't throw anything else bad at me, it's not fair.

I tried to picture him.

Nath, where are you?

I paused, gathered myself up – literally drew my head and shoulders up and sat tall in my chair. *Stop panicking. He's fine. Keep it light for Scotty.*

> He hasn't been in touch. When did he go missing? I hope he's OK. x

> I'm sure he's ok. He's only been gone since 7 this morning. Let me know if you hear from him. Hope you're ok. Thanks Cara.

Shit. He's properly worried about him.

> Will do, promise. Likewise, let me know if you hear from him. x

> He's probably just wandering about in a bit of a state. He'll be fine.

I rang Nath's number. Straight to voicemail. His voice – warm and deep – hit me like a ball of heat and life. 'Nathan, it's me. Ring me back, we need to talk.' Too much left unsaid, unfinished. We couldn't leave it like that. *I* couldn't leave it like that.

I concentrated on keeping calm. He'd taken his gran's car?

He'd *driven* somewhere?

Where?

Why?

I swallowed back bile.

Mum made me pancakes with maple syrup and scooshy cream – the best thing in the universe, possibly. Afternoon shift at the salon. I'd already had to call in sick twice; no way was I missing this week. Sandi, the owner, all cloying sympathy, had hinted I needed to actually show up if I wanted to keep my job. Anyway, I was looking forward to it – looking forward to the banter, looking forward to some stress-free hair-washing. *So much more fun than sitting about in this misery-fest, let's be honest.* All that time at home was like slow suffocation, the air paper-thin. For the first time, I understood what claustrophobia was.

I tried Nathan again.

'*Hi, Nathan here. Leave a message and—*' I hit the red button. My heart hammered.

Where are you?

Little Maddie was booked in first, bless her.

'So, tell me all about Scarlett and Ebony, and whoever else they hang about with. Remember our deal?' But my heart wasn't in it. I felt for my phone in my pocket.

She told me everything there was to know, about Maya and Violet and Arabella and Sanchez, about Sapphire and Acorn and Cherry Blossom.

'Have you got a boyfriend?' she said, the hum of a hairdryer almost snatching the last word.

I hesitated. 'Um . . . No . . . Well, sort of. Yes. I sort of did – do – have a boyfriend.'

Do I?

'Is he nice?'

I forced a smile. 'Yes, he is nice.' I paused. 'I was angry with him because of something he did . . . But— It's complicated, and . . . I like him, and he is nice.' I realized I was thinking out loud.

I miss him. I miss you, Nathan. I really, really miss you.
I still hate you, though.
How can I not hate you?

I waved goodbye to Maddie and Horse, and the unthinkable, nameless fear was still there, percolating. I pinched the bridge of my nose. Another headache.

I pulled out my phone – no notifications. Sent Scott another message.

Any luck?

The reply came almost instantly.

Nothing, Cara. Sorry.

Valentina handed me the salon phone – I'd just started shampooing the next client's hair. 'For you,' she said. 'Someone called Diane?' And in a lower voice, 'She said it's important?'

'I'm so sorry, excuse me.' I dropped the showerhead and stepped back into the corner. Valentina caught my eye and frowned in concern.

'Cara, it's Diane here – Nathan's mum. I'm sorry to bother you.' Lovely Diane, her voice tight. Stone-cold dread – pure, hard – washed over me, and I got a flashback to that terrible, terrible day, walking along the corridor with Mr Thomas, the whole thing surreal. Diane sounded like she was trying really hard to keep it casual and upbeat, but she was clearly in a state. *Please don't be bad news, I can't take any more bad news.* 'I've been trying to get hold of Nathan. Is he with you?' she asked.

'I'm really sorry, Diane,' I said, feeling like I was inflicting physical pain on her. 'I haven't heard from him since he—' I didn't finish the sentence; didn't need to.

Her voice deflated across the line, but she sounded small and scared, not surprised. 'I can't get hold of him, Scott doesn't know where he is, Damian doesn't know, he's taken my mum's car. He's been pretty low, Cara. I'm worried—' Her voice faltered and cracked.

My eyes welled and I fought to hold it together. We swapped numbers and I said I'd think of anywhere he might have gone, promised to ring her the second I heard anything. She did the same.

'Bye, Cara.' Poor woman sounded distraught.

I shuddered, trying to think where he could be. His mum, his brother, his gran, Scotty – no one knew.

Where are you, Nath? Don't do anything stupid.

Where would he go if he was feeling stressed, down, desperate? His mum – was she saying he might be suicidal? I shuddered.

A railway? No. A bridge? No. A cliff?

I pictured him, curled up in a ball, nestling into the side of a hill, amongst the heather and the bracken and the sheep and the hares. A crisp breeze, blowing his hair around. When I zoomed in, the forlorn figure looked more gaunt – pale, staring, almost lifeless. *No.* I banished the thought from my head. It was nonsense fabricated by my mind. I mentally fattened him up, gave him a jolt of strength, dismissed the gaunt image, ordered it to get up and walk. But still it returned and still it returned.

I grabbed my raincoat. 'Sorry,' I yelled.

Valentina, who was massaging the client I'd abandoned's head, excused herself a second. 'Message us to let us know you're OK,' she said, squeezing my arm. The client, lying back, her head in white-foam peaks, looked over. Magda, the senior stylist, nodded at me from behind her half-head of foils, her eyes solemn.

I'm being ridiculous. Am I?

The vision of him, now standing at the edge of a cliff, no emotion on his face – nothing – sailed into my head, like a postcard through a letterbox. I couldn't shake the image nor the sickening lurch – had to get there. Was he planning something stupid? I could see how his logic might have got skewed.

Where are you, Nath? Arthur's Seat? The Pentlands? Where would he go if he was feeling . . . ?

I rang him again. His voice, warm like syrup. *Why aren't you answering?* I left a panicked message. 'I'm coming, don't do anything.'

Still, I could see him, standing there.

Where?

Where?

Come on, Cara.

It took a moment to match the image. *Of course.* I saw it, clear as a snapshot. Claythorpe. His favourite place on Earth – a place he found peaceful, enchanting even. *I love those cliffs.* That's what he'd said.

I clicked my seatbelt, typed 'Claythorpe' into the satnav.

I love you, I love you, I love you, I love you, I love you, I love you, I love you.

I flew into fifth gear.

I completely love you. I'm completely in love with you.

I heard the voice of David Bowie in my head. 'Absolutely,' it said, 'not completely. I absolutely love you.' *Whatever you say, David.*

Driving into the car park, I looked around. A handful of cars, but I had no idea what his gran's was like, did I? I slammed the door, ran down those steps, three at a time, ran onto the beach, scanned desperately. Something bobbing in the water – I gasped – just a buoy. I rewound, scanned the panorama again, slower, taking in every detail, then right round, 360 degrees. There were dots – people and dogs – but nothing that looked like Nathan. I paused, looked up at the cliffs, remembered him talking about how rugged, how sheer, how magical they were. My breath laboured, I ran back up the steps then up the coastal path.

As I approached the brow of the hill, I was sure I'd find nothing there. An empty cliff, standing there facing the worst the sea could throw at it, as it had done for millennia.

I stopped just over the brow. I bent double, caught my breath. Nothing. I sat down and quaked. Was I too late? I didn't even want to think it.

I wiped my eyes, breathed, looked again along the path that dipped a little then continued a gentle rise. I stared. Then, no, there *was* something, *someone*, there. My heart flipped. It was him. I just knew.

I ran, fast, then slowing. Better to get there as quick as I could, or better not to give him a fright? Don't jump, I willed him, reciting it inside my head like a mantra. *Don't jump, all right? Just don't.*

But the someone stood up and it wasn't him. I looked around in all directions, getting more and more desperate. Had I got it wrong? Was he at the Pentlands after all? Or the bottom of the Forth?

No, don't think it.

I caught up with the figure. He shook his head when I described Nathan.

'Sorry,' he said.

Chapter Thirty

Nathan

December, Claythorpe

In a clump of heather by a big tuft of grasses, something shone for a moment. A tiny, purple figure bent down and picked it up. I couldn't see it – it was 400 metres away at least – but I didn't need to, to know it was blue and smooth with a cold silver bit sticking out the top.

The small, purple, brown-haired dot – a wee girl? – seemed to talk to a bigger, blonde-haired dot – her mum? – for a few moments, then launched her purple self along the rocky path like her life depended on it.

A high-pitched voice yelled – the mum, screaming at the girl to come back – then gathered up her bags and half ran, half lurched after the girl. But the girl was fast. She streaked ahead, getting bigger, still clutching the blue, smooth thing.

My inhaler.

Great.

'Billie!' The mother's voice was a barb on the breeze. The girl ignored her, her face coming into focus now, pure resolve. She pumped her wee arms and furrowed her brow and huffed and puffed through the circle she'd pushed her mouth into. How old was she? Five, maybe?

Had she seen me?

Over the crest of the hill, a whip of sea air carried a feather and a smell of salt. My throat stung with the taste of it. She was bigger now. She was heading right for me. *Shit*. She belted up the last bit, breaking into a full-on sprint – strides longer. *Eat your heart out, Bolty. Random thought of the century.*

She stopped right beside me, to my left, breathing in gulps.

Wee girl, no – not now.

I fixed on a dot on the horizon – a ship, presumably – and let my eyes blur.

She stood there, said nothing.

The sound of the sea and the wind danced in my head.

Go away, wee girl.

Still there, to my side.

Wee girl, can't you see? It's not a good time.

I breathed, and let my eyelids rest.

It's nothing personal, it's just—

'Excuse me,' she said, hesitant, then louder: 'Excuse me, is this your nin-hayla?'

The thin, white line of the horizon stretched to the edges of my awareness and beyond. Or maybe the line stopped at the ends, like a measuring tape marking out my peripheral vision. Was there an even finer black line beneath the white line? I swore I could just make out the curvature of the Earth. I was a grain of sand in an almighty universe. Nearly nothing.

A wee girl? This was not in the plan. She was nowhere in the plan. I scanned the mental picture I had of this moment. Nope, definitely no wee girls.

Go away, wee girl. Back to Mummy. You're not supposed to be here.

The drive, the petrol station, the ice cream, the walk up here; it had all been just like in the picture that had filled my head for days, filling it, like expanding foam. The car park, the overfull bin, chucking my inhaler. Even the weather, the clouds. No wee girls, though, not one.

I can't keep blanking her. She's only a little kid.

'Yes, it's mine,' I said, taking it from her outstretched hand.

Now you can go back to Mummy.

But she was still standing there.

'Look! Your mummy's wanting you.' I nodded towards the clobber-laden blonde woman hobbling up the path in her white sling-back heels and leggings. Cara looked pretty damn hot in leggings. I chided myself: *Stop thinking like that. You killed her brother, remember.*

Cara.

The wee girl was still there. Still staring at me, her head tilted, an intense look in her eyes.

Time to go, wee girl.

She was going nowhere. She was looking into me, reading me, reaching right into my soul. I had no idea little kids could do that. I shielded my thoughts – they weren't right for a wee girl.

Wee girl, you don't need this. Go back to your mummy.

The mum was nearly there now. *Great.*

'But, don't you need it?' she piped up. 'Don't you need the nin-hayla?'

So that's what she's looking for. Of course.

I sucked in a puff.

'I'm better now,' I said.

She beamed. 'OK, bye!' And she was off.

Wee girl.

Wee girl.

Wee girl, come back. Come back, wee girl.

I ran after her. The mother had her now, shielding, wary. She wasn't quite bearing her fangs, but she did let out a tiny growl, or I thought she did. The mother literally placed herself between the wee girl and me. She had the girl clamped in her arm.

'Thank you,' I said, looking past the mum at the big innocent eyes, the tilted head, the brown hair hanging in tails. 'I never said thank you.'

'You're welcome,' the wee girl said, in her sing-song voice.

She looked up at her mum, little face all serious.

'I saved his life,' she said.

Chapter Thirty-One

Cara

December, Claythorpe

I ran on, over another rise. Still nothing.

I fell on my knees and raked at the ground. *No. Stay calm.* I stood up again, breathed.

Where are you? Please be alive. You need to be alive.

I stood stock-still, scanned the land. I didn't look to the sea; didn't want to acknowledge that possibility. Then I registered a movement ahead, along the clifftop. It was him this time. It was. He wasn't standing like in the vision. He was sitting side-on to the path, gazing ahead of him, his knees resting in the crooks of his elbows, hugging himself, his clothes blending into the landscape.

I ran. Closer now. Didn't take my eyes off him. Ashen-looking, he was.

He jerked up like a jack-in-the-box, looking straight ahead

of him. The movement stole the breath from my lungs; it was so incongruous.

He looked out at the vast expanse of sea in front of him.

'No!' I screamed, the cords of my throat pulled together, gripped in a vice.

As though in slow-motion, he turned to look at me. He didn't seem to recognize me.

Then his features reordered themselves and a fragment of something edged its way to the corners of his eyes, then his mouth. My heart exploded with joy.

He was alive. He was happy to see me. He wasn't going to jump.

I flew the last few paces, grunting with the exertion. I tackled him to the ground and gripped him with such savagery it was almost violent. The pair of us blubbed like babies.

'What's the point in you dying, too?' I said, surprised by the anger in my voice. My whole body felt charged with enough electricity to light up the night sky. 'D'you think Si would want that? What about me?'

I gripped his arm so hard and then pushed at his chest, almost punching him. The warmth of his heart travelled into my fists.

'You were going to kill yourself.' It was half-question, half-statement, a verbalization, an admission to myself.

His face crumpled. 'I'm sorry.'

We lay there, holding each other, wind buffeting over us.

'I'm sorry I killed your brother.'

I wept and wept, in the arms of the boy I loved.

'You're not looking so pretty,' I said, when at last I could speak. He was like a black-and-white photocopy of himself.

'You are,' he said.

'You know how fine you are to me, Robert MacGregor?'

He managed another almost-smile.

'Do you know how fine you are to me, Mary MacGregor?' He reached into his jeans pocket and pulled out the grey and white periwinkle I'd given him, down on the beach.

I breathed out, so slowly, breathing out the trauma of the last half-year. The space filled up with something softer: hope, perhaps. Permission to be happy with this boy I loved, perhaps? Si, saying it was OK, he forgave me? Tension lifted out of me, and the warmth of Nathan seeped from his heart into mine.

We sat in the car, me in the driver's seat, him in the passenger seat, and I buckled myself into the chair like it was a funfair ride that was about to throw me up and about without a moment's notice. I had one hand clutching the door handle and one hand clutching the handbrake. There was no hiding the clunk when I pressed the button to lock the doors. Nathan looked over, and my cheeks burned.

'You choose,' I said, handing him my music on my phone.

He took ages.

Finally, the sound of the revs was interrupted by Aimee Mann, her voice melting and lifting the atmosphere in the car.

'Aw, thanks,' I said.

My eyes welled and I kept them directed at the road, at the silver Audi in front. I hadn't liked the album at first, but time and familiarity had morphed it into one of my very favourites. The seed was just a seed but grew into something beautiful.

Our perceptions are just that, I thought: perceptions. Fluid, transient, imperfect, subject to change, to evolution with the inevitable passing of time and changing of views. Even your opinion of a person was just a transitory view that could change, if you remained open to that possibility. Or even the possibility that there was no definable identity for a person, that people cannot be boxed; that we all have infinite possibilities if only we'll give ourselves and each other permission to explore them.

You couldn't cling for ever to a good past, to a former you. At some point, you had to accept your new reality, embrace it, and start living again.

At some point, you had to forgive and move on.

At some point, you had to acknowledge you couldn't live without him.

I looked over at Nathan.

At some point, you understood: we *will* make this work.

He met my eyes. His were pools.

'I'm sorry,' he said.

I pulled into a layby. I had to know.

'Were you actually going to—?' The word 'jump' stuck in my throat.

I took a shuddery breath, tried again.

'I know you, Nath. I thought: where would he go? Then I pictured you, here, and I knew.'

The sadness welled inside me.

He sobbed, his shoulders moving silently.

'What stopped you?' I said. He needed to answer me; I deserved an answer.

He couldn't speak.

I said it again, louder. 'What stopped you, Nathan? Tell me.'

Still, he couldn't speak.

Any anger flared out and flattened into calm. 'You wouldn't

have done that to me, would you? You wouldn't have done that to me a second time? You wouldn't have wanted me to lose you, too?' And I wiped my cheeks with the heel of my hand, my lungs starved.

'No,' he said, after a pause, eyes down.

'You know I don't hate you. I never hated you – not really.'

He looked at me, then straight ahead.

'I love you, Nathan.'

'I love you, too.'

A tear tracked down his cheek.

'I love you so much it hurts,' he said, in a whisper.

He sighed, looked down at his hands, then back up.

'There was a wee girl, and she was so full of hope and innocence. And I made a deal with Scotty. And the thought of never seeing you again . . .' His voice tailed off, brimming with shame, and he looked again at his hands in his lap, then out the passenger window. He tried to speak again, but his voice faltered. Then he looked straight at me. 'And, you know, Mum and Damian and Gran.'

I slipped my hand into his.

'Any time, day or night,' Nathan mumbled.

'What?'

'Any time, day or night. I promised. I promised Scotty I'd ring him any time, day or night. If I needed, you know, to talk or whatever.'

I leaned in and took hold of him and sobbed into his shoulder. Then I looked up at him.

'We'll just have to work at it.'

'You'd do that?' he said. 'For me?'

His face melted.

'Ring your mum. Tell her you're on your way home.'

He texted her.

We fell back into an exhausted, blotchy-eyed quiet, as we continued our journey.

The silence between us was interrupted as we pulled into his drive. His mum came running out in a fluffy dressing gown, her face a mess.

She wrenched open the door, toppled in, her body buckling, grabbed him, quaked and quaked with sobs like thunderclaps.

She hauled him out of the car and stood with him on the drive. Nathan was bent over, shoulders stooped: the physical shape of apology.

I'm sorry, his body whispered. *I'm sorry, Mum.* But still, he didn't speak.

'My baby, my baby,' his mum eventually whispered. I ignored the tiny wave that nagged at me – that his mum was getting this opportunity when my mum hadn't. I let it roll away – truly glad, so glad, that she had her little boy back. That last thought, though, formed a feather in my throat. But I sat with it; felt it tickle; didn't try to dislodge it. I was becoming used to accommodating sadness and joy, grief and love together.

I did that thing with my mouth that you do when you understand someone's pain but can't express it any better with words. I pressed my lips together, pulled my cheeks into a sort of smile thing. Nathan's mum grabbed me.

'You absolute angel,' she said. 'Thank you.' And she let go, sobbing.

I put my hands up.

'I'll go. He's exhausted. I'll come back tomorrow. I'll be

here tomorrow, Nath,' I said, and kissed him on the cheek.

He reached and grabbed my hand, then let it drop. His eyes held mine for a second, then he lowered his gaze, put his arm round his mum and started walking with her towards the house.

Damian stood outside the side door, like he didn't know what to do. He looked away when I caught his eye and kicked a stone along the path that ran down the side of the house.

Chapter Thirty-Two

Nathan

December, Edinburgh

I am happy to be alive. It's a revelation.

I collapsed into my bed and slept for eighteen hours straight.

Mum cooked me a massive fry-up. Bacon, sausages, eggs, mushrooms, tomatoes, tattie scones, haggis – the works – with a big squeeze of tomato ketchup. Man, was it good.

'Mum?'

'Yes, love?' She leaned back, took off her glasses, rubbed her temples with the heels of her hands. Black discs for eyes.

'I'm sorry.'

She blinked.

'It's OK, love.'

'No, it's not OK, Mum. I'm so sorry.'

I bolted around the table and hugged her, almost toppling her.

'I'm so sorry,' I whispered.

I caught Damo out the corner of my eye, at the doorway, his feet planted apart.

'What, you don't think I was worried, too? You don't think I give a shit?' He started off slow and deliberate, but his voice swelled, like some raging genie ballooning out of the bottle. I knew he had more. His chest and shoulders rose and fell. He was pumped.

'Damian—' started Mum.

'You didn't once stop to think about me and Mum?' he screamed. It was a full-on yell, his voice splitting, going high and low and high again, from boy to man to banshee.

I stared. So did Mum. The three of us, staring at each other.

'I'm sorry,' I said, this time to him. I took a step towards him.

He twisted round and bowled the rubber ball he'd been squeezing with all his might. It caught me on the hip.

'Ow!' I said, doubled over. 'Jesus.'

His eyes bored into me, as though challenging me to a fight.

Mum walked towards us, but I held my hand up to say: No, it's fine, I'll deal with this.

'I'm sorry,' I said again. 'I'm sorry, Damian. I'm really, really sorry.'

Still, he glared.

'I know it's not enough,' I said, half under my breath.

I stepped forward again and he turned and legged it up to his room. I put my head in my hands.

'Sorry, Mum.' I hugged her again. 'It's going to be all right. We'll get through this.'

'I know, love, we will.'

She peeled herself away and silently climbed the stairs to Damian's room. I heard the knock and the muffled reply before she went in.

I made the three of us tea. I took two cups up on a tray, plus two orange Clubs, knocked Damian's door, and slid the tray just inside, on the carpet, then pulled his door closed.

Mum came down, then Damo slunk down, too, and we sat together in the kitchen, drinking tea and listening to Radio 2 – Mum's choice. I got the old box of Lego from the cupboard, all dusty, and put it on the floor in front of Damo, kneeling down opposite him. We built a weird-looking building and he added a Stormtrooper and Baby Yoda. We added wonky bits over each other's additions until it got top-heavy and collapsed. We both laughed. I looked up, and Damo looked right back at me.

Later in my room, I picked up my bass, played along to Lana Del Rey, then old stuff: Prince, Police, Bowie, bit of Chili Peppers. Impossible. I watched the bass dude tutorial for 'Death of a Martian' and played along. I could watch it all day. Damian came in and sat on the end of my bed, drumming my mattress with his hands. He seemed to have grown a foot. When did that happen?

I fetched crisps and nuts from the kitchen. Damo punched me on the shoulder to say thanks. I kicked his foot.

He picked up a plastic water bottle that happened to be two-fifths full – the perfect amount. He looked at me. I knew what he was thinking. He flung it. It landed with a thud, on its side on the carpet. On the seventh go, it landed the right way up. 'Yesss!' He swung it back and flung it, again and again – nineteen out of 100 – then handed it to me.

Eleven out of 100. Sounds rubbish, but it's actually the best game ever. I'd only ever beaten him twice.

Ping. A text. I checked my phone.

'On my way x'

Cara.

I sat on the garden wall and waited for her. We went and sat on a bench in the Meadows and talked and talked and held hands, and a warmth spread through me, even though it was two degrees.

Monday morning. Grandparents in the park, manhandling small kids into bucket swings. Some guy juggling Irn-Bru bottles. A bus, swinging open its doors and spitting out a man with a beard. A cluster of mums with buggies laughing at the edge of the Meadows.

I pushed the rotating door, walked into the Blood Donor Centre. My third donation. I sat down, filled out the form, handed it back to the nice lady in the light blue uniform.

She asked if I felt well, and it was true, I did. Then she asked if I minded which arm, and I froze. How could I have forgotten about the scars? Could they even take my blood?

I took a deep breath, rolled up my sleeves, told her about the cutting – the evidence was clear to see. She asked a lot of questions about how I was feeling, if I felt depressed or suicidal, when I'd cut myself. She was so matter-of-fact about it. The tightness lifted as I talked to her – someone professional, who didn't know me for any other reason, who wasn't judging me. She asked how I felt about the act of giving blood – was there something relieving or cleansing about it?

'Like cutting?' I said. 'No.'

She said she just had to check it wasn't another, a smaller act of self-harm for me, since self-harm was a way of masking other unresolved issues that I might need help to work through.

Giving blood, I said, was my tiny act of saving, of giving something. *Of atoning for the blood that had pooled on the tarmac round Simon's chest.* But maybe I did – yes, clearly, I did – have some issues to work through.

'I'm really sorry,' she said. 'We won't take blood today. You need to concentrate on getting yourself better. Thank you for coming in – you've already helped people with your two donations – and I'll put a note on the system to send you an appointment in a year and we can review your situation and if you're well and you haven't cut yourself again, we might be able to pop you back on the register.' For a second time, the matter-of-fact way she talked about cutting took me by surprise – in a good way. If only everyone was as open about these things.

'Sorry for wasting your time,' I said. 'I should have realized.'

She reached out and touched my upper arm. 'Listen, son,' she said, quieter, 'you've been through the mill. There are excellent support services – have you sought help? You can request an urgent referral.'

I promised to seek help.

'Have a seat over there and I'll get you a cup of juice and a biscuit,' she said, but I didn't feel I'd earned them.

The day was bright. I walked home, nearly colliding with a cyclist when I crossed the road at Rankeillor Street. Mum was ready, waiting for me. Time to face the music and go back to Claythorpe. Mum drove, Gran in the passenger seat, me in the back. The car smelt weird, like fake pineapple mixed with acetone – it was my first time in it. We cruised through the streets, stopped at the lights. A man in white overalls was cleaning windows. A DPD van pulled up and a wiry old woman ran past with some sort of greyhound-type dog.

It was only when Mum pulled onto the A1 that I felt myself start to sweat.

She put on Radio 2. There wasn't any more to say, for now.

But she took the slip road at Claythorpe and turned into the car park and parked beside Gran's wee Clio – still there – and my heart thumped. The violence of it – of what I'd been planning to do – hit me. It hit me with force, and I was stunned that it hadn't occurred to me before.

Mum and Gran looked at each other. Gran put her hand on Mum's. Mum switched off the ignition, bent her head forward and sniffed – I hadn't realized she was crying.

She stepped out the car and opened my door. I let her pull me out. Gran was still in the passenger seat.

'You wouldn't harm a fly, Nathan,' Mum said. 'Ever since you were a wee boy, you'd catch spiders with a glass and a piece of card and you'd take them out and wander around until you found a perfect-looking stone or leaf and you'd tip them onto it so gently. You couldn't bear to hurt anything.' She sniffed. 'You were upset all summer after you found a baby bird that had fallen out of its nest. We dug a hole and buried it in the garden, and you picked little daisies and put them on its grave.'

And yet. And yet I was going to kill myself. How appalling.

I reached out and pulled her to me and said I was sorry over and over. We both cried. Eventually, Mum pulled away.

'Aren't you going to say anything to Gran?' she said.

I walked round to Gran's door. Out she got.

'I'm so sorry,' I said.

'I know you are, love. I just hope you're OK and I want you

to get the help you need. You need to, for you and your mum. Damian, too.'

'Yes,' I said. I stepped forward, gave her an awkward hug. 'Sorry I took your car. Sorry I . . . abused your trust.'

She waved her hand. 'For goodness' sake, to hell with that, Nathan. It's not the car I'm worried about.' Her pale eyes welled.

I nodded. 'Thanks for looking after me,' I said.

'I'm glad you felt you could come,' she said, and ruffled my hair. 'But enough. Please don't ever put us through that again,' and she shot me a warning look.

'I won't, I promise,' I said. I looked up and Mum was there, sitting on the bonnet, looking out to sea, listening.

Gran leaned over her windscreen and pulled something from under the wiper. A fine and a towing warning.

'I'll pay that, Gran,' I said, reaching to take the notice from her hands. She pulled it away.

'Och, it's just a fine,' she said. 'Away home and look after your mother, OK?'

'OK, Gran.' We waved her off – key still in the ignition. She didn't need the spare after all.

Mum didn't get back in the car.

'Where did you go?' She gestured with her arm. 'Where were you?' She looked at the ground, her face full of tears. 'Where were you standing? I want you to show me exactly where you were standing. I want you to tell me exactly what the little girl said, exactly where Cara found you.'

I hadn't realized she needed to know.

Shame filled every crack as I led my mum – the mother who had given birth to me and loved me and fed me and done everything for me all my life – up the path to the clifftop.

We got to the point, and I paused, looked at her, sat down. I reached out and pulled her hand. She kneeled beside me.

'Here,' I said. 'It was here.'

She nodded, kept nodding, for a long time.

'Here, where I . . . Where the wee girl gave me my inhaler. Here, where I came back to after the wee girl left – where Cara found me.'

'What were you thinking, wee Nathy?' She gripped my hand like she was about to fall. 'What was going through your mind?'

The air was tight in my lungs. The mirage of calm I thought I'd felt last time I was up here had evaporated. It had only been two days, and it was such a strong sense of déjà vu, but in a way it felt like forever ago. Everything had changed, in my head, anyway. 'I . . .' But the words didn't come. I couldn't think of the words to express why I'd gone so far as to actually drive out here, to chuck my inhaler, to walk to the edge of the cliff.

I took Mum's hands in both of mine and took a deep breath.

'I'm sorry. I . . . I was just sitting here looking at the horizon, and I was thinking I'm finished, I've caused too much pain, I've made a mess of everything.'

'Nathan, you had a crash. You killed a boy. It was an accident.'

'Exactly.'

'You're still processing what happened. That's what this was about – your grief for Simon Paterson, your grief for the life you could have had.'

The heaviness of the air lightened as her words settled.

'For Cara, too,' I said, hoarse. I cleared my throat.

'For Cara, yes. But feeling you were finished for this world, that's nonsense. You have to understand you have to go through this grieving process. It'll take a long time. It's completely natural you feel terrible but it's something you have to go through to heal and move on.'

'I understand that, Mum.' Until that moment, though, I don't think I had. 'But how do I know it'll ever go away?'

'It won't go away, but it absolutely will – I promise it will – get easier, less intense.' She touched my cheek. 'Promise me you won't ever do that again.'

'I promise.'

'I'm always here for you, Nathan. I tried to talk to you, but you shut me out and I didn't know what else—' She breathed in, shuddering with a succession of sobs.

'There's nothing else you could have done, Mum. It was me. You did everything right. Plus, you had Damian to sort out. None of it's your fault.'

'No. But still, you do wonder. I can't help thinking is there anything else I could have said, something I should have done, some place I could have taken you? I should have been more, I don't know, proactive, more insistent, maybe – I should have kept a closer eye on you.' She picked a blade of grass, threw it up for the breeze to catch. I pulled my knees to my chest, rested my head against her shoulder. 'I knew you were struggling, I knew you weren't coping but I sort of let you get on with it. I should've seen you needed me to be more like when you were wee.'

'You tried.'

She sniffed, bobbed her head about. 'I'm your mum – I should be able to get through to you.'

'Nobody could get through to me. I couldn't get through to myself.' I laughed a sort of non-laugh. 'You don't deserve this, Mum. You deserve better than this.'

She sighed. 'I've got everything I want in my two beautiful boys. You know that, don't you?' She looked into my eyes. 'I'm sorry for going behind your back but I'm taking you to the doctor after this, and then I'm taking you to a psychotherapist. You have an appointment. I've spoken to Scott about it too. Please don't try and—'

'I'll go, Mum. I love you. I'm sorry.' I breathed in, my chest still juddering.

'Oh, thank God.' Her shoulders dropped. 'I was worried you wouldn't go. They'll be able to help you through it. It's too much for you to deal with on your own. And I'll try, too.'

She was a blur, and then she was the world, hugging me, then the blur cleared and we both looked out to sea, and this time I saw a choppy, dark sea, with unwritten things on the horizon. Not hope, exactly – that was a long way off – but something.

Chapter Thirty-Three

Cara

2 January, Graveyard

The grey-green spears of the snowdrops I planted pushed up through the blue-white earth. I reached out and touched their rubbery tips. Fat snowflakes fell on a silent world.

Happy birthday, little brother.
Miss you so much.

Chapter Thirty-Four

Cara

January, Eildon Hills

I'd never lied to my parents before – not about anything big, anyway. OK, there was the climbing wall, but that wasn't exactly major.

It was Nathan's idea: to go back up the Eildons and build a cairn for Si.

We walked and walked and talked and talked – how messed up we both felt, the churning, relentless guilt that cement-mixed my insides daily; Nathan's inability to even put into words how bad he felt.

'I tried so hard to hate you,' I said. 'I really wanted to hate you; it would be so much easier.' He nodded, his face almost blank. I didn't need to explain – he got it, I really felt that.

His hand was warm in mine: warm and sure. I knew what we were doing, the significance of it, but it didn't stop me feeling happy, so happy. I had Nathan back.

I pulled his hand into my chest, kissed it, this precious hand. There was nothing else for it, nothing to debate; we'd just have to work it out, somehow. We couldn't live without each other, so we'd have to work at it. I hadn't come clean about it yet to Mum and Dad.

The heather and turf and mud sparkled. We crunched through glittering puddles, kicked tiny pockets of frozen groundwater with the toes of our boots, smashing them into broken mirrors. Holding hands, we walked on, the wool fibres of my mitten sticking to the Velcro wristband of his glove. The contours and humps of the hill fort were more prominent, clad in white. When we got to the top of Eildon Hill North we looked at each other. I sighed – a real, vocal sigh – and took in a big breath.

'This was his favourite hill.'

We gathered stones and built the small mound in silence. I wept freely. I didn't miss the tragic irony of it. I hoped Si would understand; thought he would.

I stepped forward, to be on my own a moment. Nathan took a step to the side, understanding instinctively.

'I wish you were up here too,' I whispered to Sibo. 'I hope you're OK with *this*.'

Two clouds separated – at different heights – to reveal a beam of sunshine. It slanted onto the shoulder of the hill then fell away into the glen.

'Are you? Are OK with this? Tell me you're OK with this? You'd like him, I promise.'

A buzzard circled over the forest – a dark-green strip down to our right.

'He didn't mean to kill you. He's sorry – really sorry.'

The buzzard swooped out of sight then rose again, soaring over the hill.

I sighed, smiled through the chain mail that constricted my every breath.

I put one last stone on the top. A nice, smooth, round one.

'I love you for ever, little brother,' I said, sobbing, my chest tightening, forcing my breath through a tiny channel.

Stepping forward, Nathan pulled me into his chest and kissed the top of my head through my hat.

Then he knelt down and pressed his hands together to his chin, like he was praying. He stared at the cairn, and the wind wheezed and swirled around us. He breathed out a deep, guttural breath, then reached out to touch the top of the top stone, his index and middle fingers resting on its curved surface. Then he fumbled in his pocket and placed a small brown ammonite a little further down, tucked into a crevice. He'd brought it specially?

'From Claythorpe – from the rock pools?' I said, through tears.

He nodded.

'I'm sorry,' he said, to Si. A snatch of wind caught him off guard, and he lifted his hand and stood up.

I leaned my head into his shoulder, and neither of us spoke for a while. We just looked at the stones piled into a mound.

Si's cairn.

At the same moment, we turned and looked into each other's eyes and had a conversation without words. Nathan's sorrow, his guilt, etched deep into his face, into the creases at the edges of his eyes. But also in his eyes, and in his mouth, was a softness, a request for mercy, as though he couldn't grant himself forgiveness; it had to come from me.

'He would have liked you,' I said, matter-of-factly. 'He would be OK with this. He wasn't one to hold grudges.'

He closed his eyes – again, as though he was in prayer. There was nothing at all he could say to make it better – he knew that. Nathan had an instinctive understanding of when it's best to simply say nothing. And for that, and for many other things, I loved him with all my heart.

I dropped my head so my pompom would jump forward and hit him. 'Did I get you in the forehead?'

'Right between the eyes.'

I smiled, and he allowed himself to, too.

Above the horizon, a waning crescent moon sat in its hammock, reflecting the light of the sun. Moon, custodian of peace.

I kissed Nathan and we held hands all the way down.

I dropped him at his bus stop and drove home. Dad held his finger up to his lips in a hush gesture when I opened the door and announced I was home. Mum had gone for a nap.

'Cara!' Mum called. Dad gave me a look. I ran upstairs and poked my head round their bedroom door.

'You'll be all right, won't you, love?' she said. 'All this stuff has been taking it out of me.'

'It's OK, Mum.' She never used to nap, but now it had become a daily ritual.

I popped my head round Si's door, crept in.

'It should have been you,' I whispered – up there, on his favourite hill, enjoying the January sun and the frost.

Back downstairs, and I'd only just sat down.

'Cara.' It was Dad, and it was a statement, not a question.

'Yes?'

'Where were you?'

I didn't answer, avoided his eyes.

He paused a moment, breathed out. 'How about we go for a walk together, up Venlaw, through the woods? Si used to love spotting squirrels up there when he was wee, and you did, too.'

'I remember, Dad.'

I had a feeling this wasn't any old walk. It wasn't a walk; it was a *walk*-walk. Dad rarely suggested either – Mum was always the main instigator.

We sat in the car, winter sun slanting across the fields in great shards. Dad backed into a space beside what I thought was a road-kill pheasant, but when I stepped out the car it scurried off. Silently I rejoiced.

'So, what's the purpose of this, Dad?' He clicked the car locked and we started up the path.

'Mum needs a bit of peace – thought we could leave her alone for an hour.'

'Dad—'

'Well, she does.'

'I know she does. I mean what's this all about, taking me out for a *walk*?' I said it like it was fly-fishing or pony-trekking or circus skills – something obscure. 'That's not what this is about, is it?'

'You have to stop thinking about that boy,' he said.

'Thought it might be something to do with him,' I muttered, my body flopping in a here-we-go gesture.

A tirade was approaching, I could tell. The cork was popped; he was about to let it all out. I breathed in, closed my eyes, counted how many steps I could do before I started to feel dizzy. Nine. I marched them out slowly: one, two, three, four, five, six, seven, eight, nine. For ten, I had to feel the path with my foot, slide it along. It was only a half-stride, so it didn't count. I opened my eyes: instant balance regain.

'Think it through, Carabelle,' he said, his eyes restless, refusing to connect with mine. 'Say it all works out, one day you get married, have kids. Your husband and the father of your kids is the person who killed Si. I know he didn't mean to, and it was all an awful accident but that's not the point. That doesn't undo the inescapable truth that that's what happened. You honestly expect your mother to be able to hold his child – her grandchild – and feel completely fine about it?'

'I'm seventeen! I'm not thinking about children! What are you talking about?'

He carried on as if he'd rehearsed this. 'You want grandchildren to be an uncomplicated thing, where you love them unconditionally, but just imagine it.'

'Uncomplicated? D'you think I chose this, Dad?' My voice was higher, tighter, than usual. My chest was tighter too. 'D'you think I *chose* complicated? Has it occurred to you that maybe every day, every hour since finding out Nathan killed Si, I haven't thought why did it have to be him? Why him? Why couldn't I meet someone else? No, why couldn't he be himself, before this nightmare? I didn't choose it, Dad. But I do love him.' I breathed out. 'He's a bastard for checking his music that day, for driving too fast. But he's not a bastard, Dad, he's kind. And I can tell you for certain that not a minute has gone by since the accident that he hasn't regretted it with his whole being. Beaten himself up about it. He has nightmares about it. He tortures himself. What if he hadn't arranged to meet Scott in town? What if he'd taken more care? He knows Si could be alive today. But it did happen.

And there's nothing any of us can do about it, except try to accept that and move on.'

'I understand how you feel, Carabelle,' he said, stopping and leaning his hand against a tree.

No, you don't. You don't understand. His grey-black hair tufted out of his neck, like a werewolf or something. I'd never seen it like that before.

'But it's impossible for you to understand the future and how you'll feel in ten, twenty years' time. You think you'll forget, but what if you never forget?'

'I never said I'd forget. I said we need to move on. Of course I won't forget it was him who killed Si, but perhaps the pain won't always be this intense; perhaps we can put it in the past.'

He huffed and puffed. 'Or perhaps being with him would be a constant reminder. Perhaps you'll meet other boys, realize there are other good boys out there. Perhaps he could meet someone else – someone who doesn't remind him daily of the thing he spends every day trying to forget. Perhaps the kindest thing you can do for everyone, for Mum, for yourself, and especially for him, is to forget about him – I'm not saying it'll be easy – and gradually, after a year or two passes, you'll be able to move on, as you say.' A freezing trickle passed through my heart, and I felt like a little girl who's suddenly discovered her dad's not the big, strong protector she thought he was.

Dad blew out, then stopped and looked at me. 'You're young, you're intelligent, talented, beautiful – you've got loads going for you. You've both got your whole lives ahead of you, to live. You both need to move on, but not together. You'll both meet other people, you'll see. You won't want to think about that now, but when it happens, you'll know it was all for the best.'

I broke away from him.

'It pains me to see you hurting,' he said, louder, 'but it also pains me to see your mother hurting and it'll be more painful over the years to watch you continue to hurt because this thing, I can promise, will never, ever, ever, go away completely.'

A pigeon flapped out from the holly bush and I jumped away.

'And how do you think *Nathan* –' he spat out his name '– is supposed to get over what he's done, with you as his constant reminder?' He struggled to control his voice. 'It would be kinder to him to move on, however much it hurts him now.'

My chest burned. I turned round. 'No, Dad, I can't. I won't.'

'You will,' he said, yelling now, his voice scaring me. I huddled into myself, pulled myself tight, my head curled down and my fists pressed together against my nose. 'You'll tell that bastard to leave us all alone!'

Dad had never sworn at me. Never threatened me. If he was losing his temper, he'd grab his coat and head out on his own. I stared at him, before the tears pricked in my eyes. I ran.

'It's killing your mum. It's killing her,' he shouted after me. 'Cara! Cara!' But I kept running – running away from my dad.

I turned round.

'No, Dad. I will not forget about him. I've tried to, and I can't, can I? You can't just stop loving someone. It's not that simple. I'll see you at home.' I turned back round and ran.

Dad cried out. I stopped and ran back.

'What're you doing?' It wasn't a question – not really. I saw what he was doing from the way he held his fist and gaped in pain: punching and kicking a tree.

'For God's sake, Dad, it's not the bloody tree's fault, is it?'

He crumpled into me and I gripped my lovely dad, hugging him so hard.

We took a side path and sat on a bench. The gunmetal sky darkened a shade with each minute as twilight beckoned.

'My boy.' He sniffed, leaning forwards a little, his hands wedged under his legs. 'It's not meant to happen. It's all wrong. Wrong way round.'

My face caved in, and I hugged Dad tight and we sobbed and sobbed.

Dad scraped a sodden leaf off his right boot with the heel of his left. We sat there in silence, hugging, sniffing, and the day closed in around us.

Chapter Thirty-Five

Nathan

February, Edinburgh

I was a bit surprised how chilled the psychotherapist was. Guess I'd expected someone all stern in a suit. This guy – Ben – was definitely at the casual end of smart-casual. Grey troos – just outside jeans territory – a rainbow-striped canvas belt and a polo shirt. I hadn't worn one of those since primary. Looked comfy. He leaned back in his chair – some sort of cool, designery red thing – cracked his back over the edge.

He started off asking about my interests, sports I liked, music – that sort of thing; a blether with a mate rather than a therapy session. I knew he'd do this, and I was grateful for this momentary pause, like the ceasefire before battle commences.

Then he adjusted his knee, glanced at his notepad and a more serious look crossed his face. Game on. My body started to coil like a spring.

'So, Nathan, can you describe the thirtieth of June last year . . . Except in this version, you're driving along, no issues, no boy, you meet your friend like you'd planned.'

I did as he said, relaxing as I told him about meeting up with Scotty in Ocean Terminal, buying a pair of sunglasses, eyeing up some girls, going for coffee like a pair of granddads.

'How do you feel about the Nathan you've just told me about?'

'I hate him,' I said, adrenaline buzzing in my chest, surprised at the ferocity of it. 'He has no fucking clue.'

'Why do you say that?' he said, his tone gentle, like he'd one hundred per cent expected me to say that. 'Why do you think he has no clue?'

'He's a fucking idiot. He's just swanning about. He has no clue how lucky he is.'

He nodded. 'OK,' he said. 'OK.'

He paused and looked at me. There was no hurrying in psychotherapy sessions, I was getting to realize. 'It sounds like you're feeling some sort of anger, or bitterness, or resentment towards him?'

'I guess,' I said.

'Can you describe him for me – this Nathan you're seeing.'

'He's very suave, obviously,' I started, going for humour as a crutch.

Ben indulged me with a weak smile, and suddenly I was aware of the sweat in my armpits. His look also communicated to me to please be a little more serious. I imagined the lecture: 'You'll only get out what you're prepared to put in, Nathan.'

'He's happy and carefree,' I admitted after a while. A giant sob erupted from my chest, like a big bubble in a lava lamp that had no physical choice but to come up. I wiped my eyes. 'He's happy. He's so happy. He's just finished school, it's sunny out, he's with his best mate.'

Nodding seemed to be Ben's go-to.

'How d'you feel about his best mate?'

'Scotty? He's a bastard,' I said. 'He's just swanning about, too, talking about some shit that doesn't matter.' I frowned. I looked up at Ben. 'I don't mean that,' I said. 'Honestly, I don't mean that.'

He put his hands up as if to say 'It's OK'. For a second, I felt like Ben was tricking me, getting me to say shit I didn't mean. But maybe a fraction of me did mean it.

'This is all very natural, Nathan,' Ben said, doing the first-name thing that I'd expected. 'It doesn't mean you don't like your friend, Scotty; it doesn't make you a bad friend. It's just something you need to process – and going back and exploring is unearthing some painful and unexpected feelings. In daily life, you don't get to express this – we often don't even realize it's there until we explore it. That's all we're doing.'

I nodded, noticed the clock at forty-two past the hour and some sort of modern abstract-art thing on the wall, all bright colours and bits jutting out. Snowflakes landed on the window outside, turning instantly to water. They seemed to slow down and circle before they landed, like they had a law unto themselves.

'Is the Nathan you just described to me – the Nathan who was happy and met up with Scotty and went shopping – is that the same Nathan as this one sitting before me?' He gestured at the whole of me with both hands.

I had to think about it.

'More no than yes,' I said. 'I'm changed. I'm different. It's changed me.'

He asked about the bits that had changed, then the bits that hadn't. 'Is there some essential part of that Nathan that's still there, inside you, do you think? Can you try to find that part of you that's still you?'

I shrugged. 'I don't know,' I said.

'There must be something you like about him,' he said, insistent. 'Tell me what you like about him, find a connection.'

The silence swelled and filled the room, pressing into the walls and ceiling, but it fitted the backdrop, with the snow falling in slow-mo outside. Then came an image of younger Nathan shushing Damian, and on the whispered count of three bursting into Mum's room to sing Happy Birthday and present her with the card I'd made and the happy box we'd put together for her in a shoebox lined with fuchsia crepe paper. Younger Nathan sitting stroking Mimi, who was curled up on my bed, purring her heart out, me babbling away some nonsense or other. Nathan bringing old Mrs Morton's bin back in for her. Nathan stepping in when the Fountainbridge crew picked on that poor emo kid they were always tormenting – and getting a black eye for his trouble.

OK, so maybe he wasn't twenty-four-carat arse.

Valentine's Day. I sent Cara a beating-heart emoji – toyed with the idea of a message, too, but nothing seemed right. She sent a beating-heart emoji straight back.

Two days to go.

February sixteenth. The date that had been looming ever closer in my mind.

Judgement Day.

Weirdly, it wasn't like it was one hundred per cent dread. Yeah, there was quite a lot of dread, but a bit of something like atonement, too. Say, seventy-eight per cent pure dread – mostly to do with seeing her parents, seventeen per cent atonement. And, yes, admittedly five per cent excitement to see Cara. I'd kept my distance the last couple of weeks out of, I dunno, courtesy, I guess – hadn't seen her since our walk up the Eildons. Shameful and fucking insane to be feeling even a scrap of excitement, I agree.

And we'll have to adjust the figures, cos I forgot about relief. Relief to finally be there, getting it over with, once and for all. Working out the shape of this new 'destiny' that I was having to mould myself to fit.

Part of the dread was an absolute terror at the possibility of going to prison. I'd had to go to Pinstripe's office and go over all the stuff that might come up, even though it wasn't actually him who'd be doing the talking. He dropped it in then, that a custodial sentence was 'possible, but highly unlikely'.

'A custodial sentence?'

'Detention in a Young Offenders Institution, Nathan.'

I wished I'd never watched all those films about what happens to people in jail.

Time sort of slowed.

'How long?'

'Depends on what level. Lord Gilchrist will be as lenient as he can within the sentencing range. It carries a maximum penalty of life imprisonment, but it's usually more like four years, out in two for good behaviour. The minimum is two years for a level C of seriousness, and you'd be out in twelve months. But they hardly ever send anyone under twenty-five down these days, unless it's murder or rape – you're covered by special guidelines. Far more likely is a community payback order – lots of unpaid work and a course. It's all very complicated.'

Four years. He said it like it was like getting a bit of Blu Tack off your shoe. A minor inconvenience.

'Don't worry, we'll push for death by *careless* driving, not death by *dangerous* driving.'

'What's the difference?'

'Lesser penalties. I wouldn't worry, Nathan, the judge will be soft on you.'

So here I was, walking up to the court. Grand sandstone building.

When you picture your life, you don't imagine yourself standing outside the High Court at your own trial.

Mum grabbed my hand and led me up the steps. Déjà vu. It was like following the police officer on the day of the accident. PC Mooney, he was called – he did have a name.

Mum had bought me a suit that she said would double up as an interview suit. Plain black. I pulled at my throat and wriggled my shoulders, trying to get comfortable. How anyone could choose to wear a suit every day was beyond me. A shirt and tie was bad enough.

The tie was dark blue with a fleck through it in a brighter blue. Navy with electric blue. It wasn't a funeral, but Mum said I needed to dress respectfully. *No shit.*

'Good luck, love.' Mum gave me a quick hug, then held me at arm's length by the shoulders. 'You'll be fine. Just—' She took a sharp in-breath. 'Just be you. You have the courage. You just have to stand there and tell the truth, love. OK?' She stroked my hair away from my eye.

I shrugged, though my skin prickled with sweat.

Mum had to go and wait in the witness room until she testified. Gran had offered to stay with her but they both agreed Gran should sit in the public gallery. 'I don't want Nathan all alone in there,' Mum had said. Damian was happy for once to be at school – between him, the guidance teacher and Mum, he seemed to be getting himself sorted; he'd been getting better grades. He would have been allowed in the public gallery, but even double Biology was more appealing. I was glad; didn't want to put him through this.

The din shrank to a hush as I walked in. Ten-thousand eyes were on me, or that's what it felt like. The macer – the court officer – led me to my chair. The dock.

Murmurs floated around the room.

'Court,' announced the macer in a clear, well-spoken voice. Everyone stood as the judge entered in a grand red gown, his wig pushed forward below his hairline in a row of tight sheep-curls.

A jolt of fear passed through me like an electric current. My stomach dropped and that giant fist squeezed again. My vision did funny things, too – the judge was there in my focal point then zoomed right out – and the noise around me muted. We'd had a school trip in third year to a courtroom and had acted out a scenario. All I remembered was laughing the whole time.

This was different. This was real.

I glanced over my shoulder to the gallery, found Gran. She did a weird sort of surreptitious wave that didn't seem very appropriate. I caught Cara's eye, held her gaze for a moment before turning back to the front. Her grey-green eyes brimmed with too many emotions battling it out – but mixed in with the love and the anguish and the guilt was something small and vulnerable: fear.

My chest bubbled and fired my love and pain for her, and there she was, on the other side of this whole thing. Her mum was like Cara but tiny and ghostly pale. Her dad was red-faced, a big bull-head, and looked like he wanted to deck somebody. No prizes for guessing who. I nodded and looked at the floor in front of me.

The prosecution lawyer, the advocate depute, called PC Mooney as a witness.

PC Mooney confirmed I was the driver of the vehicle that fatally struck Simon Paterson.

He confirmed Simon Paterson was pronounced dead at the scene of the accident.

'At what speed was Mr Blake travelling?' asked the advocate depute.

'The vehicle Mr Blake was driving was travelling at thirty-four miles per hour moments before it struck Mr Paterson,' said PC Mooney.

A few intakes of breath. I glanced around, my hands squirming in my lap. A sheet of cold wrapped itself round my torso and a tendril coiled round my heart.

'Could you repeat that please? The accused was travelling at what speed?'

'Thirty-four miles per hour – a little less at the moment of impact.'

Right from that moment, I knew we'd lost.

I would have hated me, too.

If I'd been going at twenty-four, he'd be alive.

'Can you confirm the speed limit on that stretch of road?'

'Twenty miles per hour.'

'Twenty. Yes. A busy area with shops and flats and restaurants.' She brought her eyebrows together in a peak.

The noise started to heat up in the room. The judge called for quiet. I squeezed my eyes shut for a second. I was like one of those cicadas on *Planet Earth* that only comes out every seventeen years, and before it's halfway up the first tree, gets grabbed and munched.

The advocate depute referred to several Crown productions and label numbers, and the jury, to my right, studied photographs and the pathologist's report. I closed my eyes and saw the close-ups of Si's face, his body lying in a dark pool, his earbud, his blue lips, his white hand. The eyes. The images that had haunted my sleep. I started to shake. I swiped at the tears with the heels of my hands, reached for the tissues Mum had stuffed in my pocket and blew my nose. I had to control the retch as my belly heaved its reaction to proceedings. Thank God I hadn't been able to stomach any porridge.

'Analysis of Mr Blake's mobile phone confirms it was in use at the time of impact,' PC Mooney said, responding to a question from the advocate depute. 'Mr Blake was adjusting his music on his mobile phone.'

A murmur of disgust came from everywhere, like it was on stereo.

I'd never felt more ashamed, and shame was something I'd been good at those last seven months. Expert, even. The psychotherapist had helped me to see that.

'Is there any other relevant information pertaining to Mr Blake's driving that day?'

I felt like an animal.

She paused for effect. 'Mr Blake didn't jump a red light – nothing like that?'

'Miss Colquhoun!' The judge glowered at her. 'You know

perfectly well: no leading questions.'

'Apologies, My Lord. Was Mr Blake doing anything other than *adjusting his mobile phone* when he struck Simon Paterson?' She enunciated every syllable like she was spelling them out to a small child.

There were a couple of coughs.

'Mr Blake travelled through a red traffic light two point eight metres before impact. Simon Paterson was crossing the road at the pedestrian crossing on Leith Walk where Gayfield Place turns into Haddington Place.'

A volcano erupted behind me. I felt every eye in the gallery drilling into my back.

The advocate depute leaned forward on her arms, her hands splayed on the desk.

'Thank you, PC Mooney,' she said. 'I have no further questions.'

I hung my head.

Truth is, I'd had no idea I'd gone through a red light until Pinstripe told me a few weeks after the accident. When I think back, right enough, I see traffic lights, but they're isolated images – stills. The angry guy with the crew cut and the man with the ponytail, with a set of traffic lights behind. My brain hadn't fully made the connection: that the images represented reality, my hideous reality – that I'd jumped a red light. Guess I hadn't wanted to face that truth.

Mr Lucas, my defence counsel, didn't ask to cross-examine PC Mooney. I'd only met Mr Lucas once before the courtroom, a meeting set up by Pinstripe, with Pinstripe literally sitting between us like a middleman. Pinstripe had done all the groundwork but couldn't defend me since he was 'only a solicitor', he'd said. He was training to become a solicitor advocate like Mr Lucas. To be honest, I was relieved not to be Pinstripe's first case. At least Mr Lucas looked like he'd been about. Silver hair. Serious look.

I studied the tip of my scar that I could see in the open bit above my shirt cuff, above the buttonhole. Still red. Pinstripe gave me a grim grin. Mr Lucas had barely shown any reactions during the questioning. Just another day at work – that's what his body language said. He'd scribbled a couple of times, but other than that, he could have been watching a nil-nil match.

Five witnesses were called, all of them describing the accident. One may have been Crew Cut, I wasn't sure. If it was him, he looked completely different to the picture in my head of an angry man, shouting and swearing and shaking his fist. The guy looked quite respectable in a suit and was softly spoken. Mr Lucas didn't question any of them. We weren't denying the fact I'd killed Simon. We were denying dangerous driving, even though it was clear to everyone in the room including Mr Lucas, including Pinstripe, including me, including Gran, including the judge, including every member of that jury, I was sure, that speeding, jumping a red light and anything to do with a mobile phone constitutes dangerous driving.

I'd told Pinstripe I wanted to plead guilty. He said that wasn't the way the system worked. Witnesses often fall through, he said. We'd go for not guilty, he'd insisted, push for a lesser charge. I should have ignored him, but he was a lawyer, and what did I know?

I closed my eyes a moment, and lime green blobbed around behind my eyelids.

Then what I'd been dreading most: 'I wish to call Ross Nathan Blake to the stand.'

Chapter Thirty-Six

Cara

February, Edinburgh

'Love you. xx' I'd texted him that morning. What else could I say? Good luck didn't quite cut it.

They led him in, and I felt more ashamed than I'd ever felt in my life. Ashamed that here was this boy who'd killed my brother, and here was me, sitting next to my parents, totally in love with the boy who'd caused all this. The boy who'd killed my brother, come to face trial; come to hear what the judge saw fit to do with him.

What was I thinking? Had I always been so selfish? And could I really, truly deal with this? Dad had said it would never go away; it would always be this thing between us – this big, ugly, painful thing. I'd convinced myself we'd find a way – but was I still so sure? It didn't help that he was looking beautiful, vulnerable.

It would be so much easier to hate you.

PC Mooney told the court Nathan was driving his mother's car at thirty-four miles per hour 'moments before it struck Mr Paterson'. It was the word 'struck' that did it. It struck me with the force of its own meaning, in the chest. Nathan struck Si, at thirty-four miles an hour – so hard he died instantly. My little brother. I couldn't stem the tears. They welled and overflowed, and I sobbed and saw blurs and shapes. Sound went funny, too – like underwater.

How could I have done that to Si? How could I have kept on loving the boy who'd killed him, once I knew?

Blinking fast, I stared at my hands then closed my eyes while I breathed in.

PC Mooney said Nathan had gone through a red light. I honestly thought I'd been stabbed. Between my shoulder blades. I slapped my hand over my gaping mouth – I think I'd let out a sound – then Mum grabbed my wrist and pulled it to her lap.

Nathan never said he'd jumped a red light.

He never said.

I looked at Mum and Dad, but they didn't seem shocked, or surprised. They'd gone over and over it all with the police – every last detail. I hadn't read the statements. Si's absence from our home was all the statement I'd needed.

I looked from Mum to Dad, back to Mum. They were destroyed. I was destroying them all over again.

I tried to look at Nathan.

I can't look at you.

I was shocked at my own reaction. My reaction to what I was hearing. Imagining I didn't know him. Here was this boy, clearly cut up about what he'd done, but still. He'd killed my brother. It thumped me in the chest, that fact.

I actually couldn't breathe for a bit, I was that stunned.

I wished I'd never gone to Em*pour*ium. Never met him. But as fervently as I wished it, I knew with a clarity that seared into my soul the pointlessness of if-only thinking. It got you nowhere. Just mugging around in a never-ending bog of regret.

I lifted my eyes and found the back of his head bowed, his shoulders slumped. I had no bitterness, no anger; only sadness. A heavy, heavy sadness that sank into me. That familiar sadness that had already almost crushed the spirit out of me.

But I was Cara Eva Milne, and I must go on.

Chapter Thirty-Seven

Nathan

February, Edinburgh

'Mr Blake, why did you consider it safe to fiddle with your mobile phone while you were driving?' said the advocate depute.

I was a statue cast in stone on the outside, fluttering and convulsing on the inside. 'I . . . I don't.'

Pinstripe scowled.

'Why were you travelling at *thirty-four* miles per hour on a busy *twenty* miles per hour limit street – *seventy per cent* faster than the speed limit?'

I looked at her. I didn't have an explanation, and she knew it.

She paused, for a time. She was good. Her mid-brown hair hung thinly to her shoulders. Her skirt suit shouted: I am a woman to be reckoned with.

'And how,' she started up again, 'did you come to ignore

a red light and plough through a pedestrian crossing, striking and instantly killing an innocent thirteen-year-old boy, who was out in the morning sunshine, about to enjoy his summer holidays, blissfully unaware that it was to be the last day – the last *moment* – of his life?'

I hung my head and wept.

'No further questions, My Lord.'

'Nathan, I have questions for you, too,' said Mr Lucas.

I released a breath. *I can do this.*

'Dangerous driving is a very problematic term. It carries a range of interpretations. It is, by definition, a subjective term. Nathan, were you texting as you drove?'

'No. I never text and drive.'

'Nathan, how have you felt since that day?'

I glanced at Cara now. I found her hands on her lap first, to make sure it was her; to make sure I didn't accidentally look at her mum or her dad. Her face was a pencil portrait of pain.

'Terrible. Guilty. Wishing I could turn back the clock.'

'Have you continued to drive?'

'No. I've driven once only since that day, and I've decided never to drive again.'

'Once only, you say? Why did you decide to drive on that one occasion?'

No. I don't want to do this. I did a tiny shrug.

'Nathan, what made you decide to drive on that occasion? Where were you driving to?'

'The coast. The seaside.'

'Why were you driving to the seaside?'

'I felt like it.'

'Were you planning to drive back, Nathan? Were you?'

My face crumpled and I couldn't look at him. I sobbed silently, tasting the sea air, then looked at the ceiling.

'I'm sorry, Mum,' I said, in little more than a whisper.

I could see what he was doing, and it was working. A couple of women in the jury dabbed their eyes.

'Were you planning to drive back from the seaside?'

'I don't know,' I said. Then, quieter: 'No.'

'Tell us about your nightmares, Nathan.'

'My nightmares?' *Jesus, it was all coming out, wasn't it.* I sighed, took a few breaths, looked at Mr Lucas. I had a choice: resigned myself to going with it.

It was time to be honest – with myself, with everyone. Plus, I'd sworn to tell the whole truth, hadn't I?

'I've had them since ... the day of the accident. I kept seeing ...' I couldn't say it, not in front of his parents. Not because I couldn't, but because it was too brutal to say. 'I kept seeing Simon's face, like in the photographs.'

'Thank you, Nathan. I would like to read a statement from Nathan's mother, Diane Blake. He pulled his reading glasses from his forehead to his eyes. '"Nathan woke up screaming, sweating, yelling out, yelling *No*, many times a night, every night, for months."' Someone cleared their throat. "I would have to go through to him, hold him, soothe him. He woke up looking exhausted. It improved a little, but he still suffers from his nightmares once or twice a week." Do you agree that's a fair statement, Nathan?'

I looked at Gran, stiff and unreadable – wanted to unscrew her lid little by little and let it all out.

'Yes,' I said.

He continued to read from Mum's statement. '"Nathan's

asthma also got a lot worse. He's suffered some really bad attacks – I had to take him to hospital twice last summer."' Mr Lucas looked up at me and pushed his glasses back onto his forehead. 'Had you ever had to go to hospital because of your asthma before?'

'Objection, My Lord!' said the advocate depute. 'Do we really need to hear Mr Blake's full medical history and details of every bad dream he's had?' She threw her hands in the air and shook her head.

'Objection sustained,' said the judge. 'With respect, move on.'

Mr Lucas raised a hand in acknowledgement. 'Nathan, can you roll up your sleeves, please, and show the judge and the jury your forearms?'

No. No. I can't.

'I'd rather not.'

'Why don't you want to show us, Nathan? It's only forearms.'

'I'd really rather not.'

My arms were pinned to my sides.

'But we all have forearms. Yours will be just the same as everyone else's. Won't they?'

I nodded.

'Unless there's something about your forearms that you prefer to conceal.'

'Mr Lucas, you can see your client is distressed,' said the judge. 'And he has repeatedly stated he does not wish to show us his forearms.'

Mr Lucas nodded and pursed his lips. 'Nathan, have you ever cut yourself?'

'Enough! Mr Lucas, unless this is demonstrably pertinent to proving or disproving Mr Blake's culpability—'

Mr Lucas raised his hands in surrender.

I couldn't quite believe it was over.

The advocate depute called more pieces of evidence – reports from Mum's car, analysis of my mobile phone. She talked the jury through each item and my stomach gnawed.

Finally, it was Mr Lucas's turn. He called up Mrs Morton – the old lady from number 84 – and she said she'd always watched me from her window playing football in the street and I'd always been a 'very nice, well-mannered wee boy,' and I wheeled her bin back in for her every week. She looked out of context. I gave her a tearful nod.

'My Lord, this is irrelevant,' said the advocate depute. 'We're not here to determine Mr Blake's character, we're here to determine the quality of his driving that day, and why the Crown considers it dangerous. I frankly fail to understand how this got agreed in the first place.' She motioned towards Mrs Morton.

Mr Lucas was like a lizard. Unblinking, motionless and displaying no signs of reaction or vitality.

He called up Mum. She looked ghostlike, walking up.

'Who taught Nathan to drive, Mrs Blake?'

'I did.' She looked at me, tried to smile some reassurance.

'How would you describe Nathan's driving?'

'Nathan's a good driver,' she said. Her voice was wobbly and breathless. She breathed in a couple of times. 'Sorry,' she mumbled. She looked at me again. I sent back what was supposed to be a 'don't worry' look.

'It's all right, Mrs Blake. Thank you. Try to relax.'

Jesus! Try to relax, Mrs Blake.

'Have you ever known of Nathan to text while driving?'

'No, my Nathan would never do that,' she said. 'Nathan's a responsible, caring boy.' Then she lost it and couldn't speak.

I thought of Cara, sitting behind me. My heart fluttered.

'Thank you, Mrs Blake,' said Mr Lucas. 'I appreciate how difficult this must be for you.'

Mum hurried to join Gran in the gallery.

The judge adjourned for lunch. Possibly, the third most horrendous lunch hour of my life, after the accident and the funeral. Though of course there was running away from Cara that day, too, and the day I drove to Claythorpe, which had actually been quite peaceful in a fucked-up sort of a way. I'd banked up a few, pretty shitty lunch hours, come to think of it.

I sat with Mum and Gran in the room we'd been told we could go to – didn't want to go anywhere where there was any risk of seeing anyone from the courtroom. Pinstripe led us to the room and Mr Lucas followed, clutching his briefcase. Thankfully we had our own toilet off the room, or I think I'd have had to hold it in for fear of bumping into Cara's dad in the gents.

'You're doing fine, Nathan,' said Pinstripe. He looked almost fatherly. I felt bad for thinking he was an arse.

Even Mr Lucas gave me an encouraging smile. 'Judges hate this sort of case,' he said, 'when you're clearly not a criminal who's a public danger. He'll feel sorry for you, like everyone else in that courtroom does.'

'Not everyone,' I said. 'Anyway, it's the jury who'll decide.'

'But it's the judge who'll sentence. They don't want to put away good people who've made momentary mistakes, Nathan.'

I nodded.

The door clicked shut behind them. Gran sensed she was surplus to requirements, too, and said she needed to get out 'to stretch my legs'. And she fancied a bridie from the pie shop round the corner where she used to go when she was a wee lassie, apparently. Even though she wasn't a bridie sort.

So, it was just Mum and me.

'Oh, love, c'mere to me,' she said. She pulled up a chair beside hers, hugged me to her chest and rocked me back and forth, then she started humming 'Bobby Shafto'. Then at the verse she started singing the words, then at the chorus, I joined in. Our favourite song that she'd sung me for years at bedtime, just before she'd tuck me in, tucking the edges of my covers right under me until I was cocooned like a mummy, and I'd be laughing my head off every time. How I'd loved it when Mum tucked me in. Made me feel safe.

She kept hugging me after we'd finished singing. Then she pushed me away, so gently, and held her forehead against mine, and wiped my tears away.

'This is the most difficult thing you've ever had to do in your life, Nathan,' she said. 'And you'll get through it. And these have been the most horrific few months of your life. But you got through them. It wasn't pretty . . .' We both laughed, for some crazy reason. I wiped my nose. 'But you got through them. And you'll get through today, and tomorrow, and however long the trial takes. And you'll get through the next week, and you'll get through the next year. And you'll never be quite the same again and you'll never completely get rid of the guilt, but you'll build a new you and you'll find a way to live your life and to have a good, meaningful life, even if it's not the one you imagined it would be.'

I nodded, my mouth a squiggly line.

'Thanks,' I said, when I found my voice. 'I love you, Mum.'

'I love you too, Nathy. My baby.'

It was like her words gave me a jolt of strength to get me through the next bit, like when she'd held my hand as a child when I was tired, and said she was passing her energy through my hand and up into my arm and into my chest and it was pumping all round my body and into my legs, and I would feel that energy, that surge, and I would think it must be magic. That's what my mum gave me that lunch hour. So it started off as the third worst lunch hour of my life, and turned into something sad but beautiful. I must have been going soft in the head, but I really did feel protected by my mum's love. It was a strong, invisible bubble around me, and only so much of the atmosphere's toxic rays could penetrate it.

Chapter Thirty-Eight

Cara

February, Edinburgh

Closing speeches time. Nathan sat, a fraction less hunched, staring straight ahead. I just wanted it over, so we could go home. My neck pinched and my back ached and my belly and soul felt hollowed out. My head was so heavy, and it was too warm. Blinking was an effort. I closed my eyes a moment and allowed myself the luxury of imagining a giant, plush bed, with the world's comfiest mattress and the world's softest duvet.

'That Mr Blake caused the death of poor Simon Paterson while *speeding* and using his *mobile phone* – in other words, *dangerous driving* – has already been established.' The prosecution barrister's voice jolted me back into full consciousness. 'There is nothing to debate. Whether Mr Blake is a nice chap is immaterial – that is not what you are here to deliberate upon. Of course Mr Blake regrets that day. That doesn't change the fact that you *must* find him *guilty* of causing *death* –' Nathan's chest puffed out – 'by dangerous driving.'

For a moment, I saw Nathan at the beach, his eyes bright, looking into mine, saying 'I love you, I love you, I love you' and my heart swelled.

Mum let go of my hand and blew her nose. I breathed in and held it, unable to release the breath.

The prosecution barrister tilted back and put on her best nonchalant look. 'Mr Blake was distracted *long enough* –' she slowed for dramatic effect – 'to fail to notice he'd driven through a *red light*. A red light on a set of traffic lights with a pedestrian crossing. A pedestrian crossing at which Simon Paterson and several members of the public – some of whom we have heard from today – were innocently waiting to cross the road. The red man turned into a green man, Simon began to cross the road, and Mr Blake hit him, killing him instantly. Of course, Mr Blake's cavalier attitude towards pedestrians and other road users and his flagrant disregard for the laws of the road has no bearing whatsoever on his *character*.

'It was an entirely preventable, fatal accident. Had Mr Blake been paying attention, had he been obeying the legal speed limit, Simon Paterson would be alive today and none of us would be here in this courtroom.'

A loud, ugly sob burst out of me, and I rocked forward and back, my heart squeezed tight.

She added, in a lower, slower voice. 'Nobody in this room can begin to comprehend the suffering endured by poor Simon's family.' She looked over to us, her shape blurring. I breathed out, sniffed.

Nathan started to rise to say something, but his lawyer made a strangled noise and shot him a look that said sit down now.

What did he want to say?

'Nathan has been literally cut up by this,' his lawyer said. 'Since that tragic day, he descended into severe depression, took to self-harming and became suicidal. There is no soul in this courtroom nor on the planet who regrets more fervently than Nathan does getting into his mother's car that day and adjusting the volume of his music. Find your humanity and give this young man a second chance.'

He approached the bench and spoke with the judge. The judge shook his head, the tails on his wig shifting.

Nathan's lawyer walked a circuit round the floor, a silent tour. I scanned the faces of the jury. Solemn, concentrating on every word.

'Simon Paterson was a bright, popular young man with his life ahead of him,' he said. 'Of course we'd love to be able to bring Simon back. His family aches for their son. But nothing will bring him back – no prayer, no magic spell, no prison sentence.'

Mum let out a low wail, her face a sheet of tears, and my own blurred again. I clung on to her arm, both of us shaking.

'My client has no previous driving convictions. We're not looking at a thrill-seeker who races on the roads and does stunts for kicks. We're not looking at an aggressive young man. My client is an inexperienced driver who made a mistake – a fatal mistake. My client feels awful, has been plagued by nightmares and certainly isn't likely to reoffend. The court has heard that he was indeed careless on the morning of the thirtieth of June last, but he is not reckless. He is absolutely not dangerous.'

He looked around, paused.

'Sending *this* young man to prison to serve years behind bars will not bring Simon back. Sending *this* young man to prison will achieve nothing at all but waste another young man's life, a young man who has much to give the world, a young man whose heart aches with regret and the overwhelming will to turn back the clock and not get into that car that fateful Thursday. But alas, turn back the clock we cannot.'

A couple of coughs interrupted his flow. He waited.

'What we can do, however, is to understand that here is a young man with his life ahead of him. He has a terrible thing he must learn to live with, but we must allow him to move on. We are not looking at a young man with malicious intent. We are looking at a young man, well thought of by his teachers and peers; a boy who tragically killed another boy in a momentary lapse of attention in something that I will say one more time was simply this: a terrible, tragic accident.'

Nathan pulled at his shirt cuff.

'Haven't we all done things from time to time by accident, things that we've later regretted? Fortunately, for most of us, the things we regret are nothing compared to the gravity of what this young man regrets. A moment's distraction. A lifetime of regret.'

It was so quiet I could hear my breathing.

'Dangerous driving is a very serious crime,' he continued. 'One of the determinants of seriousness, as they are called, is a prolonged, persistent and deliberate course of very bad driving. Another is consumption of alcohol or drugs. Dangerous driving is not a matter of opinion. *Dangerous* driving is much more than *careless* driving. Dangerous driving is by definition prolonged, and of far greater severity than three seconds of careless, if fatal, inattention.

'Nathan Blake is not a criminal. I urge you to exercise your compassion and reach your verdict: not guilty.'

The prosecution barrister shook her head in a slow, exaggerated way and laughed to herself. It all seemed a bit distasteful.

'The evidence is overwhelming,' she said. 'Mr Blake is guilty.'

Chapter Thirty-Nine

Nathan

February, Edinburgh

'Court.'

The judge flowed in like a bride in a blood-red gown.

'Members of the jury, I believe you have reached a verdict?'

'We have,' said the burly man who was their spokesperson.

I looked at him, looked at them all. What were they thinking?

'Do you find the accused, Ross Nathan Blake, guilty, or not guilty, of causing death by dangerous driving?'

I turned, caught Mum's eye. She held her fist against her chest, in a 'be strong' gesture. I pressed my lips together. She looked over at Cara, gave a small nod. Cara, her head hung, acknowledged the nod with a tinier nod. She glanced up and locked eyes with me, gripping her mum's hand. The three of them were there in a line – a united front of grief. It was the first time that I'd been confronted by the magnitude of their misery;

the first time I actually saw and felt their pain – this horrific presence in the room. An acute awareness shook me: I wasn't part of this little unit. How could I be? How could I ever be part of their lives? How could I have deluded myself into thinking it might be possible? How astonishingly, jaw-droppingly self-absorbed had I become?

What a wanker. I turned back to the front.

Silence expanded into every corner of the courtroom.

'Guilty.'

Noise burst in the room like a sonic boom.

My heart seized. I wanted to look at Cara but couldn't look anywhere near her parents. Let them have this moment, the three of them. But I found myself turning anyway. Cara looked dazed. Her mum and dad had their heads buried into each other, her dad's arm clutching her mum; her mum's arm limp by her side, as though she was one of those wooden dolls with elastic inside their limbs, and her arm had stopped working.

Mum was a mess, sobbing into her tissues. Gran was doing her best to console her. Thank God Damo wasn't here.

I closed my eyes, held onto the wood in front of me, turned to face the bench. It was the only way to avoid seeing. Or so I thought. But then I saw *him*, didn't I? Si, come to see his court case. But he wasn't looking pleased or anything – just a little helpless.

Then I looked at Pinstripe, and at my hands, and a feeling something like peace fell about me – a feeling I hadn't had since it happened. This was what I'd wished for, as I'd sat listening to the closing speeches: to change my plea.

So, this was justice.

Eventually the din calmed when the judge called for order and released me back on bail.

Three weeks, he said. Three weeks we'd have to wait for the sentence, at another hearing. Three weeks for Pinstripe and Mr Lucas to put together their plea in mitigation. Three weeks for Miss Colquhoun to add anything else damning.

Three more weeks for me to sweat.

Chapter Forty

Cara

February, Edinburgh
Guilty.

Good.

Good, but . . . You know.

I was pretty sure Nathan thought so, too.

We stepped out into a volley of flashes and clicks. A sea of reporters, big lenses rapid-firing like machine guns. We stood in a line, arms linked, Mum, as always, in the middle.

Dad gave them what they wanted. Miss Colquhoun, too. Sound bites galore.

'How d'you feel about your boyfriend being found guilty of killing your brother?' a man's voice shouted.

How did he know?

'It wasn't murder,' I shouted back.

'Leave her alone,' said Mum, unlinking her arms and hugging me. 'Shhh.'

PC Rhona had told us there's not usually much fuss around death by dangerous-driving cases, but the media were going crazy over us because of the circumstances. A media circus, she called it.

Outside, and it felt like spring, sunbeams leaning across the sky.

In the car on the way home, Dad voiced my thoughts.

'Thank God,' he said.

'Yes,' said Mum.

He looked at me in the rear-view mirror. 'I know you must be feeling terrible,' he said.

'Yes,' said Mum.

'I know it's tough on you,' he said. 'But it was the right judgement. Si could be sitting next to you if wasn't for him.'

'Craig—'

'It's OK, Mum. I never said I wanted them to find him not guilty, did I?'

Chapter Forty-One

Nathan

February, Edinburgh

The house was so damn quiet when we got home. Pinstripe said I was lucky to get bail – the judge could have remanded me in custody.

Mum stopped and got us all fish and chips for tea. When I walked into the kitchen, Mimi sidled up to one side of me and Damo sidled up to the other.

'Well?' he said.

'Guilty,' I said.

He paled and blinked, then backed away and ran out the room.

I let out a long, jagged sigh. What had Damo done to deserve this? Not exactly the most fun February break ever.

I stepped to the foot of the stairs. 'I'm sorry, Damo. I get that it's a shock for you.'

He punched his punchbag – I heard the rhythm of it: jab-jab-jab-hook. He really slammed that hook. I could feel his knuckles, throbbing with the impact of throwing that punch so hard.

'Three weeks until I get sentenced,' I shouted up the stairs.

More punching.

'I'm getting us some popcorn, big D.'

It wasn't just sweating I did a lot of in those three weeks, as it turned out. It was not sleeping. And sleeping. I'd either sleep sixteen hours straight, or not at all. It was like half of me was finally relieved to be found guilty, and the other half was utterly terrified at not knowing what was going to happen. I kept imagining being frogmarched out and driven off to jail.

The nightmares were back, but different. Now, I was in prison and the guy next door rapped on my door and said, 'Welcome, kid,' in a weird, jokey voice, and I looked up, and it was Si.

Chapter Forty-Two

Cara

February, Drumleith

Next day, moping around. Hot chocolate with whipped cream. I poked the cream with the long spoon.

A movement flashed outside.

Nathan, in our drive.

Oh my God. What was he doing?

I flew upstairs to swap my scabby cardi, check the mirror, check my teeth. I spied on him from my bedroom window. He stood there scanning the house, his glance shifting to take in the upstairs rooms. I ducked, I don't know why.

I straightened a little to see. The top of Dad's head lumbered towards him from the garage.

'No!' I screamed, and flew back downstairs and out the front door.

I ran after Dad, barely able to breathe.

I didn't even know he had a crowbar. I didn't know I knew what a crowbar was. But he'd stormed out the garage clutching it, and I knew without a doubt what it was and what he wanted to do with it.

Please, Dad. Please.

Dad stood before Nathan, the crowbar raised in his right hand, his face a thundercloud of pain and fury. Nathan stood statue-still, not even cowering. Come on, then, do what you're going to do, his body language said.

Dad kicked the ground in front of Nathan. 'You took my son,' he said, his voice ragged, 'and now you want my daughter, too? You've got some nerve coming here.'

'I came to say sorry.' Nathan looked Dad straight in the face. 'I'm so, so sorry.'

'Put it down, Dad,' I said, in my calmest possible voice. I reached towards him.

Mum screamed in the background. 'Craig! Craig! Oh, Craig!' She ran down the two steps at the front door.

Dad roared – a feral roar – and lunged towards Nathan. Still, Nathan stood rooted, though he flinched. Dad swung round like a shot-putter and hacked the crowbar into the gravel, then fell to his knees, his shoulders quaking.

'No!' Dad wailed, throwing back his arms and arching his face to the sky, a strangled plea. He looked up at me, like a lost child. His face softened when he registered mine.

'I'm sorry, love,' he said between gasps.

'God almighty, Craig,' said Mum, crouching down and grabbing him.

'I'm so sorry,' said Nathan, weeping, his voice hoarse. 'Your daughter's the most amazing person I've ever met, and your son obviously was, too. I'm sorry for what I've done to your family.'

Mum pulled Dad up. He looked at Nathan, scrunched up his eyes, turned away.

I left Mum and Dad to embrace and walked past them to Nathan.

I looked right into his eyes, right into his core.

I forced out the words, even though every fibre of my being screamed *no*.

'I can't do this,' I said, my chest swelling, flooding, drowning.

He paused and studied my face, looking from one eye to the other and back. He nodded, understanding.

'Beautiful angel,' he said, almost to himself. 'I love you. I'm sorry.'

I left him standing there in our drive. I left him and turned. I put a hand behind the backs of my parents.

'Come on,' I said, and walked them into the house.

I heard his footsteps, a spontaneous sprint along the pavement. Then a sound, like an animal wailing.

I held Mum and Dad, at the doorway of the kitchen. The wet nose of Pixie poked at my ankle.

And I went and sat on my bed and hugged myself. And I picked up my hot-water bottle and breathed in the smell. No trace of Nathan. I read through our text thread for the fiftieth time.

And I leaned my head back against my wall and wept – for the two boys I loved so much.

I went back down to Mum and Dad. We'd found some old videos of Si in nursery and early primary. Dad pressed play. Si, so tiny and cute, his hair much lighter – golden in the spotlight – walked on stage in a crescent-moon costume. He looked momentarily paralysed, then he started to sing. Dad turned it up to max volume. We all leaned in to hear – you could just make out this tiny, clear voice, singing, 'When you wish upon a star, makes no diff-yence who you are, anything your heart desires will come to you.' He swept his arm in front of him as he sang and pointed at the camera on 'you'. Then he was surrounded by other tiny kids with big silver stars pinned to their tummies, all singing 'Twinkle, Twinkle'. My chest was so tight with love for this little angel. I pulled Mum and Dad close and we wept and sniffed together.

When the three of us were hugged out, and the afternoon had faded into frosty February dusk, I went to talk to Si. I sat on his grave, touched the letters of his name, like I'd done the last time. Something about the shape and feel of them was comforting. Solid and permanent. I picked a blade of grass, dropped it. Gravity, air resistance, wind – the forces that determined the way it fell back to earth. The laws of the universe were still operating, albeit in a forever distorted way, like a circle that had been nudged and could never be a perfect circle ever again, however much you prodded it.

'I'm sorry,' I gasped between breaths. 'I'm sorry I got this so wrong. I don't know how I ever thought, even for a moment, that it might be possible for him and me to be a thing. I'm so sorry, little bro. I guess I lost my mind for a while. Or at least, I'd already fallen for him when I found out all that – fairly inconvenient, it has to be said – *stuff*, about the idiot who killed you and my boyfriend being the *same person*. You couldn't make it up.' I laughed, despite myself. Sibo smiled out of the ground at me – such a forgiving soul. I sobbed again. 'You're meant to be raging at me.' I narrowed my eyes at him.

'It's OK, sis,' his voice said, so clearly. 'It's OK.'

I thumped the ground twice with the heel of my hand, like a heartbeat.

I thought of the bodies under the gravestones: cold, decomposed, eaten by worms. They'd all had lives.

One day it would be my turn to be under the ground. But for now I was going to live my life.

Chapter Forty-Three

Nathan

March, Edinburgh

Like every other has before, the day came.

Pinstripe had told me to say my goodbyes and pack a small bag just in case – boxers, socks, trainers, sliders, cash, a battery-operated radio, pen and paper, envelopes and stamps, a book maybe. No phone, he said – you're not allowed a phone in detention.

In detention.

I said goodbye to Damian. *Just in case.*

'In case I don't come home,' I explained.

He looked at me blankly.

'In case the judge sends me to Polmont.'

'Today?' His eyes widened. 'How long for?'

'I don't know.' I shrugged. 'A year or two.'

'Jesus.' He didn't know what else to say.

'Damo? I love you, man.' I'd never told him that before,

but it was true, wasn't it. I hugged him – it was like hugging a mannequin, not that I'd ever done that, either – and off he went to school.

Me and Mum hugged for ages in the kitchen, and again before we went into the courtroom. She couldn't stop sobbing.

I looked up at the judge.

Cara's mum sat, red-eyed, in the middle, same as last time. Her dad stared straight ahead of him, with the look of a wild animal that had been tranquillized. Cara was a picture of grace, all in black.

Lord Gilchrist looked at me over his glasses. 'This is a tragic and difficult case. You have been found guilty of causing death by dangerous driving. It is my job to assess all aspects of the offence and the offender and balance all mitigating and aggravating factors to arrive at a sentence that is fair and proportionate.'

The advocate depute said it was a 'clear level A offence' due to a combination of factors: greatly exceeding the speed limit, ignoring a red light and being distracted with a mobile phone.

Mr Lucas read out two statements. The first was from Mr Meikle, my headteacher. *Jesus.* He'd made me out to be some sort of saint or something. The second was from 'Scott Adair, Nathan's friend.' Good old Scotty. 'Nathan's the best friend anyone could ever have,' it said. 'He's been absolutely destroyed by this.' It sounded just like Scotty. I may have wiped my eye. Mum sniffed and half smiled at me. Luckily, I couldn't really see Cara and her parents without turning.

Mr Lucas repeated all the stuff he'd said during the trial about my character and said he considered it a level C offence. 'The speeding was of a very temporary and non-deliberate nature and lasted a matter of seconds, and the failure to notice the red light was an unfortunate result of being avoidably distracted, rather than a deliberate contravention. My client also stopped immediately and cooperated fully.' I touched the bottom of my lip. My finger had a dot of blood on it from picking at the skin. I straightened up in the chair, snapped a loose thread from my trousers. 'Do not let him be a scapegoat for people texting while driving. He has the right to be, and in a moral sense deserves to be, sentenced in his own right, with no contrivance to use him as an example to deter motorists from texting. That very valid objective, of which I'm sure all present would be in favour, should be undertaken by other means.'

'Be assured no such contrivance will occur in my courtroom.' Lord Gilchrist sighed and pulled off his glasses. He looked right at me. 'Simon Paterson was crossing the road in Edinburgh, looking forward to his summer holidays,' he said. 'You drove your mother's vehicle at seventy per cent in excess of the speed limit, you drove through a red light and you were adjusting music on your mobile phone. You struck Mr Paterson fully in the torso and chest, whereby he was sent into the air before sliding down your vehicle and onto the road. He sustained fatal injuries, with extensive bleeding to his heart and internal organs, and a very short time later he was pronounced dead on the scene. Immediately after striking Mr Paterson, you stopped and got out of the car.'

I could barely breathe.

But I was the one still breathing.

'I consider your driving falls within level B of the sentencing guideline, that is, driving that created a substantial risk of danger, due to your excessive speed, disregarding road signals and use of your mobile phone – an avoidable distraction, albeit a brief one.'

I nodded, noticing the veins on my hand, bulging.

'On the other hand, I accept that your dangerous driving was short-lived and not prolonged. I accept that you cooperated with police at the scene and have continued to cooperate. Your age and lack of driving experience are also mitigating factors. Being under twenty-five years of age, the law considers you to be less able to exercise good judgement and more disposed to take risks. Rehabilitation must be a primary consideration when sentencing a young person; however, your maturity exceeds your young age, and your youth does not diminish the centrality of the harm caused to the victim. I accept, too, that you have genuine remorse and that you will carry the guilt of what you have done for the rest of your life. Indeed, I understand it was your desire to plead guilty.' He looked at Mr Lucas and raised his eyebrows a fraction, then looked back to me. 'I take into account that you are a young man of good character. You have your life ahead of you and I do not consider you to pose a danger of reoffending.'

Someone sniffed and blew their nose.

Lord Gilchrist continued, gesticulating as he spoke. 'No sentence that I impose upon you can, or is intended to, reflect the loss suffered by Simon Paterson's family and friends, who are left forever bereft of a young man, so very much loved and with so much more to give. The victim impact statements from his family are eloquent of their dignity in the face of such a devastating loss.'

The sobbing started off quiet then amplified. I saw them out the corner of my eye – the three of them in a huddle. Cara and her parents. My chest was so tight I had to focus on breathing. The three of them, and me, Mum and Gran; six of us unable to get a satisfying breath. All because I'd been momentarily obsessed with turning up Muse. All because of three seconds of inattention. I turned and looked towards Cara. My mouth sprang down at the edges, as did Cara's as she looked back at me, like a reflection, her shoulders drooped. I nodded at her parents ever so slightly, then closed my eyes.

The judge paused, too. When I opened my eyes, he bowed his head in their direction, then looked back at me. 'I have considered all that has been said on your behalf. Primarily, however, I must consider your conduct that day. Your driving fell far below that to be expected of a competent and careful driver. You presented a serious risk to other individuals. My duty is to discourage others from such irresponsible conduct. I must also mark the gravity of what happened.'

The judge put his glasses back on and pressed his hands together to his mouth, as if praying.

'Balancing all of these factors, I sentence you as follows.' I forced a deep breath, looked up at the reporters. 'In respect of the charge, I am satisfied that only a custodial sentence is appropriate. I would have imposed a sentence of four years' detention. I shall discount the sentence by five months – about ten per cent – due to your age, your lack of driving experience and your remorse. The sentence is therefore one of three years and seven months. You are disqualified from driving for six years, nine months and will be required to resit an extended driving test should you wish to hold a driving licence thereafter.'

Three years, seven months. Three years, seven months. I heard my pulse in my head. Steady, a bit fast, but nothing crazy. I thought I'd be hyperventilating but I wasn't. If anything, my chest relaxed as I realized I'd known all along what he was going to say, like it was the only logical end point to the whole thing.

Cara's dad was on his feet, shouting, lunging towards me, a policeman restraining him.

'Three years something for my son's life? *Three years?*' he said. 'And he'll be out in half that. You call that justice?' And to the policeman, 'You said to leave it to the law.' And he broke down, squirmed out of the officer's grip and marched towards the door, pulling Cara and her mum out with him, one with each hand; the three of them a fresh picture of grief. Cara broke away and ran towards me. She launched herself at me and gripped me so hard I lost my balance.

I looked into her eyes and her face streamed with tears.

'I love you!' she said.

'I love you too,' I said, and kissed her hair, sobbing so hard my breaths were gasps. Then she was being pulled away, her face melting into a blur. My heart ripped out of my chest. A strangled sound came out of me, and I collapsed to the floor.

'Would the escort take the prisoner down please,' said Lord Gilchrist, quiet but firm.

'I'm sorry,' I shouted after her parents, my voice hoarse. 'I'm sorry.'

Mum reached out to me with both arms. 'Nathan!' she said, with such anguish it kicked me solid in the belly. I kept my eyes on her as I was led towards the corner of the room, Gran supporting Mum.

'Sorry,' I said, sniffing.

'I love you.' She struggled to get the words out. And all I heard when the door swung shut behind me was her wail, and the snap of the handcuffs. I stared at my wrists, winced at the cold solidity of metal.

'Standard procedure,' said the escort.

The officer took me down to a holding cell, unlocked the handcuffs. No windows. A smell of piss and bleach. Black benches either side, a urinal at the end, lots of graffiti.

I threw up in the urinal. I wasn't prepared for this, at all. I thought I was, but I wasn't. Mum's voice sailed into my head, singing, '*Pack up your troubles in your old kit bag and smile, smile, smile.*' How could I? It was her little ditty to help me if I was worried about anything.

The officer left me on my own.

My own silence, to contemplate this new beginning.

Chapter Forty-Four

Cara

March, Drumleith
So that's it.
He's gone.
It seems a long time.
I can't stop picturing him, in a prison cell, looking lost.
My heart's been snatched, kicked about, doused in petrol and set alight – just to be sure.

Chapter Forty-Five

Cara

Fourteen years and two months earlier, Tweedshaugh
I'd never been away from Mum overnight.

'Isn't he beautiful?' Dad said.

Beautiful? *Beautiful?* I stared into the tiny face. It was white and wrinkled, like the next door neighbours' pug dog. Ugly, like a shrunken old man. And completely bald! But I looked at Dad and nodded.

I waited. Two weeks later, I plucked up the courage.

'Are we keeping it? All the time?'

What was so funny?

'But it doesn't *do* anything. It just sleeps and poos and gets sick. Why don't we get a puppy instead?'

So we got a puppy, as well, and I was given the Very Important Job of picking the name.

'Pixie,' I said. My parents always said I was a decisive wee thing.

The baby kept watching me. Sometimes I'd take a sneaky look, just to check. He was always watching me, if he was awake, anyway. There was something quite nice about the way he looked at me, like I was the best thing ever. And he wasn't as ugly or boring as when they'd first brought him home.

Then he started to smile.

Chapter Forty-Six

Cara

29 June, Drumleith

My dearest little brother,
I can't believe a year has gone by since I last saw you. For a long time, I wanted to go back to a year ago, and hug you and hold you and stop you leaving the house. I would have broken your legs, if that would have stopped you leaving.

I miss you so much. The house has been so cold and empty since that awful day. Tomorrow, Mum, Dad and I are going to get up at 3 a.m. and come and see the sunrise with you. We're going to bring a picnic blanket and sit with you.

I want to thank you, for adding so much to our lives. You were the best little brother in the whole world. From the moment you first smiled at me, I loved you more than I can ever say. It seems so wrong to talk of you in the past tense. Mum still sets the table for four sometimes.

I'm crying again now. I still struggle every day, but I'm through the hate and the anger. There's a long way to go, and life will never be the same without you, but I know you'd want me to be happy. I've started to feel that there is some future out there. One not blessed with you in it, so it will always be missing your Sibo spark, but I'll try to do something with my life. For you. You wanted to save the world. I can't promise that, but I promise I'll do my best to make you proud of me.

I'm so, so proud of you. I will always miss you, every day of my life, until the day I'll be lying beside you. Mum and Dad have bought the plots next to you. OK, it's a bit morbid, but . . . ! Look, a great smudge. Do you like how I've turned it into a caterpillar?

You have given us all so much. You brightened our world. You were the brightest star of all.

I love you for ever.

Your big sis, C xxxxxxxxxx

Chapter Forty-Seven

Nathan

January, two years later, Edinburgh

Mum and Damo were waiting at the gate and it was so weird walking out, like I was doing something illegal. Freedom – even the word felt odd. I hesitated. I went for the passenger door out of habit, sensed Damo's uncertainty, climbed in the back seat. I guessed the passenger seat had been Damo's all that time. He hesitated, too, then climbed in the back beside me.

We got home and it was so weird, I can't explain it. The kitchen, the smell of our house. Totally surreal. I wandered round, taking in every detail. I walked up the stairs and found my room, all tidy and hoovered but the same. I picked up my alarm clock, put it back down on my bedside table. I leaned back against my door a second, blew out a couple of breaths, pulled myself together before going back down to Mum and Damo. And Mimi, poor old Mimi, sniffed and pawed me, wondering how I'd come back from the dead. Gran came over, too – her usual, chirpy self.

I was a mess those first few weeks. On what inmates call the 'outside'. It was The Outside. I really felt that. I'd served my time, and now I was allowed Out.

I say The Outside, but I stayed in my hovel pretty much all day every day. Too much of a shock, to be free. Then, on the first of April, I decided I was bored of doing nothing, bored of being a waster. I got out my pit, went to the park, came back and looked up a couple of courses – I'd missed the deadline by miles, but worth a try in case there were any spaces, eh. Mum had announced on Good Friday, to stunned silence: 'Simon Paterson wouldn't have wanted you to waste your life.' Maybe that's what did it.

It took me three days solid to fill out the first application, a day and a half to do the second. Biomedical engineering. Strathclyde and Dundee Unis. Learn to design new kit, develop stuff that works. Most people can tick the 'no' box for criminal convictions. I hit submit, wondered, *will they give me another chance?*

It was Mum's birthday, and me and Damo were cooking chicken korma. Mimi wasn't allowed on the worktops, but she was trying it on anyway, pawing at the cupboard door. I nudged her away. I don't know if it was just the raw chicken, or the unprecedented sight of the two of us doing something in the kitchen other than eating.

I hated chopping chicken breasts. There was something about them, firm and fleshy, like your forearm. But it was Mum's favourite, and she was getting her favourite that day.

Our cake was rubbish and sunken, but we'd stuck a gold candle in the middle and red ribbon round the edge, that we'd found in Mum's gift drawer.

The look on her face when she walked through the door. God, we obviously weren't very good sons. She just welled up and hugged us. You'd think we'd given her a house and a car and a lifetime guarantee of joy and happiness.

She took my face in her hands.

'Is that my boy back?' she said, looking from one eye to the other. 'Is that you?'

My chin may have wobbled.

Mum's boyfriend Colin came round, too. He sat on my chair at the kitchen table. Damo relaxed and joked with him, discussing the Man U game as I served up the korma. Mum looked from one to the other of us and smiled. I sat at the chair that had always been empty, where Mimi sometimes napped. When I caught Mum watching me, I started singing 'Happy Birthday', and Damo and Colin joined in. We lit the candle and filled four champagne flutes with Mum's favourite Prosecco. It was all a bit weird, but good-weird. We chinked our glasses and Mum tipped her head back and laughed like she used to. The way her face lit up, it felt like we were a real, actual, almost even normal family. For the first time in a very long time.

'You look great, Mum – really great,' I said.

'Thanks, love,' she said, blinking, smiling. She closed her eyes like she was making a wish, then blew out the candle.

I lifted Mimi onto my lap and stroked the bald patch where she'd been shaved. The scar was still red – shiny and new. The rest of her was getting a bit scraggy. She licked the back of my hand with her sandpaper tongue.

Outside, a giant bumblebee with a beige bum daundered about the place, half-asleep. I took down the laundry from the line, played a mad combo of keepy-uppies and donkey with Damo, then sat on the garden bench in the evening sun. A new beginning.

Chapter Forty-Eight

Cara

May, Drumleith

'Just me, hon.' Shell's head appears round the door, her hair swinging in a high ponytail that reaches halfway down her back. The light catches the pink and turquoise of the new scallop-shell tattoo on her shoulder, the pearl shimmering as she turns. She's dressed for sun, in a black racer-back top. Optimistic, you could say. Capitalizing on life, I'd say. She's the best flatmate ever – these past five months have been so much fun; such a laugh. I love it. I couldn't do our original plan of finding somewhere in Edinburgh – couldn't do that to Mum and Dad. But we have a sweet wee place on Chapel Street, five minutes from home, and we've been busy painting and putting up pictures and nice fairy lights and stuff. We've got a double room each and we share the bathroom. Second floor, lots of light, and plenty of stairs to keep our glutes tight.

There was this guy I quite liked at the climbing club. But he wasn't Nathan – didn't come close. I went for two months two years ago, but then I stopped. Stars are more my thing.

'You OK, hon?' says Shell, studying my face.

'I'm good,' I say.

The coconut-vanilla scent of gorse wafts through the open window, and I breathe it in, smiling at its warmth.

It's there always, a stone polished smooth in the pit of my belly, slowly, so slowly getting smaller – imperceptibly, infinitesimally – with every year, every hour, every minute, I suppose. Smoothed by the relentless tides that usher in and out. I'm not aware of it every moment. I do forget sometimes. But it's there, dark and glossy, like a chilled kidney. Sometimes, a tidal wave picks me up and throws me under, flooding my lungs, drowning me, just about. Sometimes it's flat calm. Always, the tide comes in and the tide goes out, smoothing, polishing the sharpnesses, turning crags into knowes.

Mum and Dad though . . . you know.

I picked up Dad and we went to see Si. I put my arm round Dad and together we wept. I picked a posy of flowers I found dotted around the place and put them on the grass, roughly where his heart would be. Dad patted the stone like it was Si's shoulder.

I don't think there's anything more I can do for Mum and Dad on the Si front. Just be there myself. I see them most days. They need me, and I need them. That's the way it works.

Bobby's really helped them. Never has there been a more doted-on dog. They've poured all their love into him – every last ounce. I'm so glad they got him when they did – three months before Pixie died.

On my phone, a notification pops up: *'Three years ago today'*. And there's Si, stuffing marshmallows into his mouth until his cheeks are bulging, then trying to speak without laughing. There's a picture of him pulling a hat down so that his ears stick out, pulling a funny face. I scroll down and there's another video of him cuddling Pixie, both of them looking happy as. There's also a clip of him playing fiddle with his quartet. He's incredible. Such passion, such talent.

I think back to the eulogy I wrote for Si's assembly.

I see his face, beaming with life.

I have to live every day. I have to make it count. I have to make it count doubly. That is my meaning.

Chapter Forty-Nine

Nathan

June, Edinburgh

I run, up Salisbury Crags, round Arthur's Seat, past Dunsapie Loch, down past St Margaret's Loch, taking in lungfuls of fresh air – crisp for June – my heart thumping in my chest and ears, my feet pounding, my veins pulsing. Cliffs, seabirds, clouds. Earth below, sky above. I look up a moment – the vastness of everything. I'm here, now: part of all this.

I sprint along the flat stretch, buzzing all over, then wander back and watch the swans and their cygnets sailing about. Folk are throwing bits of bread at them, even though there's a sign saying *Do not feed the birds*. One of the swan parents is getting well stressed, then breaks away from its family and heads towards a couple of kids, flapping and honking. The kids run away, shrieking, the dad scolding. I bend down and pick Mum a teeny wee purply-pink orchid – she'll like that.

After my shower, I lie down on my bed for a bit, think about what I'm going to say to the senior boys tomorrow at my old school – I offered to go in and speak to them about mental health and Mr Meikle jumped at it. Guess I'll just be totally honest – y'know, if it helps just one boy and all.

Mimi clambers up and nuzzles into my neck, purring like an engine when I scratch behind her ear. Her whiskers tickle my chin and her skull feels fragile through her fur. She's skin and bone, but she's still soft, lovely Mimi.

In the kitchen, Mum hands me a postcard and gives me a funny look. A picture of a star. I turn it over. *POLARIS*, it says. I reach behind me and hold the worktop. I'm back on the roof of the Observatory, with Cara, gazing up, reaching for her hand, warm in the cold air, our breath forming shapes in the dark. Polaris – she pointed it out. We looked at it together. And here it is, in my hand.

The postcard is blank except for my name and address. *Cara's writing.* I see her, sitting down at a table, writing it, her head bent forwards, her hair hanging down, fingers splayed across the card.

I read the print at the bottom left.

POLARIS, the North Star, Alpha Ursae Minoris, widely used in navigation, being 0.7 degrees from the north celestial pole. The naked eye sees a single star, however Polaris is in fact a triple star system comprising a yellow supergiant in orbit with two smaller companions.

I turn back to the photo of the main star on the front.

A yellow supergiant in orbit with two smaller companions? Si? Si's the supergiant, and me and Cara are the smaller companions, linked in the stars? Is that what she means? In orbit together?

I smile. *Thank you, Cara. Thank you, thank you, thank you.*

I let my focus soften, taking in the depth of black around the stars. Cara's voice floats into my head, that time we lay in the woods and stared up at the sky. 'It's not just about the things we can see,' she'd said. 'What's there, that we can't see? It's not nothing, is it?'

It's not nothing, Cara.
It's not nothing.

Playlist

https://open.spotify.com/playlist/4kYqNxVcTQgjnq9Ofs0LB4

'Starlight' – Muse (Nathan)
'Beam Me Up' – P!nk (Cara)
'Price Tag' (acoustic version) – Jessie J (salon)
'Read My Mind' – The Killers (Nathan)
'The Lion Sleeps Tonight' – The Tokens (Cara)
'Vienna' – Ultravox (Cara)
'In the Ghetto' – Dolly Parton/Elvis Presley (Cara)
'Coastline' – Hollow Coves (Cara and Nathan)
'Stargazing' – Myles Smith (Nathan and Cara)
'Seven Nation Army' – The White Stripes (Damian)
'Lose Control' – Teddy Swims (Nathan)

'Canon in D Major' – Johann Pachelbel (Si)
'Running' – Norah Jones (Nathan)
'Figure It Out' – Royal Blood (Nathan)
'Thursday' – Jess Glynne (Shell)
'Time After Time' – Cyndi Lauper (Cara)
'I'm Gonna Be (500 Miles)' – The Proclaimers (Majorca)
'Polaris' – Jimmy Eat World (Nathan and Cara)
'Absolute Beginners' – David Bowie (Cara)
'Save Me' – Aimee Mann (Nathan and Cara)
'Stubborn Love' – The Lumineers (Nathan and Cara)
'Candy' – Paolo Nutini (Nathan)
'Gotten' – Slash featuring Adam Levine (Cara)
'Sometimes It Snows in April' – Prince (Nathan)
'Death of a Martian' – Red Hot Chili Peppers (Nathan)
'Sing to the Moon' – Laura Mvula (Cara)
'Sometimes' – James (Cara)
'This is How It Feels' – Inspiral Carpets (Nathan)
'Someone Like You' – Adele (Cara)
'Waiting for My Chance to Come' – Noah and the Whale (Nathan)
'Leave a Light On' – Tom Walker & Red Hot Chilli Pipers, The Quay Sessions (Cara and Nathan)
'Sigh No More' – Mumford & Sons (Nathan)
'The Cave' – Mumford & Sons (Nathan)
'Days' – Kirsty MacColl (Cara)
'Paradise Stars' – Noah and the Whale (Cara, Nathan and Si)
'I Can See Clearly Now' – Johnny Nash (Nathan and Cara)

Support

If any of the issues raised in *A Beautiful, Terrible Thing* are directly relatable, here are some organizations in the UK that may be able to help you.

Childline • childline.org.uk • 0800 1111
A 24/7 helpline for under 19s. Calls are free and the phone number won't show up on your phone bill.

Harmless • harmless.org.uk
A support organisation working to address and overcome issues related to self-harm and suicide.

harmLESS • harmless.nhs.uk
An NHS guide for anyone who has contact with young people who are self-harming, designed to help you talk about self-harm so that you can decide what support might be helpful.

Mind • mind.org.uk • 0300 123 3393 • Text 86463 • info@mind.org.uk

A mental health charity which offers help with finding specialist support.

Movember • uk.movember.com

A men's health charity that works on suicide prevention, mental health and learning how to 'spot a bro who's feeling low'. Their website gives advice on how to talk about low feelings and encouraging a friend/family member to open up if you're worried about them.

Papyrus • 0800 068 4141 • Text 88247 • papyrus-uk.org • pat@papyrus-uk.org

A national charity that provides confidential support and advice to young people struggling with thoughts of suicide, and anyone worried about a young person.

Samaritans • samaritans.org • jo@samaritans.org • 116 123

A 24/7 listening service that offers support but does not provide intervention or advice. There is also a self-help app to track your mood and find practical tips and techniques to look after your emotional health.

Shout • giveusashout.org • Text SHOUT to 85258

A free, confidential, 24/7 text-support service.

Students Against Depression • studentsagainstdepression.org

A service that offers support and information for students who are depressed, have a low mood or are having suicidal thoughts.

The Campaign Against Living Miserably • thecalmzone.net • 0800 585858

A resource for young men who are struggling with mental health.

YoungMinds • youngminds.org.uk • Text 85258 • Parents' helpline 0808 802 5544

A mental health charity for children, young people and parents, working to help all young people get the best possible mental health support and have the resilience to overcome life's difficulties.

Talking to someone you trust

If you don't want to speak to someone on a helpline, you could talk to:

- a member of your family, a friend or someone you trust, such as a teacher or a community or sports or religious leader
- your GP, a mental healthcare professional or another healthcare professional.

Support for bereaved parents and siblings

Cruse • cruse.org.uk • 0808 808 1677

Care for the Family • careforthefamily.org.uk • 029 2081 0800 • mail@cff.org.uk

Hospice UK's Dying Matters • hospiceuk.org/our-campaigns/dying-matters

SLOW (Surviving the Loss of Your World) • slowgroup.co.uk • 07532 423 674 • info@slowgroup.co.uk

The Compassionate Friends • tcf.org.uk • 0345 123 2304 • helpline@tcf.org.uk

Acknowledgements

To everyone who has helped in any way, big or small, with this book, thank you. In particular . . .

Everyone at David Fickling Books, especially brilliant and hawk-eyed editors Liz Cross and Meggie Degurney. Also Bronwen Bennie, Phil Earle, Alison Gadsby, Fraser Hutchinson, Ruth Sanderson and freelance publicist Liz Scott – the whole team, in fact. I am immensely grateful to have landed in your warm and expert hands. It's no exaggeration to say the DFB and Arvon Search for a Storyteller competition has been life-changing for me: winning it has opened a whole new world. Thanks also to Arvon for your wonderful support.

Cover designer Michelle Brackenborough, for a superb and thoughtful job.

My crit group girls the Critters: Rachel Davison, Moira McPartlin, Elizabeth Frattaroli, Claire Watts, Caroline Deacon. Eternal gratitude and friendship. Also, readers of various drafts or chapters along the way, including Kristin Pedroja,

Helen MacKenzie, Cormac Moore, Eve Hepburn, Marcus Sedgwick, Sheila Averbuch and Michael Edwards.

My writing buddy, first reader and friend, Joan Haig, a great big hug. Joanday is my favourite writing day.

Janis Mackay. This story was borne from your course.

Those who shared our magical YA course at Moniack Mhor (students, tutors Cat Clarke and Martyn Bedford, staff).

Writers' Workshop (now Jericho Writers) Self-Editing Your Novel tutors Debi Alper and Emma Darwin.

Cornerstones Literary Consultancy and editor Becky Hunter.

The Royal Literary Fund, for being brilliant.

SCBWI Scotland, the greatest and most supportive community of writers and illustrators around. Also Children's Books North, Society of Authors and Scottish Book Trust; WriteMentor, Searchlight and Bath Novel Awards, for championing emerging authors.

For advice or information relating to the ambulance scene, policing material and trial or any other medical, police or legal matter: Paul Fettes, Russell Duncan, Matthew Strachan, David Moran, Maggie Pettigrew, Yvonne Davidson, Simon Wotton, Marian Brown, Jennifer Veitch. Especially David and Jennifer: thank you for patiently tolerating my endless Oh, and one more thing ... ad infinitum, until it actually was my very last question. Also Police Scotland; Scottish Courts and Tribunals Service; Crown Office & Procurator Fiscal Service; Judiciary of Scotland; Faculty of Advocates; Scottish Sentencing Council; Scottish Prison Service; Disclosure Scotland; Victim Support Scotland; Inside Time and HM Inspectorate of Prisons for Scotland. A doff of my hat also to Samaritans Media Guidelines. Deep respect to the emergency services people who have to perform these vital jobs in real life, with care and sensitivity. Thank goodness this story is fiction.

A note: Regarding court procedure, police process and medical details, a little artistic license was used, to avoid procedure stifling story. The same goes for my places, which are a blend of real and imagined. I have chosen story over strict accuracy or likelihood a number of times, but have always tried to retain broad authenticity.

Royal Observatory Edinburgh and Institute for Astronomy, University of Edinburgh, a nod.

My shelf of craft books on writing, a passing wink.

Readers: it's all about you. Thank you.

And to my nearest and dearest, my family and friends, my brightest thanks, and my love.

About the Author

Miranda Moore writes fiction and non-fiction. She works as a freelance editor and writing coach. She is also a Royal Literary Fund Fellow, supporting students with their writing. Before books, she worked in newspapers as a features writer and section editor.

Miranda won DFB and Arvon's Search for a Storyteller 2024 and the Wells Festival of Literature Book for Children 2023, and has been twice shortlisted for the Scottish Book Trust New Writers Awards.

She lives with her family in the Scottish Borders.